MW01420567

Kathleen:

You are the

Key.

Thank you for a

perfect cover.

Love

[illegible signature]

Euphoria Zone

Eight Keys of Light

A novel by
ALAN LEE BRESLOW
Co-authored by Maia Shaffer

authorHOUSE™
1663 Liberty Drive, Suite 200
Bloomington, Indiana 47403
(800) 839-8640
www.AuthorHouse.com

First published by AuthorHouse 04/29/05

ISBN: 1-4184-7375-8 (e)
ISBN: 1-4184-7373-1 (sc)
ISBN: 1-4184-7374-X (dj)

Library of Congress Control Number: 2004094597

Printed in the United States of America
Bloomington, Indiana

This book is printed on acid-free paper.

Library of Congress Cataloging-in-Publication Data
Breslow, Alan
Euphoria Zone: Eight Keys of Light/Alan Breslow

1. New Age. 2. Visionary Fiction. 3. Spirituality. 4. Inspirational. 5. Science Fiction. 6. Adventure. 7. Self-Help. 8. Eastern Philosophy. 9. Cosmological.

Cover design, illustrations and book consultation: Cathleen Shaw

For my wife, Maia
The eye through which I see God.

ACKNOWLEDGMENTS

I fill with joy when I ponder acknowledgments.

How could I leave out my parents—or my fun sisters, Mona and Lynda! Growing up in New York City, being exposed to an array of characters and experiences provided me an expansive foundation.

One schoolteacher inspired me. I can't remember her name but she was the pretty, eighth-grade teacher who "loved" my short story, *Corky Goes to the Moon*. From that day on, I continued to write stories.

Maia and I were living in Alachua, Florida, in our proverbial cabin in the woods when I started writing a short story about a wonder child named Leon. We were attending the Temple of the Universe and were mesmerized by Mickey Singer's talks about the applications of yogic wisdom. These talks greatly influenced the spiritual principles referred to in the *Euphoria Zone*. What started as a short story, literally poured out of me and did not stop until it became this novel.

For over twenty years, I've had a sporadic fascination with *The Urantia Book*. Much of the scientific information, astronomy, as well as the details of Jesus' life were taken from this cosmological masterpiece. I also used some of the book's compelling phraseology.

I wholeheartedly thank editors: Stephanee Killen, Victoria Giraud and Patrika Vaughn. Ah, if only the book had poured out of me perfectly written!

I thank my countless teachers and their books. To mention a few: Lao Tzu, Buddha, Jesus Christ, Dr. Wilson Tilley, Carl Rogers, and Jean Houston.

Finally, of my life teachers, the most influential has been my wife, Maia. Her ancient wisdom and courageous, playful spirit has shaped my life and confirmed the power of Love. She helped write, edit and market *Euphoria Zone* and was the force that got this book to completion. She earned title as co-author.

The joy of writing is to weave myself into words, then see who I am. "Peek-a-boo!"

AUTHOR'S NOTE

Frustrated by the course of humanity, I have been compelled to write and invent solutions. In sixth grade, I redesigned the school curriculum instead of doing the assigned homework. Needless to say, everyone thought I was just, well—nuts. My mother said, "Alan, why can't you just go to school? Why do you have to reinvent it?"

This book is my overt expression of a lifetime of creating divergent solutions; its fabric, after-all, is an invention—a method to live life in direct Soul connection.

I based Aaron Ardo's character on myself. He expresses my personality, theories, growth methods, and my improvisation techniques (yes, *Beach Ball* really is a process that I begin my groups with, and you can discover why in our documentary, *You're a Genius, Stupid*). And Leon? He's based on my evolving capacity to access higher levels of Self. Josie Ardo's character is based on my beloved wife, Maia—(Zelia the fairy really did heal Maia and take her *Soul Journeying*).

The seven year process of rewriting *Euphoria Zone* was fun and painstaking. But it was worth every minute! I have actualized in book form, what I have spent a lifetime doing as a facilitator—making personal growth entertaining and adventurous.

One final note: Since Leon speaks in quotes, I have taken creative license with the punctuation—instead of using the single quotation mark enclosed with a double quotation mark, as per *The Chicago Manual of Style*, I have placed the quotes in italics with one double quotation mark. This was done to make for an easier read.

Many blessing on your journey to Euphoria!

Alan

Table of Contents

Prologue

"It's time," Modeen sang as he burst from the void.

Nine hundred Angels rocketed to the same spot forming a single twinkling star. Delighted by the spectacle, Modeen emitted waves of golden light as he let forth an outrageous high-pitched yodel. "AhhhhhEeeeeeee."

The Angels surrounded Modeen like children around a raging campfire. Only Angel Dimron hovered on the outskirts of Modeen's antics. . .wondering why ragtag angel oddities were "chosen" by the Master himself!

Master Modeen shattered the moment with another yodel, then he thundered, "Proclamation of Divergence!"

Angels recoiled in disbelief. This meant they would be breaking Angel Rules, which was forbidden! Modeen watched the quivering specks as they pondered the paradox. It was a momentous moment for all Angels with consequences even Modeen could not fathom. His plan required novice angels. Their spiritual naiveté was imperative so that Modeen could mold them to fulfill the incredible task at hand.

"In my final physical incarnation," Modeen whispered, causing the Angels to move in even closer, "I was Ryana, the Story Priestess." Ryana was a legendary three-brained mystic from the Orvonton superuniverse. She ended a war that had raged for ten thousand years by telling a ten-minute story. The Angels listened with trembling curiosity. "The tale I am about to tell is a Ryana remedy," Modeen revealed. "A cosmic thriller on a planet called Earth."

Angels froze. They'd heard about Earth, the infamous speck at the edge of nowhere. They feared an assignment on a planet where humans were so out of touch with their Souls and so bound by the illusion of form. Look at what they had done to the Christ!

"Infamy is our business," Modeen reminded his students. "True, wisdom eludes most earthlings because they fixate on form, but that is what the physical plane is for." He smiled and added knowingly, "These humans are ready for a leap."

Modeen glowed with the warmth of a million stars as he beheld the budding Angels, aware that their own leap was only moments away. Modeen emitted a third yodel that was so intense it created an explosion of light—most definitely against Angel Rules. As the swirling cosmic dust settled, every Angel beheld hundreds of spirals surrounding Modeen like jewels glistening in a crown.

"These spirals were sculpted from the very first light, the blast at the beginning of this beginning," Modeen informed them.

Nine hundred radiant coils of creation's light hung mindfully, beating like naked, knowing hearts. Every Angel knew about Modeen's *Light Laboratory*, a workshop renowned for miracles like the ones now floating before them. Indeed, the spirals were a miraculous breakthrough, just what Modeen needed to facilitate an outrageous twist in Earth and angel history—a twist that could ignite the cosmos and beyond.

"It's time," Modeen commanded.

Each spiral floated seductively before its Angel partner.

"The coil before you is your soul mate in light," Modeen affirmed sweetly.

The Spirits trembled.

"Now is forever," the Master proclaimed. The spirals began twisting clockwise except for Dimron's that spun counter. Modeen's fanning wings electrified the air.

"Faster!" he cried.

Light whirled. The Angels bubbled.

"Faster!" Modeen howled as he flapped. Spirals twisted toward the speed of light.

"Now!" Modeen rejoiced.

A spiral jewel pierced each Angel heart, lodging itself deep within its mate, spinning faster and faster, whirling to the edge of starlight. . .

"NOW!"

The spirals exploded into pure white energy hitting light speed. Angels collapsed within its currents, except for Dimron who attempted to resist the dazzling explosions of color. He knew the blasts were going deep within his field, dissolving ancient blockages. . .and that all the Angels were receiving the same healing. Finally, the light explosions stopped. . . leaving a divine tingle, even in Dimron. Only Modeen knew that this tingle would never go away.

"These coils enable you to experience the story with sights, sounds and physical sensations; you can even feel human emotions," Modeen said gleefully. "You will have feelings that no angel has ever felt."

"Angel candy?" Dimron questioned. (Angels crave sensations like humans crave sweets.) "Why feed us candy?"

"Sweetness will serve you on this mission," Modeen assured the rebel, concealing how close Dimron had come to discovering the master plan.

Dimron's spiral took the longest to synchronize. With each coil attuned to its host, they prepared to connect with one another. Simultaneously, every coil emitted nine hundred rays of light that crisscrossed, creating a grid so complex even Modeen could not quantify it. Modeen focused his mind upon a particular human. Spirals tilted; the grid tilted and touched the Master's aura at his heart. The Master asked, "Can you see Leon, the eleven year old earthling sitting with his school principal?"

The Angels experienced pulsing colors and static, but saw nothing. Suddenly, Angel wings thrashed wildly.

"Experience Leon if you dare," Modeen yelled above the flapping. "Taste our love! I was his indwelling angel."

"You are an Archangel," Dimron confronted. "How could a mere boy merit an Archangel indweller?"

"There is nothing *mere* about Leon," the Master giggled. Holding the thought of Leon at his third eye, Modeen could see Leon's past lives sprawled out into infinity.

"Forever is now," the Archangel rejoiced, emitting an outburst of love that every coil converted to orgasmic insights—eons of wisdom from a single blast.

With Spirits trembling, Archangel Modeen heralded, "Let us begin—not at the beginning, since there is no such thing, but at the Heart, where everything comes to a boil!"

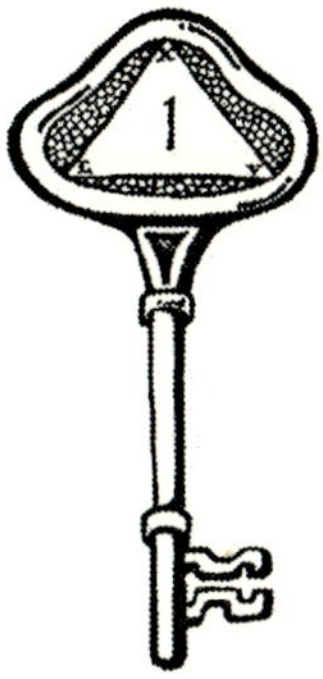

Life is a mystery to be lived...

"According to this, you have superhuman intelligence. Are you aware of being special, Leon?"

Leon wouldn't answer. He just gazed intently at Principal Snow, his silence creating an awkward stillness.

Principal Snow looked past the security bars on his window, wanting to escape the silence. It reminded him of the jail cell he'd occupied for one night, back in college, when a panty raid had gotten way out of control. *Too much booze*, he'd told his mother, as she dragged him home for "the belt."

The belt lived on the bathroom door as a reminder to be good or else. Good depended on Mother's mood and that day it had been foul. This time, though, he was eighteen and over six feet tall. Walter Leonardo Snow recalled his mother's bewilderment as he'd ripped the belt from her trembling hand. It had been the last time he'd endured her physical wrath, but her words still screamed in his head. *You stupid, fat-ass, no-good son.* Silences provoked the memory of her nagging voice and Principal Snow sensed that the child knew.

Leon sat serenely, staring at Snow.

The principal was about to end the meeting when the child finally spoke. "*Surely God would not have created such a being as man, with an ability to grasp the infinite, to exist only for a day! No, no, man was made for immortality.*—Abraham Lincoln." Leon stared at Snow like an eager puppy.

"Not another Abe Lincoln quote," the principal of Lincoln Middle School moaned. Snow bounded out of his chair and paced behind Leon, trying to think of a response. Flailing his arms nervously, his knuckles slammed the back of Leon's chair. "Goddamn it!" Snow blurted out, "Say something in your *own* words!" He looked like a ripe tomato ready to explode as he shook his chubby hand and sputtered, "Leon, aren't you afraid of spending your life isolated from people?"

Leon spoke slowly. "*Fear knocked at the door, Faith answered. No one was there.*—Hindu proverb."

The faint glow emanating from Leon's huge blue eyes scared Snow. The principal looked around the room for something to rescue him from the child's eerie stare. He was relieved by the noon bell, accompanied by the smell of macaroni and cheese that wafted through the air vent. It was Wednesday, his favorite food day. The sound of his growling stomach was drowned out by the boisterous children in the hall.

"Leon, you're gifted," Snow said, waving a bulging folder. "According to these aptitude test results you possess a three-level photographic memory, unparalleled conceptual ability, aptitude for *everything* and the emotional profile of a saint. Dr. Lambert at Washington University insists you be brought in for re-evaluation. He even wrote: 'Scores this far off the curve can be random error. However, if results are valid, you have a very rare jewel.'"

Snow sat facing the boy. "Let's explore your gifts together, Leon." Snow was now approaching his diamond-in-the-very-rough, daring to believe the miraculous. "If you could talk in your own words, it would be a great start. I need to know who *you* are." The principal strained to straighten his large frame, but settled for folding his arms onto the platform of his belly.

Leon's little head bobbed peacefully; his eyes still focused on Snow.

The principal was staring down at the stained vinyl floor. He broke the silence, conceding, "Well, if you don't want to communicate there's nothing I can do!" Snow stood and headed for the door.

"*We are different and the same,*" Leon said to Snow's curved back. "*Nurture difference, it leads to diversity; nurture sameness, it leads to understanding*—Principal Snow, June 4th assembly, after racial incident."

Snow stopped. "I said that?" Leon had never quoted him before. It occurred to Principal Snow that the child remembered every word he'd ever spoken in front of him. With quivering appreciation, Snow made contact with Leon's eyes but quickly diverted his gaze to Leon's silky blond hair. *He sees through me*, Snow thought, closing his eyes for a needed pause.

"Starting now," the principal said in a brighter tone, "I'm not going to let your quotes disturb me. I will treat them as your very own words." Snow opened his eyes just in time to see Leon's subtle rocking exaggerate into a gracious bow. Snow seized the offering. "Leon, are you aware of your mental powers?"

Leon responded, "*Do not judge potential by intellect alone. True measure is found within the Will.*—Principal Snow, March 9th assembly, on the occasion of the lowest SAT scores in the school's history."

The memory of those SAT scores still burned in Snow's mind. How would his educational innovations ever be accepted if he couldn't get those scores up? It was especially embarrassing at a school so near the nation's capitol. "I understand," Principal Snow chuckled. "You don't want intelligence emphasized. But you can't avoid your gifts," he added warmly.

"*Listen to me*," Leon insisted in a passionate voice, causing Snow to lunge back.

Listen to me was a pet saying Snow used when he wanted students to take his message into their hearts. Leon had said it, capturing Snow's high voice and inflection perfectly. The educator was spellbound by the boy's impersonation of him.

"*Affecting us as much as our best laid plans are unexpected twists and turns. Life is surprising! It can change right in front of your nose. Enjoy it. Listen to me. Life has a mind of its own, and together we can seek its wisdom.*—Principal Snow, May 3rd assembly, after shooting incident."

"Leon," Snow marveled. "Your physical rendition of me was incredible; you even touched your nose after saying nose, exactly the way I did when—" The principal's jaw dropped open. Leon wasn't impersonating. He was duplicating the past, like a video replay! Snow wasn't certain what "three-level photographic memory" meant, but he was getting an idea and wrote a note, with an exclamation point, to call Dr. Lambert.

"Leon, you seem happy. Your parents have done an excellent job raising you, considering your, uh, emotional state." Snow winced.

Leon's voice was rapturous. "*There is no difficulty that enough love will not conquer; no disease that enough love will not heal; no door that enough love will not open; no gulf that enough love will not bridge; no wall that enough love will not throw down; no sin that enough love will not redeem .... It makes no difference how deeply seated may be the trouble, how hopeless the outlook, how muddled the tangle, how great the mistake. A sufficient realization of love will dissolve it all. If only you could love enough, you would be the happiest and most powerful being in the world.*—Emmet Fox."

Snow had once recited the same passage in an acting class, but not as well as Leon. "I-I-I guess your parents loved you enough."

Leon's nodding transformed into the persona of a mother rocking a child in her arms and crooning: "*Leon, you are the most beautiful baby I could imagine, a perfect infant. Raising you to follow your dreams, that will be my gift to you. I love you more than I ever loved before—and every day I love you more.*"

Leon's intimate portrayal flustered Snow. *He has total recall of early infancy! Maybe the womb! Is that possible? What a scientific resource!* Snow's racing mind halted when Leon stopped rocking.

"*Son*," Leon mimicked, as his body puffed into a male persona, "*the most important thing you can do is keep love alive. Love is not found outside, it's found within, and that is where your search for happiness begins and never ends. Wealth and power are nothing! Love and happiness, these are things worth basing a life upon.*"

With tears in his eyes, Snow swept Leon into a hug—then quickly let go amidst waves of embarrassment. His coarse white hair offset his blushing red face. Leon's spotlight eyes sparkled at him. *This child is secure, just like the test says*, Snow thought. *Problems follow Leon, but he never complains. Leon's heart stays open while the rest of us scurry about in panic. We're the crazy ones*, Snow realized, trying to look into Leon's eyes.

"Your father is wise," Snow said as he took a relaxing breath. "I'll bet he meditates."

Leon beamed and nodded confirmation.

Snow thought about a possible meeting with Leon's parents and chuckled, imagining them to be eccentric geniuses who also spoke in quotes. Then he remembered Leon's disgruntled English teacher. "Leon, let me help you deal more effectively at school. Mrs. Henley was upset when you corrected her in class and wouldn't stop until you'd quoted the entire Shakespearean scene."

Unaffected, Leon advised, "*Sweet are the uses of adversity, which, like the toad, ugly and venomous, wears yet a precious jewel in his head; And this our life, exempt from public haunt, finds tongues in trees, trembling books in the running brook, sermons in stones, and good in everything. I would not change it.*—Shakespeare."

"Wow Leon, your accent is unbelievable!" Snow tried to respond intelligently, adding a touch of British inflection: "Adversity can be our teacher; however, we need not encourage it. Through will, we can take control of a situation."

Snow felt he was doing exactly that when Leon stood up and said in a slight New England drawl, "*A little consideration of what takes place around us every day would show us that a higher law than that of our will regulates events.*—Emerson." Leon ended with a stomp of his foot.

Confusion glazed Snow's face. *Leon's inflection, the brightness in the eyes, the...* Snow grabbed his prized master's thesis, *True Emerson*, and opened to a quote by Oliver Wendell Holmes which described Emerson's speaking style. Snow read it softly, "No one who ever heard him speak will forget the play of his features, the lighting up of his eyes with rapt inner illumination, the emphatic stamp of his foot when some weighty thought required enforcement."

Leon had stamped his foot and his eyes had lit up. My God, Leon is video replaying Ralph Waldo Emerson. How? Could Leon transport himself back in time? Trying to hide the panic in his eyes, Snow bolted from the room.

The boy plucked the thesis off the desktop and turned to the last page where an odd Emerson quote stood glorified: *A chief event of life is the day in which we have encountered a mind that startled us.* With angelic grace, Leon pulled a violet pen from his pocket and wrote below the quote: *No man thoroughly understands a truth until he has contended against it.* Then he signed it—*Ralph Waldo Emerson.*

Principal Snow returned to his office. *That kid must think I'm an idiot for running out. Maybe I am,* he thought with a chuckle. *A child with a photographic memory could have read about Emerson and produced such a portrayal. Leon's gifts are incredible but within the realm of ordinary experience.* Snow walked over to his desk and saw Leon's handwriting on the thesis and collapsed, causing his chin to hit the ragged edge of the desktop as he tumbled to the floor. From his knees, he grabbed the thesis in his shaking hand and looked again. "Impossible!" he gasped. Snow had studied every handwritten Emerson document. Reproductions of Emerson's letters were framed on his living room wall. Nothing could explain how Leon had written in Emerson's own handwriting.

"Gotta be a coincidence," Snow muttered. Then he had a curious realization: The speech that Leon had quoted about IQ was made years before the child attended Lincoln Middle School. With blood dripping from his chin, Snow stormed out of his office.

The ringing telephone startled Josie Ardo as she contemplated the correct feng shui for their new Zen garden. Her thick, reddish-blond hair fell across her bright green eyes as she snatched the phone from the receiver. She answered curtly, "Hello, yes, this is Leon's mother. Oh, oh, yes, can you hold on a moment?" Josie held the receiver and called out, "Aaron, it's Leon's school, Principal Snow. You'd better get on."

"Is Leon all right?"

"Yes, but the principal sounds upset."

"You can handle it," Aaron called from his study as he continued writing.

"The principal wants specifics about Leon's gifts. He wants to know how Leon can write in Emerson's exact handwriting."

"Tell him it's because a dinosaur farted two million years ago."

"I heard that!" Principal Snow yelled into the phone. "I can hear everything."

Josie's voice flattened. "He mentioned Leon's IQ test results."

"Test results!" Aaron lunged for the phone on his desk. "Aaron Ardo speaking."

"Yes, this is Principal Snow, and I heard your remark about the dinosaur fart."

Aaron laughed. "Oh, I meant no disrespect. It's a family joke."

"Why don't you let me in on it?" Snow asked, surprised at his own forwardness.

"Okay, but I should warn you that my views are not popular with educators." Aaron paused and took a breath. "At night, I look at the stars and wonder. . . of all the worlds and dimensions within infinite space, what do I know of them? I don't even know what's happening at my own home, let alone my planet. My God," Aaron proclaimed, "ninety percent of my own mind is off limits to me!"

He continued with soft intensity, "As I make myself small, I say to my ego mind—of all there is to be experienced and known, you know next to nothing. So, shut up!"

Snow laughed, engaged by Aaron's dramatic delivery. Then an overwhelming feeling of déjà vu swept through him.

"Mr. Snow, how many causative factors are converging right now to make this moment possible?" Aaron asked playfully, "How many? How many events have transpired since the beginning of time so we may have this conversation? Of the trillions of events, was one less important than any other?"

"Hmmm, I guess not," the principal admitted.

"So, when Josie asks a 'why' question, I tame my ego by not answering it. It's a complete shift from the ego know-it-all," Aaron said.

"Or he answers, 'Because a dinosaur farted,'" Josie interjected.

Snow chuckled. Josie caught a whiff of manure from the herb garden outside her window and chuckled with him.

"It sounds absurd," Aaron said, "but it's as good an answer as any. The reason Leon talks in quotes is because two million years ago a dinosaur farted, forcing an ape man to another tree where he met an adorable ape woman; they mated and gave birth to Leon's great, great, great. . ."

"I get it," Principal Snow interrupted. "If we believe that our limited perspective is real, we spiral into the illusion of ego mind and move from Truth. We can't know our vastness until we master our smallness."

"Well summarized," Aaron said.

It was, Snow thought, just as his insecurities staged an ambush. *You are a scholar, but it's all in your fat-ass head—ugly fool, loser, faker.* With a shake of his head, Snow abandoned the image of his mother's twisted face and said, "Well, I'm glad that dinosaur farted, because I don't think I'd be here if it hadn't."

Everyone laughed.

The principal continued with mock assurance, "Leon appears to be happy, except for the way he isolates himself with his communication, uh. . .challenge."

"Let me guess," Josie cut in with fire in her voice, "everybody is freaked, but Leon is fine. Right?"

"Exactly." Principal Snow was eager to calm her. "Leon seems secure, and his tests confirm that. I know his upbringing was first class. He shared—I mean, he impersonated your child-rearing styles."

"He did?" both parents exclaimed.

"He's never done that for anyone, not even Saul," Josie said, as if to herself.

Aaron cleared his throat. "My son trusts you. Now I need to." He cleared his throat again and asked, "We want to keep Leon's gifts quiet; could you help us do that? Please."

"I will," Principal Snow promised, unaware of the implications of such a covenant.

Aaron continued, relieved. "Leon acquired an article you wrote about children with special challenges in public school and he wanted to become part of the experiment. He promised he wouldn't do anything too out of the ordinary. We were hesitant, but we felt so resonant with your philosophy that we took a chance. Leon's been sheltered; we hoped he'd make friends, maybe stabilize." Aaron paused, tapping his nose thoughtfully. "Since school started his gifts have evolved more rapidly. Even Josie and I are uncertain what he's capable of." His voice softened as he suggested to Josie, "Maybe we should have kept him home."

"Remember the dinosaur fart," Josie urged in a cute voice. She pushed through her own anxiety to the question that she thought Aaron would ask. "You said Leon took some tests, Mr. Snow. How did he do?"

"Off the charts."

"Darn," Aaron replied, "he knows better. Mr. Snow, is anyone else aware of Leon's scores?"

"Only Washington University."

"Oh boy." Aaron knew of their reputation in educational testing. "They want to see Leon, don't they?"

"Yes, the department head wrote a personal note."

"Did you respond yet?"

"No."

"Mr. Snow," Aaron said brightly, "there are some unusual details we want to share with you, but it's not appropriate on the phone. Could we meet?"

"Absolutely. Can you come to school tomorrow?"

"Come to our house," Josie insisted. "Leon will prepare dinner."

Principal Snow hung up and gazed at a gum stain scuffed into the vinyl floor. It looked like a mountain range. It reminded him of the glorious summer when he'd climbed the Himalayas. *I'm in the adventure now,* he thought. *Hours ago I wanted to strangle Leon; now I'm his crusader. Life is full of surprises.*

Snow's nagging mommy-mind intervened. *Something extraordinary is happening. Hopefully your drinking won't screw it up—fat-ass loser, faker!*

Snow blinked the screaming thoughts away. He was determined to remain strong. His mind drifted beyond linoleum peaks to visions of Leon's mystifying eyes. He tried to visualize them but a quote popped into his mind. It was his sixties motto, one of Kierkegaard's ideas that he hadn't recalled for years. But he remembered it now, realizing that it embodied the ideal attitude to maintain during an adventure. He wrote it on the cover of a new notebook: *Life is a mystery to be lived, not a problem to be solved.*

Losing an illusion makes you wiser...

Principal Snow's old Honda rattled down the dirt road leading to the Ardo's two-thousand-acre Virginia estate. Snow managed to crack open his jammed window allowing him to revel in the canopy of trees and the surrounding scent of cedar. Birds sang as if they felt the same delight. "This is a goddamn paradise," he murmured.

Fifty yards down the bumpy road he saw a sign—*Ardo Family.* He rounded a bend and turned into the home site. Snow shrieked, slamming on the brakes, "Holy shit, it's a flying saucer!" He gawked for several minutes at the huge object nestled among towering hardwoods before realizing it was a circular dome house with eye-shaped windows and a glass roof.

He felt relieved as he made his way along the tree-lined path. The smell of jasmine filled the air as he climbed the steps and noticed the two red front doors. They were adorned with beautiful gold symbols that looked like letters from a lost time—Atlantis maybe. He was studying them when his foot touched the deck and the doors swung open.

"Welcome to Ardo-land or, as some people call it, Weirdo-land," Aaron announced as he greeted Snow with open arms. Aaron was wearing white silk pants and a soft gold shirt in contrast to Snow's cheap polyester suit. Josie was wearing a simple denim dress that made Snow feel less embarrassed about his own clothes.

Snow was taken aback by their appearance. They were around his age, about 50, but they had an unusual ageless quality. Snow's mind raced, *I thought they'd be in their thirties. I thought they'd be poor. I thought...*all of which stopped when they ushered him into a circular room with violet walls arching forty feet to a glass cupola ceiling. Daylight set the enormous room aglow.

"This place is unbelievable," Snow marveled, as his mind flashed to his cramped efficiency apartment. The acoustics of the room added crispness to his voice, and it startled him. He noticed the absence of outside noise. "It's like being in an immense womb. This room is huge, yet I feel contained. I know! It's the interplay of aesthetic opposites." Snow tilted his head, studying the room as he would a work of art. His eyes settled at the room's center where turquoise couches formed a circle around a blue coffee table. The arrangement resembled a big eye looking out through the glass ceiling. "I love how minimal the furnishings are; yet the feeling is homey. The floors are exquisite. Oak?"

"Yep, made from the trees we cleared from this very spot," Aaron said with pride, beaming at his wife.

Snow scanned the room, making a complete turn. "It's so tranquil."

"Curves have that effect." Aaron's brown eyes sparkled as he added proudly, "Josie designed the house."

"The challenges we faced creating a round building in a square world were unbelievable," Josie volunteered.

"Builders like straight lines." Snow chuckled.

"Exactly," Aaron said. "It took her a year to design it and two to build it." Aaron reached for Josie's hand and pulled her close. "She wanted me to have a harmonious place to work. I'd say she out-did herself. She—"

"Enough, Aaron," Josie interjected as she flung her hair off her face, luring Snow with a pretty smile. "Want the grand tour?"

"I'd love it."

Aaron noticed Snow looking at the paintings. "Josie painted them. Wonderful, aren't they?"

Snow nodded, scanning each painting one by one. "I can feel them flowing together; they seem to be telling a story." He was drawn to the central canvas: a mythic goddess reaching into a swirling vortex of purple heavenly light.

"That's her first oil," Aaron said. His thin body seemed to glide towards it. Josie followed him, shaking her head. She didn't want a long speech about this, Aaron's favorite painting in the world. Aaron held back and Snow filled in the silence.

"Everything belongs exactly where it is. Moving anything would be tragic," Snow expressed as he walked around the room as if in a trance.

"The ultimate compliment," Josie acknowledged with a humble bow. Aaron was about to explain, but Josie interrupted, "I used feng shui—the Chinese art of placement. It begins by positioning the house properly on the land—then tremendous care is given to the layout of space and furnishings. If everything is aligned, a tangible feeling of well-being prevails."

"I sure feel it," Snow agreed, returning the bow. "I even smell it."

"Aromatherapy." Josie pointed to a small atomizer. "Lavender is intensely soothing," she said in a dreamy voice.

Aaron escorted Snow to the back of the huge room which flowed into a corridor of doors. "My office is first," Aaron said, opening the door to reveal a burgundy Persian rug, a majestic oak desk, and glass doors that led to a wooded garden. The bright room was lined with built-in bookcases.

"What do you do?" Snow inquired, scanning the vast library for a hint.

"I'm writing short stories right now."

Snow read a plaque on the wall—*Sterling Ardo, Positive Pursuits, National Book Award.* His face flushed. "You're *the* Sterling Ardo? I thought your name was Aaron—pen name, right? Oh, wow! Oh, wow—oh, I already said that." Snow nervously flailed his hands. "I gotta tell you, *Positive Pursuits* changed my life. It's the core of my educational philosophy." Snow shook his finger at Aaron and said in a squeaky voice. "That's why you were attracted to my program. They're *your* ideas! I stole them!"

Aaron laughed.

"It's true," Snow insisted. "I run a Positive Pursuits group at school. It's transformed my educational philosophy. It's the hope of my life, and the kids love it beyond words. Goddamn!"

Snow couldn't shake the shock of being with one of his few intellectual heroes, let alone with a celebrity notorious for seclusion. He cleared his throat to avoid the squeak that always came on when he was overly excited. "I loved the way you used an improvisational acting troupe as a metaphor for what our civilization might become. More than anything, I love the way you always provide specific solutions as you peck away at social problems. And the movie, *You're a Genius, Stupid,* was wonderful—the first film in history to come with an instructional pamphlet. I heard on

CNN that thousands of theater groups started because of it." Snow took a deep breath, then sang out in a rich baritone, "*Now that I found you, distant stars are exploding into dreams come true.*" He looked at Aaron. "You wrote that song, didn't you? *Positive Pursuits* was my favorite TV show ever. It was the first Positive Reality Show, wasn't it? Aaron, the whole concept was so innovative. Oh, sorry. I'm rambling!" He was also squeaking again. Snow bit his bottom lip to squelch embarrassment.

"Continue!" Aaron bowed graciously. "I don't get much attention these days."

Snow reached in his breast pocket for a cigarette although he'd quit smoking ten years before. He remained fidgety with excitement as the trio explored rooms active with purpose, each opening to a serene wooded park. At the end of the corridor Snow's excitement yielded to caution, reflecting a similar change in the Ardos.

"This is the forbidden zone," Aaron stated.

Josie opened the door to Leon's room. Aaron peeked in, then led Snow over the threshold.

"What the ding-dang-doodle?" Snow asked, blinking at a mayhem of futuristic looking devices that were flashing, beeping, and humming. "This looks like the set of a science fiction movie."

Lining the walls were portraits of extraterrestrials, each with a face that looked holy, as if these were the shamans of their planets. "I'll bet Josie didn't paint *that*," he asserted, looking at the image of a lizard-faced alien priest. Snow stood in amazement as he looked around the room filled with crystal artifacts and odd colored stones. "Where did you get all this?" Snow asked.

"We didn't," they answered simultaneously.

"We wake up every morning and poof, there are new objects in Leon's room," Josie explained. "We have no idea where he gets them or what they are."

"The mechanical objects," Aaron pointed out, "began appearing after Leon started school."

Snow was attracted to a sphere resting on a metallic base. It looked like a magic crystal ball.

"Touch it," Aaron dared.

"Oh, I've seen things like this," Snow remarked, stepping back.

"No you haven't!" Aaron insisted, urging Snow forward with a boyish nudge.

Carefully, the principal placed his hands above the globe. It immediately responded with a golden glow. "It feels buoyant; it's pulling my fingers toward it." Ever so gently his fingers touched the surface. "It's hot." A rush swept through him like a drug high. He pulled his hands back.

"It's safe," Aaron assured him. "Leon plays with it."

"I've seen enough," Snow said. He wanted to leave the forbidden zone. Its madhouse of objects had shocked him back to his purpose. "Tell me, does Leon talk in quotes when he's home?" Snow asked, stepping back into the hall.

Josie nodded. "Occasionally he speaks without quoting, but never more than a remark."

"In a way there is no Leon, because he has no formal ego structure," Aaron confided, tapping his nose as Josie nodded her agreement.

Scalding puzzlement produced a profuse sweat; Snow reached for his hanky just as the sound of a gong rumbled through the intercom. Leon announced, "*Le diner est servi dans la salle principale.*"

"Ooolaalaa, we're dining *au Français,*" Josie declared in a flirtatious French accent. She grabbed Snow's shaky arm and escorted him to the second floor balcony above the rooms they had just explored. A dining area and open kitchen sprawled beneath the clear glass roof. The stars were becoming visible and Snow could see a crescent moon with a bright star at each tip. Josie directed him to the seat with the best moon view. Dining indoors beneath a celestial wonder contributed to Snow's already surreal mood.

Three elaborate settings adorned a rustic wood table. Josie sat at the head, while Aaron and Snow faced each other on each side. As Snow put the cloth napkin on his lap, he noticed that its white on white design was a crescent moon with a star at each tip. "Far out," he whispered, fantasizing that Leon had arranged the stars to coordinate with the linen. He was going to ask about that coincidence when he noticed there were only three place settings. "Isn't Leon joining us?"

Josie looked at Aaron, who nodded permission. "Leon doesn't eat. There are documented cases of breatharians, people who do not require food. I did research." Josie caught herself being defensive and softened. "Leon doesn't eat, but he's quite a cook. In fact, he's planned a dessert performance in your honor."

Before Snow could ask what a dessert performance was, Leon appeared in medieval attire carrying the main course. The platter held a crepe soaked in a red sauce, surrounded by vegetables and turquoise edible flowers. A wonderful fragrance, like a night blooming Eden, filled the room. Snow started salivating. He swallowed.

Josie and Aaron closed their eyes and started breathing deeply.

Following their lead, Snow closed his eyes. *Oh God, I hope they don't do a ten minute grace ritual,* Snow thought, peeking. After five aroma-filled breaths, the Ardos plunged into the intoxicating flavors and colors. Snow was so enthralled by the minty, rose sauce and crunchy texture that he overlooked his need to know what he was eating (mostly tofu, nuts, aromatic herbs, and flowers). He didn't know that the food preparation was a mystery so profound even a dinosaur fart couldn't explain it.

After several minutes of silence broken by occasional moans of pleasure, conversation ensued. The threesome talked about the lack of good restaurants and their mutual love for experimental theater. A warm liking developed as Leon watched joyfully. No one saw him put on the wizard's cap and black robe.

Suddenly, Leon wheeled in a cart filled with lit candles and a stone bowl surrounded by thirteen containers. He clapped his hands and the house lights went off. As their eyes grew accustomed to the candlelight, gold lines on Leon's robe came alive and he made dramatic movements to accentuate them. The dance ended with his hands wrapped around a squeeze container.

As he raised it above his head and squirted its contents into the center bowl, wispy strands of pastel smoke wafted up. He took a different colored powder in each hand and sprinkled them above the bowl; twinkling lights exploded as the powders drifted down and coalesced. Next, he flung in what looked like glittering crystal candies: streaks of rainbow light flashed. The light show intensified along with Leon's dramatic movements.

Leon probably grew up in Aaron's improv classes. That explains his creativity and physicality, Snow surmised.

Abruptly, Leon froze. He focused his laser eyes on the last container. All three adults held their breath. Slowly, he lifted the gold creamer and poured a clear syrup that sizzled the instant it touched the other ingredients. Red smoke rose from the bowl and began to swirl like a tornado. When the swirling smoke coalesced into a throbbing red heart, Leon lit a match and touched it to the surface of the dessert. Flames shot up. Heat swept across the room.

Snow gasped.

Leon leaned into the blaze. Wild flames wrapped around his face, creating a heart-shaped halo of fire above his head. He smiled angelically and stated in a thick French accent, "*Heart's Delight* is the name of this dessert; you want it 'hot' I presume."

As the fire subsided, the tenderness that remained on Leon's face was more amazing than the fact that his skin was not burned. *It's true,* Snow thought, watching the after-glow rise from the bowl, *there is no Leon, no ego.*

There is nothing to burn. "Can I talk to Leon about this?" the principal asked, pointing at the dessert placed before him that resembled a lumpy, vanilla swirled, chocolate custard.

"Not really," Josie replied. "For Leon, the ceremony is over."

"When you're not past or future oriented, you have profound energy to channel into the present," Aaron explained. "It's how Leon functions. For him, time is the center of a circle, not a straight line; he focuses right at the center, which means all temporal possibilities are available within a multi-dimensional moment."

Josie suggested, "What works with Leon is being present within your feelings. Let me show you." Josie smiled broadly, pulled her chair out from the table and braced herself. "Leon, honey, Mama is feeling a love burst."

Leon ran across the room and leaped into Josie's arms, nestling like a contented infant. She stroked and kissed his head. "You are such a perfect child. I love you more than I ever did before." Josie was totally present and Leon received her hugs and kisses as if they were all of Creation.

My mother never showed love, Snow thought, as an image of her brooding face appeared. A tear fell from his left eye landing beside his dessert. He shook his head, then chuckled at the sight of a red heart radiating above the bowl. He snatched a taste and groaned with delight. The Ardos turned and laughed as Snow licked his pinky and pointed to the heart holograms above each plate.

Josie and Aaron tasted the dessert and moaned expressively which brought on more laughter.

"Leon strikes again," Aaron boasted as he wielded his glass into a toast.

Following his lead, they all acclaimed, "Leon strikes again!"

Leon began laughing with complete abandon. For an instant, he seemed like a normal boy. He even took a bit of dessert and placed it on his tongue.

With his stomach aching from laughter and food, Snow bellowed from a full mouth, "What is this stuff?" Then he started singing to the melody of *God Bless America.* "God bless the dinosaurs/they once roamed free. If one hadn't farted/we'd be parted/and perhaps there wouldn't be dessert for me."

After hearty applause, Josie and Aaron joined in, making up verses beginning with "God bless the dinosaurs."

"This feels like a Positive Pursuits improv," Snow commented. Josie and Aaron agreed as they plunged into the crunchy nut custard, a perfect blend of bitter and sweet. With each delicious bite, the hologram heart above each plate faded. When the last bite was taken, it was entirely gone.

"Aaron is thin, and I'm, well—almost thin," Josie said, rubbing her bulging tummy. "This dessert is eighty calories and it's healthy. The entire meal was organic, low in fat, and high in fiber and protein. Leon is a vegan cook; everything is from plants. No animals are harmed or inconvenienced around here," she said proudly.

After a freewheeling conversation in which Snow confessed his macaroni and cheese addiction, the principal turned the talk back to Leon. "I'd like your advice on deepening my relationship with your son."

"You don't need it," Aaron encouraged with a mad-scientist glint. "Improvise!"

The principal slumped. He wanted to be mentored by his hero, at least a little.

Aaron conceded. "Okay. You've read *Positive Pursuits* so I can use the jargon. You know I believe in Soft Control."

Snow nodded. Soft Control was a core idea in *Positive Pursuits*, and Snow was very familiar with it.

Aaron continued. "Remember the scene when Ken Kenton talks with the president of the United States about Soft Control? Kenton says, 'Control is a drug; you always want more.' Then he looks into the president's eyes and says, 'You're drunk with power now—tomorrow comes the hangover!'"

Snow nodded enthusiastically; he loved that part.

"I feel it's best not to influence you right now, but since you want my advice—"

Snow straightened his posture and gave Aaron his full attention.

"Let go and be yourself, like when you're leading a Positive Pursuits improv class. Get into the flow with Leon; it's easy because he has no mental or emotional baggage. Just get out of your head," Aaron urged with a wink and a rap dance step. "When you're in the know, just go with the flow."

"Let's give them some time alone," Josie suggested, grabbing Aaron's arm and pulling him down the stairs to the huge main room.

While waiting for the right moment to approach Leon, Snow became enthralled by how the squares in his cut-crystal water glass captured the moonlight, and he slowly turned the tumbler creating a moving universe of twinkles. He looked up from the play of light to see Leon's huge eyes staring back.

This kid never stops looking; it's like he's recording everything. Snow recalled the strange portraits hanging on the child's wall and thought, *Maybe Leon is an ET spy, and his eyes are cameras connecting to the leaders of distant planets. My God, I'm being broadcast intergalactically!* When the principal's mind calmed, Leon moved within reach and Snow impulsively pulled him into a hug. The child melted into Snow as he had with Josie a moment ago. The intimacy flustered Snow. He pushed Leon away and the boy left as easily as he'd come.

(Earlier in the day Snow had been playing a favorite game: he would open a book to a random page, then read whatever his eye fell upon. He'd learned the technique from a psychic who believed the first words you see are a prophetic message, not an accident. Snow had opened his favorite meditation book, Ram Dass' *Journey of Awakening*, and noticed a quote. It was perfect for this moment.) He began reciting it to Leon with the skill of a Shakespearean actor: "*I had heard about a superior type of man, possessing the keys to everything which is a mystery to us. This idea of a higher and unknown strain within the human race was not something I could take simply as an allegory. Experience has proved, I told myself, that a man cannot reach truth directly, nor all by himself. An intermediary has to be present, a force still human in certain respects yet transcending humanity in others. Somewhere on Earth this superior form of humanity must exist, and not utterly out of our reach. In that case shouldn't all my efforts be directed toward discovering it?*—Rene Daumal."

After bowing to acknowledge that he understood, Leon gracefully raised his arms indicating something special in response.

Snow watched intently.

Leon searched his corduroy pants pockets frantically, exaggerating his movements like a mime. The child's face expressed profound relief when he found what he was looking for and reverently raised it into the air.

Snow gulped. He saw a key made of golden light—its triangular top held purple gems forming a mysterious letter like those on the red front doors of the dome. Leon waved the mysterious key over an imaginary object on the ground, indicating its boundaries with his hands. Deliberately, he inserted the key into the invisible treasure chest.

Lunging for his notebook, Snow wrote at the top of the page, *Key of Light.*

Leon turned the key and slowly opened the chest. The child glowed at the sight of its contents, then flung the key which disappeared into thin air as he called out, "*Losing an illusion makes you wiser than finding a truth.*—Ludwig Borne."

The quote struck Snow at his core, even overshadowing the disappearing key effect. He repeated the words to himself. "*Losing an illusion makes you wiser than finding a truth.*" Finally, he asked, "What illusion must I lose?"

"*It's all illusion!*" Leon stated, then quoted from his father's book: "*To know Reality and find your Soul, you must let go of yourself bit by bit until there is nothing left. Release feelings, desires, and beliefs. This will make you so light you'll float away, taking nothing but Truth. Truth and God are the same, and they await at your core, at your all-seeing eye.*—Sterling Ardo." Leon's index finger traced a circle in the air while his other hand drew an eye within the circle's center. Snow was looking right into it as Leon said, "*The eye with which I see God is the same eye with which God sees me.*—Meister Eckhart."

Leon had strung three quotes together to express a deep truth, and Snow responded with sincere humility, "I should be *your* student."

The child became very still; his eyeballs disappeared behind half-closed lids as his face settled into a motionless peace. Communication was over.

Always avoiding Leon's stare, this was the first time Snow had actually looked at Leon directly. He allowed himself the moment. The child's skin was like fine porcelain, and Snow realized this beauty grew out of an absence of stress. Snow even saw a faint halo around the child—or was it the moonlight? *You're a grown man! Why are you letting this child control you like he's a fairy godmother? You're the teacher. Take control,* his mother's voice screamed inside his head.

Snow slumped down the stairs and was again taken by the immensity of the main room where Aaron and Josie awaited him. He flopped onto the adjacent couch, encountering a surface harder than anticipated; Aaron and Josie laughed as he adjusted his body using comical gestures.

Aaron continued talking about his lower back problems and proper furniture design before the conversation turned to Snow's experience with Leon. Snow described details, adding personal observations and hope as the couple listened with extraordinary intensity. Snow stopped his monologue when he noticed that an hour had evaporated.

Without conferring with Josie, Aaron proposed, "We want you to continue working with Leon, but I think he should stop attending school for a while. You can work with him here."

"I'll announce his suspension on grounds of emotional instability. Everybody will believe that," Snow offered. "I'll call Dr. Lambert and tell him the test results were a fluke and that Leon is schizophrenic."

This proposal got an enthusiastic response from the couple—anything to keep Leon out of the spotlight.

Snow's mind raced with things to do to cover Leon's trail. "I'll call tomorrow morning at eleven to let you know how my conversation with

Dr. Lambert goes." Snow agreed to return the next day to work with Leon. "It will be about dinnertime, but no dessert performance is necessary." Everyone laughed.

They paused at the front door where a large mirror hung, enabling Snow to see himself giving Josie a back-rubbing hug. "Holy shit!" he shrieked, pushing her away. Josie stumbled into Aaron's arms, leaving one of the best hugs she'd ever received.

"My hands," Snow said, staring at them, "they're gone!" His hands were trembling. "The liver spots—the spots on the back of my hands are gone. I've had them for twenty years. Just today, I noticed how ugly they were getting. I wore this dark shirt to hide them. But now they're gone. They're completely gone!"

The "liver spot miracle" was attributed to the globe Snow had touched in the forbidden zone. However, it was finally decided on a comradely note, that the *real* reason was a dinosaur fart.

Snow felt like he was floating as he walked down the steps into the outdoor paradise. He strolled beside towering trees, pinching himself—his muscle tone felt firmer, which was confirmed when he pulled open his dented car door with ease.

The instant his body collapsed into the car seat, Snow let forth a gas eruption and in the midst of its sustained chorus he was unable to roll down the stuck window. He began to laugh. As he opened and closed the car door, Snow pondered the importance of his smelly fart and how it might influence the future of humankind. A quote popped into his mind, one he loved dearly. He recited it in rhythm with the fanning door. "*To see a World in a Grain of Sand, And a Heaven in a Wild Flower, Hold Infinity in the palm of your hand, And Eternity in an hour.*" He added a line of his own. "To hear the beat of every human heart, resound within the echo of a single fart."

His laughter rocked with the car as he navigated the bumpy dirt road. By the time Snow reached the pavement, his mind had reviewed the evening, particularly his talk with Leon. Fearful he'd forget the child's extraordinary message, he tried to create a concise summary. He skidded to the shoulder of the deserted road, turned to the page in his notebook where he'd written *Key of Light*, and began writing. The words flowed effortlessly.

First Key of Light: Undoing Exceeds Doing. "Losing an illusion makes you wiser than finding a truth."—Ludwig Borne. You can find God and Truth if you are willing to lose the illusion of your lower self. Let go of beliefs, desires, and feelings and God's attributes await. They are Love, Peace, and Joy. They are Truth; they are the fiber of your Soul and exist at your core. Dissolve the illusion that it's your eyes seeing, and you will find the inner-eye with which you can see God. Then you will see God looking back saying, Undoing Exceeds Doing.

The writing flowed on. His autopilot mind recalled the *ga ga* stage with his wife—insane love had cleansed his ego. He relived his first improv class, how it had ended with everyone entwined on the floor in a laughing, ego-less heap. The lessening of lower ego mind, "the losing of an illusion," marked both of his peak experiences!

Confirming Leon's wisdom brought him within reach of the magic, and with a defiant stroke, he wrote: *Lose your lower self, find your higher Self waiting naked.—Walter Leonardo Snow.*

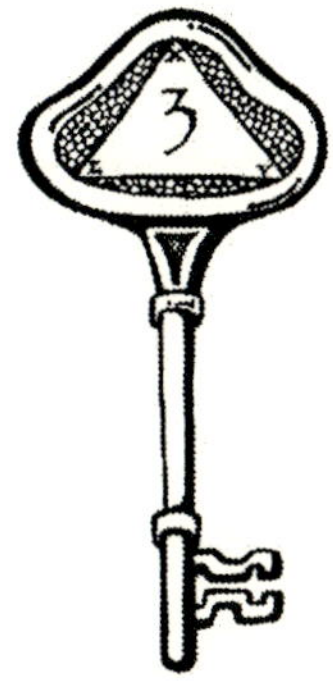

The secret to a healthy relationship is...

Josie was sitting under the cupola flipping through a decorating magazine when Saul, their gardener, knocked on the door.

"Saul, you stink worse than a gym locker in a barn," Josie said, holding her nose and grimacing.

"You'd stink if you'd been picking peppers in the worst heat wave in friggin' history." Saul was wearing disheveled jeans and no shirt. His ribs stuck out like peas bulging from a dirty, bruised pod. "Is the dude ready?" he slurred.

"Leon, honey, Saul is here," Josie called out.

Leon slid down the banister into Saul's smelly armpits, ending with a secret dance of fingers and a high five.

"Okay dude, today we dig," Saul said to Leon who was bouncing up and down like a jack-in-the-box. Saul continued his monologue as they walked outside. "I'm going to put a pond outside your room to balance the weirrrrd energy back there." Leon skipped to keep up with his only friend. Saul, a forty-year-old hippie gardener, was so whacked out from past psychedelic use that he didn't find Leon's behavior all that odd. They were a team founded upon a perfect premise: Saul did the talking, and he could talk for days about peppers alone.

"You know how much money there is in peppers? Wow! When I say pepper, you think green, right? Well, red peppers are where the money is. Did you know a red pepper is just a green pepper in disguise?" Saul and Leon laughed. "Ever eat a hot pepper?" Saul pulled one from his pocket and waved it in front of Leon's face. "Suck on this and you'll go innnnn orrrrrrbit!" He flung the limp pepper at Leon, who pounced on it. Saul grabbed Leon and amidst hysterical laughter, wrestled the pepper from the child's hand. "May the force be with you, dude," Saul exclaimed, waving the injured pepper triumphantly. Josie chuckled, feeling thankful that Leon could enjoy something so normal.

Once the boys outside quieted down, Josie could hear the faint sound of baroque music from Aaron's office. She tiptoed into his room where he was writing at the computer in his usual trance state. Josie admired his power of concentration as she leaned down and kissed his faint bald spot.

"Hi, honey," Aaron said, barely moving his lips.

"Hi, Aaronsky." She kissed him again while she peered over his shoulder and read the beginning of his magazine article entitled, *Secret To a Healthy Relationship*: "Because Josie and I are in the public, we are asked how we maintain such a successful relationship. I answer by recounting the endless therapy we both had before we met. Then I summarize with my motto: 'The secret to a healthy relationship is two healthy people.'" Josie laughed and gave him a huge kiss on the cheek and said, "I love it."

"Thanks, and I love you."

"I love you too and you know I seldom bother you when you're working, but I need to show you something." She dragged him to the window and asked, "What do you see?"

"Saul and Leon digging a hole," he responded.

"Yes, but what do you see with your heart?"

Aaron was not in the mood for guessing games so he countered, "Honey, what do you want me to see?"

"When Leon is gardening with Saul, he seems like an ordinary kid. I think it's good for him," she confirmed.

"You're right, it's grounding. Let's have Saul come every day. We want a bigger veggie garden—ooh, organic beans, kale, and ooh, fruit trees. Yuuuummy. Maybe farming will bring Leon down to Earth," Aaron said with a wry smile. "Saul!" Aaron shouted from the open window as he rubbed Josie's favorite spot on her back, "talk to Josie before you leave. We have a proposition that will get you out of picking peppers at Peter's."

Saul laughed and went back to work. He and Leon were *in the groove*, and Saul made this known when he confirmed, "If you can't work *in the groove*, it ain't worth doing." Josie and Aaron nodded in agreement, then returned to their respective passions.

Hours passed like a perfect breath.

Josie was startled from her concentration when Saul called out from the doorway, "This job is bigger than I thought. I'll need a week. I'm going with a cement pond, not a plastic liner." Josie seized the opportunity and shared her proposal.

"I get to see little dude every day? WOW," Saul howled, giving Leon a hug and kiss. "We'll plant a pepper patch and split the profits. You know, pepper farming is very—"

"Principal Snow hasn't called," Aaron interrupted. "He said he'd call at eleven; he was definite." Aaron looked at his watch. "It's past two."

"You know how things come up at schools," Josie reminded him.

Aaron agreed just as the telephone rang. He was certain it was the principal. "Hello, Mr. Snow."

"Funny you'd say that," a bookish voice replied suspiciously. "This is Mrs. Larsen, Principal Snow's secretary. Mr. Snow didn't show up at school today, and apparently, he didn't make it home last night. I'm calling you because the police are looking for him and—"

"Police?" Aaron interrupted.

"Yes, they found his car abandoned on a dirt road outside of town. I believe it was near where you live. The police suspect foul play," Mrs. Larsen said nervously.

"He was here last night," Aaron confirmed, "and left about ten. Everything was fine. He wasn't drinking alcohol."

Aaron listened intently before he hung up and explained.

Leon answered, "*Be more prompt to go to a friend in adversity than in prosperity.*—Chilo."

Aaron countered, "We can't go searching for Snow, we could get—"

"*The shortest answer is doing.*—Herbert," Leon said, challenging Aaron.

"Okay, okay," Aaron conceded looking at Josie. "I'll take Saul and Leon."

"You're staying here by the phone," Josie commanded. "I'm going. I know exactly what to do!"

As Josie made for the door, Aaron grabbed her arm. "Why can't I go? I prefer—"

"*The Great Way is not difficult for those who have no preferences.*—Third Zen Patriarch," Leon said to Aaron.

"Tell that to her," Aaron protested.

Like an actor setting up the next shot, Leon turned to Josie.

Her answer ended the debate. "Zelia told me to go."

"Zelia!" Aaron said. "Zelia is back?"

"Fairies come in times of need," Josie said emphatically as she walked to the door holding Leon's hand. "Stay by the phone. I'll keep you posted. Don't worry, I've got a secret weapon called Leon," Josie said, hugging the child. "Saul, are you coming?"

"You betcha."

Aaron returned to his office, dropped his face into his hands, and laughed. "Zelia is back! What timing!"

Leon sat in the back seat, leaning forward so his hands could rest on his mother's shoulders. When he squeezed her right shoulder, it meant take the next right turn; left meant left. This family game always ended in treasures, like waterfalls by a river lined with wildflowers. Bottom line: Leon could find things.

Saul was riding shotgun, unaware that Leon was directing. To Saul, Leon was just a "weird little dude" who listened and laughed. "Now, if we sell hot peppers directly to Mexican restaurants, we can make a killing," Saul explained, just when Leon released both hands from Josie's shoulders. Saul braced himself as the car stopped in front of an out-of-place brick warehouse on the west edge of D.C., a mile from the Maryland border.

"This was where Zelia told me to look," Josie fibbed to Saul.

Josie parked the car out of sight. The foursome inched their way along the side of the building, stopping outside the warehouse door. They assessed the situation and decided that Leon should go first and open the door. He entered the warehouse and motioned for the group to join him. When they heard muffled voices, they followed the sounds, dashing around boxes like cartoon characters. They hid and listened.

"My name is Walter Snow," they heard. "I'm the principal of Lincoln Middle School, and I do NOT know anything about the Ardo family. I just met them today—I mean yesterday. I went to their house to inform them that their son was being suspended from school."

"Why would you go to their house on a school matter?"

"Because they invited me, thinking it might benefit their son in some way. I told you, I don't know anything," Snow implored. "Leon has attended school less than a semester. He's schizophrenic. He's a very disturbed child."

"Did you see anything unusual at their residence?" the CIA agent probed. "Anything threatening?"

"I think you're the threat." Snow's face fell into his hands. He laughed to himself—he was obstructing justice which could mean imprisonment. Anchored in visions of Leon's glow, he continued the improvisation of his life. "Who are YOU?" Snow railed. "I want to know who the hell you are," he yelled as he slammed his fist down on a dirty tabletop.

"Do you think Leon is a threat?" the agent repeated.

"Oh yes, he's a big threat. Now that you have Leon, and all the other eleven-year-olds plotting world domination, I'll be able to sleep nights, which is exactly what I'm going to do. If you want to charge me, do it—or else I'm going home to bed." Snow stood up and headed for the door.

"You've been watching too many detective shows," the agent said as he blocked the way. Snow persisted and the agent pushed him back. Snow charged the door but was met with a solid blow to the gut. He doubled over, moaning, "I don't know anything; I'm a school principal. I just want to go home!"

Josie smelled moldy dust and felt grit on her hands. After her ninety-year-old Aunt Helen had died, Josie had gone through old boxes that held the same insidious smell, and she'd been sick for months. She fought a sneeze as they reached the enclosed office. All three peeked in before dropping to the floor.

Snow looked terrible: his bruised face was swollen with rage. Josie urged Leon forward and whispered to Saul, "Leon has a knock-out injection." She toyed with another sneeze just as Leon crawled behind the agent's chair.

The child raised his small hand into the man's energy field and made a clockwise circle with his forefinger.

"Wow," Saul responded, when he saw the agent slump over. "That must be groovy stuff."

Snow was stupefied! A minute ago he was being assaulted; now the agent was unconscious with Leon standing behind him smiling. The principal captured a glimpse of the child's radiant eyes.

"Principal Snow, are you alright?" Josie blurted out as she stepped into the room. "You look so much better than you did a moment ago—in fact, you look great."

"I feel great!" Snow winked, then acknowledged, "I'm an actor!"

Josie smiled appreciatively, guessing what he'd been through. "I've got a bad feeling about this situation. Let's get out of here right now."

"Leave?" Snow questioned, as he pointed to the agent. "This is the CIA."

Leon shook his head.

"They are not CIA agents, Principal Snow," Josie interpreted.

"Leon's word is good enough for me," Snow affirmed, as he stroked the boy's head gently. "By the way, my name is Walter; my friends call me Walt."

"Okay, Walt, let's go," Josie commanded. The four scampered like mice from box to box until they reached the exit. With a hand gesture Leon cautioned them to hide flat against the wall. Josie held her dripping nose as two thugs, definitely not CIA agents, headed for the back of the warehouse. The team escaped easily.

After a sneezing fit and several deep breaths of fresh air, Josie speed-dialed Aaron from the car. "Hi, honey," she sniffled.

"Who's this?" a stranger answered. Josie hung up.

Saul then called his girlfriend Duffy who lived with him in a secluded guesthouse at the back of the Ardo property. "The cops are everywhere," Duffy reported. "Aaron's been arrested—something to do with objects found at the dome."

"Wow, we'd better go to my place," Saul advised. The huge Ardo estate had a hidden road on the north side that led to Saul and Duffy's house. "No one will look for us so close to home," he maintained.

Leon agreed with Saul's plan but remained alert during the forty-minute trek.

When they arrived, Duffy had to know everything. The five talked for hours until, one by one, they fell asleep where they sat. Everyone had an unexpectedly deep slumber, even Walt Snow who at first couldn't let go of questions. *What were those strange objects in Leon's room? How did my liver spots disappear? How did Leon find me and subdue the so-called agent? What if Leon is an ET*, Snow seriously wondered as he drifted towards sleep. Shivers rippled up his neck as a smile crossed his face and he whispered, "If ever there was a time to have faith in life, this is it!" *Another Walter Leonardo Snow quote*, he thought, repeating it to himself like a mantra as he fell into a blissful dream about a blue healing stream.

Night wrapped a thick blanket around the hideout. Only the owl saw sparks shooting through the roof above the spot where Leon rested.

"Whooo! Whooo!" the owl cried when the sparks turned to bolts of light.

"Very-derry true, the question is Who?" Zelia replied as she swirled through the trees before disappearing into the night.

"Whooo! Whooo!"

Rise into the frequency of miracles...

It looked like he was sleeping, but Leon never slept. He journeyed. He'd lie in bed naked with the windows open and feel the breeze whisper across his body while listening to the buzzing night symphony. Totally present, Leon would turn inward and watch the dancing blackness behind his closed eyelids. Playfully, the blackness would turn into colors, then to an image of himself standing beside a raging river. When he could feel the moisture and hear the rumble of rushing water, a canoe would appear in his imagination, moving rapidly down the tangled stream. As the boat approached, Leon could see himself in it, and at that moment of recognition—it was so!

The currents were unpredictable, but he always managed to arrive at the magic mountain downriver. Once docked beside the heavenly peak, a unique way to the top always presented itself. Today, he simply sprouted wings and flew.

*****

Archangel Modeen halted transmission. "My part in this adventure begins now. It's small at first, but it shall expand as the drama intensifies."

The passion in his voice caused the spellbound Angels to rustle. Dimron remained motionless. "All you need to know is that I am Mo, the gatekeeper." The Archangel emitted a spontaneous surge of love before resuming transmission. The spiral implants altered their spins, enabling the Angels to double their awareness.

*****

Leon landed beside Mo. Although the child loved talking with him, today Leon headed directly for the magic portal.

"May your journey be bright," Mo heralded, as he transmitted an important insight, which Leon was not aware of receiving. It would wait in his unconscious until the perfect moment to surface. Mo offered a hint, "Remember, If something *outside* of you is bothering you, the problem is *inside* of you."

Leon nodded, then stepped into the pulsating gateway of swirling thick energy. His form revolved slowly to the right, gradually turning white. After twenty-one revolutions, a black mirror image of Leon appeared, spinning in the opposite direction. The two Leons increased speed until they were a blur of black and white spiral lines dancing at light speed. In a flash, they seared into a single DNA-like unit and disappeared. Leon's lifeless torso reappeared, suspended in the gateway.

His light-body ascended into a blue haze. Dark fragments along his aura's edge, where thoughts and emotions gripped, dissolved into trails of colorful lights. When the fireworks ceased and he felt empty and at peace, he was ready to *Soul Journey*.

On Earth, seekers travel to caves atop remote mountain ranges in search of enlightened teachers. Leon's Soul had completed those searches by the time he was six. From distant stars to dimensions veiled in darkness, Leon had pursued avatars. Today he wanted the advice of a non-breather because they had creative flare. Leon knew the Orvonton superuniverse had the greatest concentration of non-breathers anywhere.

Leaning his thoughts in that direction, Leon's consciousness caused a shift in his energy field; like a strobe light, his aura changed from red to blue, then white lightning, ending in blackness. It was within that instant of blackness that Leon could sense an endless stream of connection to everything. That feeling of oneness enabled him to warp time and space. Immediately, he encountered a great teacher.

"May the light of Spirit wash you," Ommatrin of Orvonton, the non-breather, greeted him as their energy fields met creating an ecstatic exchange.

To Leon's delight, Ommatrin assumed the form of a massive winged angel.

"What should I do?" Leon asked.

"Hmmm, do?" Ommatrin questioned. "You think you can 'do' better than the Almighty All?"

"Can I get the Almighty to do it for me?"

Ommatrin flapped his huge wings and laughed before responding. His answer did not make sense at first. "The more God-realized a life-form is, the less it affects the physical world it inhabits. That means technological cultures tend to be less enlightened than primitive ones, contrary to human belief. Dolphins and whales gave up manipulating matter millions of years ago. Do you know why, Dear One?"

Leon remained silent.

"Their consciousness expanded beyond form. Technology marries you to form. The moment you build a fire to keep warm, you unconsciously say, 'I need an external aid to control my body temperature.' You relinquish the power of consciousness for the power of technology. Dolphins communicate across Earth without a telephone. A few great ones can even transport themselves to other planets without a mechanical ship.

"These feats are unimaginable to humans because they use so little of their brainpower. Some dolphins and whales use all of both brain hemispheres. Manipulating form has many benefits, but it has caused the human brain to close to the frequency of miracles. We perceive these sea dwellers as inferior because they, like yogis in a cave, leave no physical evidence of their greatness."

"If they are so smart, why are so many killed by man?" Leon questioned.

"Do you know the great one, Jesus?" Ommatrin asked.

"Oh, yes," Leon resounded. "We are very close."

"He was killed by man!" Ommatrin emitted a soothing Om. "Have you communed with him about why he allowed the crucifixion when he could have averted it easily? In part, it was because Jesus respected the flow of life so much that he would not disturb it even to avert his own death. Rather than manipulate the world, he surrendered to it like a leaf in the wind.

"Scores of celestial beings from all seven superuniverses watched his crucifixion." Ommatrin flapped majestically. "I know a Midwayer who witnessed Jesus' end, and this is what she told me as documented in Earth's Urantia Book." Ommatrin assumed the form of the Midwayer—a half-human, half-angel.

He imitated her rolling tones perfectly. "*As Jesus saw his mother, with John and his brother and sister, he smiled but said nothing. Meanwhile the four soldiers assigned to the Master's crucifixion, as was the custom, had divided his clothes among them, one taking the sandals, one the turban, one the girdle, and the fourth the cloak. This left the tunic, or seamless vestment reaching down to near the knees, to be cut up into four pieces, but when the soldiers saw what an unusual garment it was, they decided to cast lots for it. Jesus looked down on them while they divided his garments, and the thoughtless crowd jeered at him.*

"It was well that the Roman soldiers took possession of the Master's clothing. Otherwise, if his followers had gained possession of these garments, they would have been tempted to resort to superstitious relic worship. The Master desired that his followers should have nothing material to associate with his life on Earth."

Ommatrin concluded, "Touch lightly. Avoid controlling life. Instead, channel all your resources into each arriving moment. Flow joyously with the surprises life will surely bring. Surrender and God's will shall be delivered to you!" Ommatrin let forth another soothing, "Om," then stated, "I have spoken enough."

"But Master," Leon persisted, "last time you taught me a technique. I cherish it."

Ommatrin's heart fluttered and from it an idea sprouted. Immediately he began to instruct, "Earth humanity is becoming aware of the vastness of God's physical dimension. Once, a light-year was a huge amount; now, it is but a speck. Soon humanity will discover that their newly expanded conceptions of space and reality are but a particle of the truth. How big is it all? All the inhabited worlds, all the quazillion universes spiraling in harmony, all the unfolding, enfolding dimensions—how much is there? Can you imagine what Everything is?"

"No, Master," Leon admitted humbly.

"Just as I asked you to surrender to life, I now ask you to surrender all sense of limit," the teacher prompted. "Release your limiting mind, and your consciousness will naturally enlarge. Every universe, every molecule—you can fit it all within you!"

Leon tried to surrender, but part of him deemed it a task, causing his mind to hold on even tighter. *Let go,* he demanded of himself, only creating more resistance. After several minutes of contemplating the emptiness of space, his mind relaxed and his consciousness expanded slightly. Like a roller coaster at the crest, it suddenly rocketed down. Expansion's momentum exploded in all directions, past birthing planets and erupting stars, until his consciousness blurred beyond the shallow walls of matter. Leon could hear the hiss of dimensions whizzing past like infinite cards shuffling. Suddenly he felt an opening into an endless vista of alluring nothingness.

"Om," Ommatrin sang sweetly. "Now you feel the All!"

"Yes," Leon uttered.

Ommatrin delivered the last vital instruction. "Now, take this immensity and shrink it to the head of a pin within your heart. Do it now. Now!" Ommatrin demanded.

Leon's energy field vibrated within a revelation no words could convey. Yet amidst this, his heart, kidnapped by his mind, left the moment to make a mental note: *Teach Walter Snow this technique.* The odd divergence lasted only a second, but when he returned, Ommatrin was gone.

The child floated aimlessly. "I'm a leaf in the wind," he started singing, just when a streak of woven green-pink light disturbed him.

Zelia whizzed around the edge of Leon's aura creating cosmic tickles before she dove into his field, fluffing up areas and patting down others. Leon was delighted that Josie's fairy was so adept at manipulating electromagnetic fields.

Secretly, Zelia was preparing to interrogate him. The fairy was sensing danger in Josie's future and wanted to avert it. She knew Leon was telepathic when he was *out-of-body*, and at the speed of thought, Zelia got the information she had come for.

Leon's appreciation for the fairy flowered into an idea. "Zelia, you would be a perfect inter-dimensional liaison. I could contribute more by journeying *out-of-body* full time. You could alert me if I'm needed on the—"

"Oh joy, oh glee, oh merriment and mirth," Zelia interrupted, "your next great adventure is happening on Earth!" Her high-pitched fairy voice was crystal clear, "Leon, it's time! Earth time. Seek the reason for your incarnation; it may be your last. Look for signs; look for signs!"

"Yes Great One," the boy barely uttered, confusing Zelia with Ommatrin of Orvonton.

Zelia disappeared in a flash.

Leon returned to expanding into and shrinking the unfathomable All. He was a huge pendulum swinging back and forth when, from a place not familiar to him, a hand appeared and stopped the pendulum in the middle. Leon's energy field rose an octave. "Zelia!" he called out.

"What?" the flash of light questioned before it became actual.

"I have a message for Josie. Tell her to share it with Walter Snow. Let them know this is the *Second Key of Light.*" Leon sent the thought transmission, and the fairy was gone in a green flash.

The next morning while Saul and Duffy were making veggie omelets, Josie shared the message she had just received from Zelia.

Snow transcribed every word with fanatic intensity.

Second Key of Light: Surrender to Presence.

"Rise into the frequency of miracles by replacing control with presence."— Ommatrin of Orvonton.

You are FREE the moment you can say, I will be happy no matter what life brings. My happiness is unconditional.

Ego opposes this blissful freedom by creating conditions: I will be happy if I'm rich, if I'm healthy, if-if-if-if... This if game puts you at the mercy of an unpredictable world for satisfaction! What is Ego's purpose?

It is to protect the wounds of your heart! It controls everything inside and out, trying to create pleasure and safety. Most of Ego's energy is spent shielding you from pain. Like a tragic figure, Ego is enslaved, oblivious that the heart needs healing, not protection!

Ego's province was to help your evolving spiritual essence navigate the physical plane. This survival function was overstepped when Ego froze a large portion of the brain to insure its control of the psyche. The portions frozen include psychic abilities, telepathy, awareness of inter-dimensions, and more. Much more.

How can we heal this rebellious component of mind and remove blockages to happiness and potential?

Relinquish control of life! Allow life to be a divine thriller that unfolds before you. Be spellbound!

Ask yourself: If I am not in control, who is?

Relinquishing control heals Ego; it's an act of faith endlessly rewarded. Here is how: if you let go, God, as life, automatically brings healing remedies in the form of people, places, and things. A remedy is anything that activates your blockages, enabling you to see them and thus heal them. These events will come in the perfect order to facilitate your growth, much like the peeling away of an onion.

Life whispers truth, and you can hear it when the denseness of control has been replaced by the lightness of receptivity. Flowing with life while being joyfully present will naturally cause your frequency to rise. Ever higher you can go, needing only everyday life as fuel for your ascension.

Surrender, then prepare! Mind assumes that surrendering control means inaction. Ha! Powers of manifestation are amazing as you rise in frequency. However, your actions come not from ego, but from intuition's interplay with life. Life happens and you flow with It, like dancing when no one is leading. Dance with life in this way, and the riches of the moment will be placed at your feet.

Soul-driven, not Ego-driven, your divine purpose is revealed through Life.

Surrender to presence and hear God's voice in every instant. Soar into the limitless light of miracles, where the pendulum stops in the middle and there is no right and wrong, good and bad—only Heart. It all begins now. Simply, Surrender to Presence, like a musician lost in a rhapsody.

"Boy, this sounds like it's from a Sterling Ardo book," Snow remarked after he caught his breath. "Remember our conversation about Soft Control? Isn't this the same idea?"

Josie nodded soberly.

"Let's put this Key into action," the principal suggested warmly. "Let's be present and trust that life is bringing us what we need to learn." Snow took Josie's hand. His mind drifted to the thought he'd repeated as he had dropped off to sleep the night before. "If ever there was a time to have faith in life, this is it," he said.

"Ideas do seem to be connecting, like we're in the flow," she conceded.

Snow tried to understand the synchronicity of ideas by writing them all on the same page. Even his beloved sixties motto fit. *Life is a mystery to be lived, not a problem to be solved.*

He looked at the second Key, then the first. "The first Key says to undo, and the second Key tells how." Snow's brow lifted. "The Keys are more than wisdom; they're a system!" Unable to contain himself, he squeezed Josie's hand. "Leon is providing humanity with a way to heal itself! I'm sure of it!"

Everything is perfect, but...

General Fielding was a steel-jawed, by-the-book, icon of military intelligence and he'd risen to the top for one spit-shining reason: Fielding succeeded after everyone else failed.

In a fifty-thousand-square-foot converted missile hangar, teams of scientists began analysis of the alleged alien objects found at the Ardo estate. The general watched through the window of his makeshift office. To the dismay of some scientists, Fielding had restricted their investigation: There would be no dismantling of objects until research information was gathered and a strategy formulated. *Slow and steady with no foul-ups* was Fielding's way.

This hands-off policy caused heated disagreements among the scientists, but temperatures cooled when equipment arrived and they plunged into work using state-of-the-art sound, light, and element analysis methods. The cool, however, didn't last long.

Scrapings from the objects defied all chemical analysis; it was as if the matter was void of substance, like it didn't exist. Similarly, the mechanical objects emitting light and sound had no effect on any measurement instruments. Extensive tests were performed on the globe using the most sophisticated devices, and again not a meter moved nor did its scrapings produce a particle of information.

When a renowned physicist declared the entire matter a hoax, several scientists joined him to figure out how the trick was performed. These doubters were so passionate, they contacted a famous scientific debunker whom they agreed to fly in at their own expense.

While researchers scurried about scratching their heads, Fielding "Question Probed" (a system he'd created for rapid problem solving). He closed his eyes and began to list questions related to the dilemma. The challenge was to not think in terms of solutions, just questions. Fielding's mind unloaded instantly. *What is the light machine's function? Why do all the objects resist testing? Could this be an extraterrestrial encounter? Could this be the work of a foreign government? Is Aaron Ardo a spy? Are these devices dangerous? Are they weapons? Is my staff safe?*

"Questions are answers," Fielding asserted. He planned to bring in a medical team and begin daily physical exams of the scientific staff. Studies would be geared toward isolating any changes related to exposure to the devices. This would maximize safety and create a possible avenue for researching the enigma.

Fielding surmised that the most immediate source of answers was slumped in the corner. Though Fielding and Aaron Ardo were both about six feet tall, the general looked twice Aaron's size as he paced the dingy office. "Aaron, I'd appreciate it if you'd tell me what you know. Under the circumstances," he said, pointing to the objects through the glass, "we want to keep this situation contained. With your cooperation, I believe we can."

Fielding had kept Aaron up all night in an effort to break down his defenses. When a strange sensation started buzzing through Aaron's head, he thought it was his exhaustion. The sensation increased as a crisp message rang through the grogginess. *Father, it's time for my Earth adventure to begin. I no longer want to hide. Tell the truth. It's time!*

Being a writer, it was easy for Aaron to get right to the point. He leaned forward. "My son has superhuman powers, and even I don't know their extent. One of them, I believe, is the ability to transport himself anywhere in space or time. Apparently, he returns from these space/time travels with souvenirs. Which means these objects can be anything from anywhere, anytime. We've sheltered Leon because we knew if anyone found out about his abilities, particularly the United States government, his freedom would be lost forever." Aaron closed his eyes feeling relief.

Fielding studied him, then repeated, "Where did you get those items? Are they dangerous?"

What irony, Aaron thought. *I've spent years hiding a truth that no one in his right mind would believe.*

Fielding reached beneath his desk and pushed a button four times. A special security agent entered carrying a syringe. "This will loosen your tongue."

"I will not allow you to put a toxic substance in my body," Aaron protested. "I'm chemically sensitive. I'm an organic vegetarian. This is a gross violation of my rights!"

Fielding gave the syringe a slight tap.

The needle was inching closer as Leon's angelic smile entered Aaron's mind . . . Aaron turned pale . . . Leon's face appeared in a blue mist—simultaneously, the room started shaking as a hissing sound increased to a mind-rattling intensity. Sound became matter.

"Huh?" Fielding gulped as he dropped the syringe.

Aaron's eyes opened and his arms automatically extended. Leon ran to him.

"How did he get in here?" Fielding demanded, pushing the security alarm beneath his desk as he pulled his gun. "The joke is over. I want to know how you got in here."

Leon held a fixed stare on Fielding as he stepped between Aaron and the gun.

"Stay back," Fielding ordered, faltering at the sight of Leon's diminutive size and fearless eyes.

Leon's smile broadened with every step as he reached through Fielding's powerful energy field.

"He's just a boy. Please don't hurt him," Aaron pleaded. He rubbed his nose thoughtfully. "Listen, I have an idea that—"

Leon wiggled three fingers. *WHOOSH!*

Instantly, Fielding was plummeting in pitch-blackness, and he sensed Leon falling beside him just before they came to rest on rocky ground.

"Guess where we are?" Leon teased, not giving Fielding a second to think. "You're exactly where you were standing before we took this ride."

Fielding attempted to rub his chin, but he didn't have one. His body was gone! A surprising mixture of disorientation and clarity rumbled through the general's energy field.

"Where is my body?"

"In your office." Leon paused for emphasis. "Your body hasn't moved, time has! It's now 550 million B.C., pre-animal life. You can see plants are beginning their evolutionary climb. Notice the green hue over there? It's algae," Leon said, as if talking about a departed loved one.

"How can I see if I have no eyes, no body?" Fielding asked, as he scanned the untainted terrain and realized it did look like what Earth might have been. "It's so bright," Fielding noted.

That was the inducement Leon needed to share his endless knowledge of such things. (This information was acquired from the great non-breathing scientist Ommada, Ommatrin's brother.)

"It's so bright because there is no pollution, and the Sun is emitting slightly more energy. Did you know that Earth's atmosphere receives only one two-billionths of the Sun's total light emanation? Still, if the sunlight falling upon Chicago was paid for at the rate of two cents per kilowatt-hour, the bill would be one hundred million dollars a day." Leon's energy field quivered with delight. "If you captured one second of the total heat put out by our magnificent Sun, it would bring all of Earth's oceans to a boil instantly." These fun facts were just a prelude. "There is so much about our stars and planets that science does not understand."

"You do?" Fielding asked.

Leon continued. "Of the thirty suns nearest us, three are brighter. They have the average diameter of one million miles. The largest, the stellar cloud Antares, is sixty million times the volume of our Sun and four hundred fifty times the diameter. But don't worry, there's no shortage of space in space," Leon joked. "These huge stars have as much comparative room as a dozen oranges would have if they were floating inside our hollow Earth."

"How do you know these things?"

Leon's energy field brightened as he recalled the journeys that had ended in Ommada's laboratory. "You wouldn't believe me if I told you, but you can believe this. Earth is not the center of the universe, it's out of the way—on the edge of a new frontier. If it weren't for Jesus, Earth would be scarcely known. Well, that was until 1972 when Earth became the most famous planet in the cosmos, but that's a story for another time."

"Huh?" responded Fielding, wondering how they'd gotten from suns to Jesus, then back to Earth in 1972. The general pursued something he could understand. "You're telling me there are planets with intelligent life?"

Leon's energy field vibrated like a laughing belly. "How many sperm are produced by a single male ejaculation?"

"Huh? Millions, billions, I don't know."

"Could we say an immense amount?" Leon coaxed. "How many chemical reactions occur in your body in one second? How many cells are in your body? How many atoms are in one cell? The numbers are vast, aren't they? Now, what about space? Are there not trillions of galaxies with trillions of suns and planets? Aren't the numbers unfathomable as well? Whether it is on the micro or macro level, whether it is subatomic particles or suns a million times the size of ours, one thing is certain, there is a mind-staggering profusion of it. Have you ever wondered why?"

Leon shrunk the vastness down to the head of a pin. His field rumbled as he said, "Profusion is nature's insurance policy. Nature creates billions of sperm to insure that one will reach the egg; plants create a score of seeds for the same reason. God seeds billions of planets with life. Why?"

When the general's field stopped bubbling, Leon pursued. "Do you think it conceivable that in the entire profusion-filled cosmos there is only one planet with self-aware life forms? Can you present anything supporting the statistically improbable idea that we are alone amongst all this?"

After allowing Fielding a moment to consider, Leon informed, "Some Earth beings, like yourself, believe life evolved. Others believe God created it. Both are the same! Both are true. Evolution is God's creative system! And profusion is at the heart, the perfect game for an infinite God."

Leon returned to facts. "In our local area alone, six hundred and nineteen planets are in the life evolving process. There are thirty-six planets just at the point of plant life formation and about two hundred worlds a few million years away from that. Evolution/creation is happening everywhere, on all levels. Anova, one of forty-four planets orbiting a dark hole with three suns, has inhabitants that are far more advanced than Earth's humans."

Fielding's energy field was hiccuping and Leon decided to agitate it further. "Planets, moons, and suns are sentient beings. They have life/death cycles just like us, and they possess consciousness. Words cannot describe the enlightened state of our great Earth and it, compared to other planets, is a mere infant. After eons, dear general, your Soul might evolve enough to incarnate as a planet. Planet Fielding," Leon trumpeted with playful reverence.

The general's belching mind was suspended without a thought. Leon's outrageous ideas were fogging the tower of belief that held Fielding erect.

"I'm going to tell you something hard to accept," Leon persisted.

Fielding vibrated delight between heaves. *What could possibly follow?*

"Earth is a maverick planet maintained by defiant spirits. (Only ten percent of inhabited worlds are permitted Earth's leeway.) Anyway, due to an impending devastation related to the instability of Earth's Sun, these renegade spirits, aided by beings from the planet Sirius, performed a miraculous Earth healing. It raised God's eyebrows." Leon's field emitted a light chuckle. "Their intervention prevented the Armageddon that so many Earth cultures prophesied."

Even under these circumstances the general could not accept that Earth was an experiment saved by ETs and renegade spirits.

"Remember we spoke of the mind-numbing profusion on all levels of the physical plane. Well, the physical plane is miniscule compared to spiritual realms. There are infinite dimensions—all possessing infinite quantities of differentiated spirits. It is beyond numbers."

After Fielding's energy field settled into a well modulated shaking, Leon asked, "Can you guess the thread to everything I have said? Here is a hint: It's God's gift to every living thing and humans experience only the tip of it." Leon waited for an answer but only received a loud belch. "Consciousness! Evolving consciousness is the glue of the cosmos. Consciousness is God's bequest, and it doesn't require a body, as you are now aware. Your formless Soul is pure, electromagnetic consciousness. It is immortal; you are immortal. You are God stuff and you can evolve into anything, Planet Fielding!"

The general, a devout atheist, imagined his body (a natural defense against his current formless state). Waves of pleasurable physical sensations flooded his mind as he recalled the daring dives he'd taken off the Colorado River cliffs. His awareness expanded and he could understand why an angel, if there was such a thing, would choose to experience the physical plane. Fielding's energy field lengthened, accidentally contacting Leon's—souls touched. *WHOOSH!*

"—will solve everything," Aaron cried desperately. "Just don't hurt my boy!"

General Fielding felt literally beside himself. No time had passed! Aaron was still rubbing his nose, completing the sentence he had begun before Leon had taken him. The general holstered his gun; it felt heavy and obsolete.

Leon stood motionless, grinning.

Fielding looked at Leon and was captured by the child's oceanic blue eyes. He held Leon's stare until his disciplined focus became a blissful mutual exchange. *I'll never be the same,* the general felt, as his gaze dissolved into memories of his wife's sudden death. Leon's shimmering eyes soothed him—Fielding was mesmerized. *If there are such things as angels, this child is one of them.* He questioned what he was about to do for the Ardos, but he had no doubt about the force that compelled him.

Leon broke the eye-to-eye communion to attend to Aaron.

General Fielding attempted to speak, "Wow, huh, we got quite a situation here! Wow, well? Okay. Let's see, this is um, this is how we'll handle it." Fielding was feeling clear despite his verbal disconnect. "If anyone finds out about Leon, tell them he's schizophrenic! Avoid saying anything about his powers. It's essential we keep a low profile. We do not want to fuel the fire! At least not yet," Fielding added, with an uncharacteristic twinkle in his eye.

Aaron nodded approval. This was similar to Snow's approach. All fronts were converging.

Fielding would let Aaron and Leon return home if Leon agreed to help with research related to the objects. The general emphasized, "These objects are tangible; they're the problem! They—" The general stopped in mid-sentence, his eyes jetting back and forth between Leon and the lab. "What's happening? My God!" he gasped, as he stormed into the hangar, calming the scientists who were waving their hands at empty space.

A young scientist had been holding a crystal that instantly vanished from his hand. "I guess this is a hoax too," he said defiantly to the leader of the doubters. Within two minutes every alien object had disappeared, literally faded away! Before a breath could be taken, there was a blinding explosion of light.

Fielding was the first to open his eyes and get a bleary look at the globe resting on its base as if it had never disappeared. It glowed seductively. "Holy Shimoli," General Fielding declared, as he turned to Leon and whispered, "Get your dad out of here and wait for me at your house. Promise me you won't go anywhere."

The child's nod reassured Fielding; he could feel Leon's divine integrity. As the general watched Aaron and Leon dissolve into the chaos, he noticed that the globe's luminosity decreased as they moved away. The general kept his eye on the alien device and its ever-changing light emissions throughout the briefing that followed.

The scientists were in shock, particularly the conservative doubters, so Fielding worked the group patiently until ideas began to flow. It was an intelligence officer who contended that dematerialization of matter was within scientific possibility. He'd heard rumors of classified experiments. Several other scientists eagerly agreed. Fielding supported this theory when he speculated that the remaining device could be the dematerializer.

Fielding sequestered the scientific staff allowing one call each to inform their families that work would keep them on-site for several weeks. He emphasized that saying anything related to the occurrence would border on treason. His stomach twisted in knots when he thought about calling Flint Killingsworth, his boss.

From his makeshift office, Fielding peered at the globe wanting to drift away into its warm glow. Instead, he planted his feet and allowed questions to sequence in his mind. A seemingly irrelevant question gnawed at him despite the majority of impending ones. *When I was out-of-body in 550 million* B.C., *how was I able to see?* This led to a host of speculations he chose not to pursue until the essential question was answered: What to do next!

The general picked up the picture of his deceased wife, Sylvia, and kissed it twice. As he pulled it toward his heart, he noticed a smudge and rubbed hard to wipe it off. In disbelief he exclaimed, "It can't be. My God!" He picked up his magnifying glass, and tried to focus as his arm trembled. "It is!" he yelped. It was Sylvia's squiggly signature; the way her initials hid within the tangle of swirls was unmistakable. They'd always joked that no one could forge her mark.

How Sylvia's signature materialized was another question Fielding considered as his breath constricted and his mind moved faster than his racing heart. *Is Leon an extraterrestrial? Is my wife's signature a cruel joke or a compassionate stroke?* After gazing at the tangled swirls, Roy Fielding declared it a blessing; he was unrecognizable behind the huge smile that spread across his face. A lightheaded rush overcame him, and he fought it by imagining Leon's unwavering eyes. He asked his last question, "What is happening to me?"

"We have a breaking story. We're going live to—"

Leon turned up the TV.

"This is Tom Brook for CNN with an exclusive story. I'm outside a Pentagon outpost where Sterling Ardo, famed creator of *Positive Pursuits,* is being held for questioning. He was arrested on his Virginia estate where agents found objects—listen to this—which could NOT be from Earth! Some of these items appear to be religious artifacts. Others are mechanical and produce lights and sounds. The functions of the mechanical devices are unknown. I repeat: Items found at the Ardo estate could not have been created on planet Earth! Is this the defining moment, proof of extraterrestrial life? Jane, if these items are found to be from *out of this world,* who knows where this story will lead.

"I repeat, because I still can't believe it, visionary author Sterling Ardo has been detained for questioning. He is alleged to have been in possession of objects not from this Earth. What a story! And you heard it first on CNN. This is Tom Brook with another exclusive, reporting live."

"Hey, you," Brook scowled at the cameraman. "I told you last week to shoot my right side." Brook turned sideways, pointing to his right cheek. "That's my angle. You want me to look good, don't you? Don't you?"

The cameraman didn't respond.

"Listen dirt-bag, I'm not going to let you screw this up. Get with *my* program, or I'll get someone who can! Got it?"

The technician walked away, intending to pack his camera once he was out of the reporter's firing range. Brook took potshots at his back. "You were late last week, once more and you're out on your ass." The cameraman stepped into the van as Brook ranted, "This could be the story of the century, and you're shooting my bad side, asshole!"

Tom Brook's rage softened into daydreaming about a Pulitzer. When his cellphone rang, the Golden Voice answered in his controlled announcer style. As Brook listened to his boss's lecture, the reporter plunged into the crevices of paranoia. *He wants control of the story; he'll give it to a veteran reporter. That covert bastard! Screw him! That asshole cameraman is probably Clark's spy. Screw them all! I can go to any network because I've got the informant.* He bit his lip as he listened and repeated, "Yes sir, Mr. Clark."

Brook's jaw clenched, deepening his scowl. Black clouds sailed overhead, allowing just a hint of light. He brushed back his dark, thick hair and made off in search of his informant—keeping him exclusive and productive meant everything.

Principal Snow and Josie stayed by the TV monitoring the news. Tom Brook's story was CNN's lead which meant it went worldwide instantly. It was repeated every half-hour with expert sidebars, including everything from legitimate scientists to crackpot ET abductees.

"I'm afraid of what might happen if the media discovers Leon's abilities. They'll think he's an ET freak," Josie cried as she watched an interview with a professor who claimed to have been abducted and altered with invisible implants.

"Present Leon's birth certificate," Snow recommended. "That will disprove this ET nonsense."

Josie pulled away. "We have no birth certificate. Leon's not our biological child. I'm infertile." She paused and took a deep breath. "Eleven years ago, when Aaron and I were confronting my infertility, the very day we decided to adopt, Aaron and I were awakened by a loud rumbling. We assumed it was a truck. We ran to the door, but no one was there. Then we looked down and saw a baby in a beat-up old basket. There was a note pinned to him. I've read it so many times I know it by heart. *Help me! This is my baby, Leon. I can't care for him, so I asked God what to do and he told me to bring him here. God said that you are his true parents.* It was a miracle," Josie said intently. "We kept the manner of Leon's acquisition quiet. As far as friends and family were concerned, he was adopted. You're the only one who knows," Josie revealed, taking Snow's large hand into hers.

They talked for hours until Josie dozed off. Without thinking, Snow brushed a strand of hair off her face and kissed her forehead. As he watched the innocent ebb and flow of her breath, an alarming thought blurred the moment. *Leon could be an extraterrestrial, altered human, abducted as an infant, modified, and returned to Earth. He could even be half alien, half human.*

Snow laughed. The wacky TV reports were getting to him. He knew that whatever Leon was, his purpose had to be for the good of humankind. Snow made a solemn pledge to stand by the Ardo family, no matter what.

He fell asleep with surprising ease and began dreaming about a fairy sprinkling dust into people's eyes. Josie dreamed about a pixie dancing on moonbeams. They were jolted out of fairyland when the front door slammed against the wall.

"Oh my god, you're safe," Josie screeched, running toward the door.

"*Everything is perfect,*" Leon said, pointing to a disheveled Aaron, "*but there is a lot of room for improvement.*—Shunryu Suzuki." They all laughed and fell into a heap of unrestrained hugs and kisses. Only Snow considered the elegance of the paradox as he wrote it in his notebook: *Everything is perfect, but there is a lot of room for improvement.*

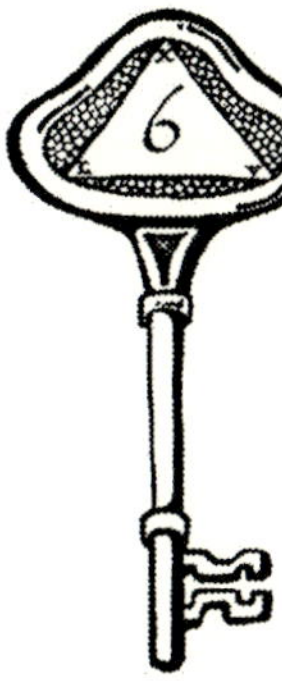

God was concealed...

Complying with Fielding's orders, the Ardos and Walt Snow returned to the magic dome where they nestled into the huge family room. Aaron was drained, so Josie turned domestic and made him herbal tea and healthy treats.

Snow felt energized and was chattering in his high squeaky voice so everyone could hear, "Aaron, you gotta see this. You're on TV non-stop! I'll bet your publishers are thrilled!" Snow ran toward the TV to turn it up, but Leon blocked his path with a dance step that ended in a flawless spin. Snow could feel the breeze. "Wow, Leon, that was *out of this world!*" Snow said, giggling at the pun.

With arms beckoning to the heavens, Leon said, "*From the moment you came into the world of being, a ladder was placed before you that you might escape.*—Diviani Shamsi Tabritz."

In the perfect mood to play verbal charades, Snow guessed without hesitation, "You're saying there is a way out of our current problem that is so obvious we can't see it?"

Leon was silent.

Snow paced, his arms folded on his belly. "It's more about life in general and less about our present situation. Right?"

Leon smiled.

"You're saying we can *escape* from our conditioning," the principal guessed again.

Leon's face brightened. Snow pursued with urgings from Aaron and Josie. "There is a ladder, a ladder, something about a ladder—a method. There is a technique we can employ to escape the grip of our conditioned consciousness?"

Nodding and smiling, Leon said, "*There is a sadhu in Hrishikesh who gets up early in the morning and stands near a great waterfall. He looks at it the whole day and says to God: 'Ah, You have done well! Well done! How amazing.' He doesn't practice any other form of japa or austerity. At night he returns to his hut.*—The Gospel of Sri Ramakrishna."

"You're saying you will show me the ladder, meaning teach me a simple technique to transcend ordinary consciousness so I can know God; however, it's important I don't cling to the ladder." He paused and considered. "Techniques are not truth, simply a tool to discover truth!"

Dropping to the floor, Leon kissed Snow's socked feet with the enthusiasm of the sadhu from Hrishikesh. Had the child not been so comical, Snow's white skin might have turned blood red.

"*Techniques are not truth, simply a tool to discover truth,*" Aaron declared. "Now Walt is making up quotes! Someone call Bartlett!"

Leon began doing a jig, becoming increasingly comical until everybody was roaring with laughter and dancing along. They were *delightened*, as Josie put it.

Zelia, the self-proclaimed queen of *delightenment*, took the cue. She hovered around Josie's energy field waving her wand, taking serious whacks at Josie's third eye portal. When the energies were just right, Zelia requested politely, "I have the next Key; may I speak through thee?"

Josie closed her almond eyes. To channel Zelia required a shift best described as *acceptance of the miraculous*. It necessitated a surrendering of self, and Zelia helped with strategic whacks of her wand.

"The *Third Key of Light*," Josie sang out in a joyous clear voice.

Aaron threw Snow the trusty notebook. They waited with anticipation, even Leon.

Zelia transmitted and Josie's thin lips moved. "*Third Key of Light: Aware of Awareness. 'The seer is the unchanging non-dual unity or Soul. The seen is the changing, visible universe and the mind.'*—Sivanada."

Josie's eyes lit up as she channeled, "*Imagine that God is a spinning wheel emitting infinite sparks, and you are one of them! Your Soul is that spark lost inside of you, and like any buried treasure it's difficult to find without a map.*"

A familiar pain shot through Aaron's lower back and he adjusted his position.

"*When you feel pain, how do you know it hurts?*" Josie continued in her trance state. "*There is pain and the part of you experiencing the pain; they are separate. When you are happy, you say, 'I am happy.' What is the 'I' who feels this happiness? What is this stream of constant awareness witnessing everything?*

"*Your body, emotions, thoughts, and sensory-based feelings come and go, but the subtle awareness experiencing them is eternal. Awareness is the tip of your Soul.*

"*To know your Soul, be aware of being aware! It is as simple as that!*"

Zelia waved her wand rhythmically right above Josie's chest portal. "*There is a proverb: 'God was concealed as a diamond in my heart.' A diamond is almost invisible, but if you know it is there, you adjust your sight to witness its radiance. So, too, you can experience your elusive Soul Awareness.*

"*Let's try right now! Pinch yourself,*" Zelia commanded through Josie. "*Can you sense that the witness experiencing the pain is separate from the pain? With practice, you can!*"

A determined Snow pinched his rubbery arm so hard he squealed. Leon sent him a loving glance. Aaron smiled.

Josie's voice deepened. "*With practice, you can reside in your Soul while living in the astounding world of form. That is how Jesus was able to hang from the cross and still love those who drove in the stakes. That is how an enlightened Master lives.*"

Zelia felt the communication channel weakening; Josie was a balloon ready to float away. The fairy located a blockage above Josie's third eye and dislodged it with a solid whack of the wand, then she continued, "*The Koran states: 'Paradise is nearer to you than the thongs of your sandals.' If paradise (the Soul) is so close, why have so few found it?*

"*The part that sees (the Soul) has merged with what it is seeing. You are not your thoughts, feelings, and beliefs. You are the awareness experiencing them.*" Josie took a soothing breath and revealed, "*You are the Light, not what the Light shines upon!*" Zelia fluttered about Josie's crown, pulling energy up and out. Snow's pen whizzed across the page. Zelia waited. The fairy had an awe-inspiring conclusion but opted for enticing simplicity. "*To fortify the inner resources needed to achieve the Keys of Light, become Aware of Awareness.*"

Josie's consciousness returned to normal. She sat motionless, feeling lightheaded and joyful.

Snow kept writing as insights collided, creating memory trails. One led back to college when he had taken awareness training and loved it. "This all makes sense, doesn't it?" Snow asked with childish innocence.

"Beyond sense," Aaron agreed.

"I know quite a few awareness techniques," Josie offered brightly. "I could put together a class for us."

Aaron gazed at Josie like a child in puppy love. His affection ignited Snow, who wagged about the room in anticipation.

Josie's initial ideas fell into place, and she was ready in minutes. Aaron and the principal settled down with seated stretching. Just when she began facilitating calm breaths, Leon clicked on the TV just as the telephone rang.

"I'll get the phone." Aaron said, running into his office.

"This is Tom Brook with another CNN exclusive," the TV blared. "An already unbelievable story has gone out-of-orbit. Yesterday, writer Sterling Ardo was detained by military intelligence for possession of objects that could not have been produced on Earth. My sources tell me these alleged alien objects have vanished! Not stolen. They literally dematerialized as two hundred scientists watched in astonishment.

"The scientists who witnessed this phenomenon have been sequestered. Now, here is the twist: One object that disappeared—moments later reappeared! The government has one alien object, a glowing globe about the size of a bowling ball. Experts speculate that this device caused the others to dematerialize.

"I repeat—Items not from this Earth dematerialized in front of two hundred scientists. One item remains! This sounds like science fiction. But, could it be science reality, a 'real' extraterrestrial demonstration? No one has a better answer. This is a mind-boggled Tom Brook, with another CNN exclusive story."

Leon hit the mute button when Aaron returned with an update, "It was General Fielding on the phone; there's been another leak. Fielding says we can't leave the house. Apparently, we're sealed in."

"How is Tom Brook getting this information?" Snow asked, after telling Aaron about the report.

Aaron ignored him. "Listen to this! Fielding wants all of us, including Leon, to go on 'Larry King Live,' tonight! King is flying into D.C. right now. Fielding says, 'The situation is explosive and we need to diffuse it.'" Aaron impersonated Fielding's curt mannerism. "He emphasized that being on Larry King is our chance to tell the truth and do the right thing."

Leon headed for the kitchen determined to feed the troops. Josie darted off saying, "I must beautify myself for Larry." Aaron ran to the shower and was dressed before Josie got started. Snow languished in the guest bathroom. When Fielding arrived, they were a well-groomed, well-fed, but not well-organized bunch of renegades.

They were all in the central living area when Leon emerged impeccably garbed in a blue pinstriped suit and a red paisley bow tie. Snow wondered how someone so odd could look so normal.

Fielding couldn't stop surveying the surroundings. "Your house looks like a flying saucer. This is not going to help us convince the public that Leon is not an alien or an ET-altered human."

Snow turned tomato red when he heard the phrase *ET altered-human.*

"The truth is," Aaron emphasized, "Leon is not an ET anything. He is a gift from God, an unbelievably endowed human, a miracle."

"Can you sell that to the world?" Fielding questioned.

Josie cut in, "Of course we can! Look at that face." Josie was still glowing from Zelia. "How could anyone believe this beautiful boy is an ET?" She said, tweaking Leon's cheek as he made funny faces back.

Fielding looked at Leon and rekindled the meaningful eye contact they'd shared in his office. "I'm convinced you believe what you're saying but that doesn't mean it's the truth."

Leon glowed with intent and said, "*Everything that is possible to be believed is an image of the truth.*—William Blake."

"What?" Fielding asked, puzzled.

"*Truth, like a rose, blossoms upon a thorny stem.*—Hafiz."

Fielding stiffened. "What the blazes is he talking about?"

After Aaron explained Leon's communication style, Fielding still insisted the child be on the show. It became clear that the general wanted to expose the truth, whatever it was.

Leon proposed a strategy in very few words. *Spontaneous fun is a direct channel to Truth.*—Sterling Ardo."

With that, it was decided to place less emphasis on planning and more on getting emotionally ready. Aaron coached Snow in a few tension-releasing exercises while Josie gave Fielding a tour of the house. By the end of the tour, the general was aglow; his billboard chest relaxed. Snow was dizzy from deep breathing. A giddy conversation ensued, and by the time the CNN limousine arrived, Fielding was enchanted by the Ardo magic. Snow, Aaron, and Josie felt oddly confident.

The limo drove the dirt road like a shiny panther slithering through dark woods. When it emerged onto the paved street, a bedlam of blaring lights and flashing bulbs blasted; stalking reporters wielded microphones like daggers. The driver proceeded slowly as the vultures spread out of the way. The limo skidded off as lights flashed.

Most of the group was frazzled, except for Leon and Fielding. Josie recuperated quickly: Zelia had been hiding in her aura, energizing centers related to truth and fun (as per Leon's instructions).Aaron and Walter sat quietly, unaware that a gifted fairy was about to renew their energy fields and that a sweet calling would lure them to the playful truth Aaron called "creative flow."

The limo zipped down Interstate 66, and before you could say, "Welcome to Larry King Live," they were there.

"Welcome to Larry King Live, and do we have a show tonight," Larry announced. His ridged forehead was unusually smooth, enlarging his lively presence. (Zelia had just completed extensive work on his energy field and was beginning to work on the producer and camera operators.)

"Tonight we have Leon, Josie, and Aaron Ardo, the family associated with the alleged vanishing ET items. You may recall that Aaron Sterling Ardo was on this show ten years ago when his book *Positive Pursuits* was made into a movie. Its huge success spawned the groundbreaking TV show of the same name. Also here tonight is Walter Snow, Leon's principal and family friend. And finally we have General Roy Fielding, director of military intelligence."

Fielding and Snow sat on a platform behind the Ardos. The family was seated around Larry's interview desk; Leon was in the middle.

Turning from the camera, Larry looked into cosmic blue eyes and asked, "Leon, the world wants to know, are you an ET?"

Leon placed both hands on his head, wiggled fingers like space tentacles and replied, "*Well, that depends upon what planet I'm on, Na-nu Na-nu.*" His impersonation of Mork from Ork, Robin Williams' ET character, was flawless.

When Larry's mouth dropped open, Leon's did the same. The cameraman got a perfect shot of the exchange (with a little help from a fairy).

Seamlessly, Leon turned to the camera impersonating Larry's voice and mannerisms with shivering accuracy as he said, "Larry, the world wants to know, are *you* an ET?"

Larry ignited into laughter. During a lifetime of interviewing, he'd never lost control of a show, but Larry couldn't stop laughing. Holding his gut, feeling oddly at ease under the circumstances, he signaled for his producer, Mel, to go to a break.

Instead, the producer cut to Leon who was leaning forward mimicking the way King sat during interviews. King's heaving laughter escalated (despite a guilty fairy, hard at work). Leon was the only one unruffled, his face luminous with a delight equal to the intensity of Larry's release. Love beams shot from the child's eyes (Zelia tried to harness their sedative quality). But Larry couldn't stop. He clutched his heart, his skin turned gray as concern washed across his face.

"Pull in tight on Leon," Mel ordered. "Cut Larry's sound; he's scaring the crap out of me. Something's happening! Look at Leon's face; it's glowing. Oh my—"

Boom! A miniature lightening bolt flew out from the crown of Leon's head.

Larry lunged back in his seat. "What the, huh, what was that?"

Leon's eyes glistened like newborn suns, as his little hand extended into Larry's field; it looked like he was turning the knob of a door while wiggling fingers— *WHOOSH*!

"What's going on? Where am I?"

"We're both *out-of-body*," Larry. But don't worry, no passage of time will be experienced on the Earth plane."

The boy was amazed how easily King had let go. The fear the interviewer held in his body, particularly around his brow, sank like dark oil. Joy permeated his countenance.

"You look like a million glistening diamonds," Larry gushed, staring at Leon's energy field. As King's consciousness opened, the blurry beyond sharpened into a clear view of a metropolis etched into pink, sparkling cliffs. Stone pyramids sprawled into unearthly city lights.

"What is this place?" Larry's field bubbled. "It looks different, but it feels familiar."

"Very true." Leon's appreciation for Larry swelled. "It is different because we're on the other end of the universe, but it's familiar because one Intelligence unifies life everywhere. No matter where you travel in the cosmos, similarities outweigh differences. For example, certain Earth animals exist on other planets and some species that are common on distant worlds do not exist here. Humanoid biology has more similarities than differences; there are one, two, and three-brained beings but their gray matter is very similar, as are their central nervous systems and organ systems.

"It is difficult to admit that there are others out there because we feel so alone inside," Leon explained compassionately. "We are part of something so much bigger than anyone on Earth has dared imagine. We have not touched the tip of the truth. Humans cling to the *next great idea* and it becomes their cage."

Leon returned to concrete facts. "Guess what all atmospheric, 'inhabited' planets share in common?"

The interviewer was eager to give an answer but didn't have one.

"Three things," Leon radiated. "All populated worlds are warmed by a sun or suns creating seasonal temperature variations; all advancing life forms participate in some form of agriculture; and the sexes, male/female, prevail everywhere.

"Male/female procreation replicates creation itself. The sacred mechanics are identical which means every conception is a miniature Big Bang!" Leon sent Larry sacred geometric images of the life/creation process. Larry was not able to assimilate them so Leon took another tact.

"Earth scientists are discovering a correlation between spirituality and longevity. On distant worlds people live for thirty to five hundred years depending upon their degree of spiritual evolution. "I've seen an entire race spiritualize overnight, and the major precursor was equality between the sexes. Women are equal to men, like left is equal to right."

Larry could feel Leon's field compress as the child continued, "On Earth, throughout the ages, countless atrocities have been committed by man in wars; yet all of them do not equal the atrocities committed by man against woman. You are living through a million-years-in-the-making shift from male domination to sex equality. Earth is poised on the edge of a spiritual awakening and it will affect every aspect of life, including longevity."

The interviewer's energy field consumed every nuance.

Leon brightened. "We are looking at the capital of the most advanced planet in Earth's local universe. I brought you here because its history is similar to ours."

The child magnetized his energy field, enabling Larry to be towed along as they visited families, schools, and government agencies; then they zoomed to an island about the size of Australia. "The population is about 140 million, a mixed race, mostly blue and yellow, with more violet than the so-called white race of Earth. These people live twice as long as Earth humans."

"It really doesn't seem that different," Larry transmitted.

"Exactly! And because they are only a small step ahead of us, we can learn from them. For example, when they confronted the crisis of their failing families, they instituted very innovative social changes. One of my favorites is Parental Schools—mandatory training for anyone having a baby.

"The average family has five children who are under the full control of their parents, as they are on Earth. Except here, birth is *creation* and parenting is holy. Orphans are rare, but if any exist, regardless of physical condition, parents compete for them through examinations and interviews. To receive an orphan is equivalent to winning the lottery on Earth. It is the supreme honor!

"Honors are associated with those things deemed vitally important by the culture." Leon paused. "Who and what do we honor on Earth?"

Larry earnestly considered the question and didn't like the answers.

"On this planet you need parental consent to get married if you are under twenty-five years of age." Leon continued, "Plus, you must give one year's notice and the bride and groom must be graduates of Parental Schools. It is interesting to note that divorce regulations are very lax here."

Larry summarized as he would during an interview, "On Earth, getting married is easy but divorcing is difficult. Here, it's the exact opposite!"

"Perfect!" Leon's full brightness returned.

"I'll bet divorce is uncommon on this world," Larry considered.

"You're right!" Leon glowed, eager to continue. "On this world it's rare for a child to be violent, depressed, or disruptive. On Earth, it is epidemic. We think it noble and wise to rehabilitate youth. We launch anti-sex and anti-drug campaigns; we spend fortunes to reduce violence in schools, then spend more to convince dropouts, the ones most likely to commit violence, to return to school. This world would think us dimwitted for emphasizing rehabilitation rather than raising children right in the first place." Leon summarized, "Only a culture dedicated to effective child rearing can thrive; then spirituality can be centered in the family, where it belongs."

"What is their spiritual belief?" Larry inquired, his field glistening.

"Peace and love," Leon responded. "That is their belief and curriculum! If you teach children to experience peace and to love, they will find God on their own. 'Each in their own way,' is the motto here."

"It's so simple," Larry sparkled.

"It is," Leon agreed, thoroughly enjoying King's radiance. "It's time to return." *WHOOSH!*

Larry's consciousness tumbled through a blue-light tunnel, spinning rapidly. He recalled being a child, how he'd go to Prospect Park and meet new people. He knew he could get anyone to talk but he had also wanted them to feel good and to grow during the process. The little boy loved the challenge of interviewing. *Love is the force behind my career, love is the force, love is the force,* he swore to remember as he tumbled.

"My producer tells me we're having problems with our lights," Larry said, feeling exhilarated and amazingly present.

"I did?" Mel nudged the engineer, who remained focused upon the afterglow of Leon's spark.

"Look at the kid's face," the engineer pointed out. "He's lit up like an angel or something."

"Camera three," Mel directed into his headset, "go tight on Leon's face. Hello, camera three. What's going on? Are you asleep?" (Zelia was just finishing up.) "My show is falling apart. Larry! Camera three! Is anyone alive out there?"

Leon was smiling so radiantly, Larry couldn't take his eyes off him. The camera three operator moved in slowly, not because he'd heard Mel's reprimand but because he was drawn to Leon's shimmering presence.

"Okay camera three, close enough. Enough! Stop you idiot!"

The camera kept zooming until Leon's eyes filled the entire frame, twinkling as if special effects had been employed.

Josie broke the Leon-induced chaos when she jumped to her feet and said, "Could this sweet face be an ET? Larry, look at this sweetie." She sat down and pinched her son's cheek.

"Tell us about Leon's special gifts and how he came by the objects," Larry countered with truth-seeking intent.

Leon's head was on Josie's shoulder, and she stroked it with her left hand. The camera then panned to Aaron, who was rubbing Leon's hand. The world was falling under the Ardo spell. Josie, swept up in the theatrical moment, assumed the accent of a helpless Southern belle and responded, "Oh, I just don't know what to say. I think my husband is better equipped to answer your question, sir." She batted her eyes at Aaron with such exaggerated adoration, the entire fairy-dusted staff began to laugh. The camera shot to Larry chuckling along with Leon.

Aaron took the lead, sounding like Clark Gable playing Rhett Butler. "This is Aaron Sterling Ardo, and I would be delighted to speak on behalf of my charming wife and adoring son." Simultaneously, Leon and Josie batted their eyes at Aaron. The crew laughed heartily along with half the world.

Returning to his own voice and to the issue, Aaron said, "It's ridiculous to think my son is an ET but I can understand why you might. He is very different, mysterious, even miraculous. For example, he seldom talks and when he does, it's in quotes. We speculate that he uses other people's words because . . ." Aaron paused, then blurted out, "there is no Leon!"

"Huh?" Larry put forth as a question.

"Leon has no *personal self*, no ego. We guess that this ego absence brings with it an absence of limitation, which enables him to access a wide range of what might be called, magical powers."

"Magical powers?" Larry's brow tightened.

A breeze swept through the room bringing a smell like the aroma after a rain. At the source of the turbulence was a pinpoint of red light which hovered above Larry's desk and began to expand. Within fifteen seconds a red blob floundered cartoonishly in mid-air, throbbing as it began to coalesce into a red, three-dimensional heart. Leon clapped his hands and the floating heart began to emit rainbow colored sparks. Spellbound, they watched the pulsing heart as its interior began swirling rapidly into a reddish-gray solidity. Just as the odor intensified, there was a burst of heat and the heart dropped on the desk making a loud thump.

Larry leaned toward what looked like a heart-shaped pink stone with a sparkling face. *It's the same color as the cliff that alien city rested on,* Larry thought, as he said into the mike, "What a trick! David Copperfield would be jealous. How did you do it?" Larry continued to stare at the rock. (Within forty-eight hours a geologist would confirm that it was not of Earthly origin.) Leon slid the stone over to King, along with a wink, and the interviewer shivered. The words *Love Is the Force* were etched into it. *It's a necessary reminder from Leon*, Larry acknowledged; he was already forgetting the journey, much like he forgot his nightly dreams. His crinkled brow felt like steel tracks.

"This is NOT a trick," Aaron assured Larry. "It's 'real' magic! Leon has the ability to manifest items. This is how he acquired the objects confiscated from our home. Gurus in India are known to have the same ability; it is not unheard of." Aaron paused and looked at Leon and Josie; their eyes burned into his naked heart. "Why must our world turn saints into freaks? Leon is a gift from God, here to show us what *we* might become. Everything about him is filled with love and wonder. He's a divine phenomenon to be honored, not an oddity to be prodded."

Leon was mimicking what Aaron was saying. When Aaron said, "prodded," Leon's face twisted into outlandish contortions causing unrestrained laughter on the set, even from General Fielding.

"Unbelievable!" Mel offered to the technician, who had cut to a close-up at the perfect moment. "Cut to Josie."

The camera picked up Josie rocking rhythmically with Aaron's words; Leon joined her. The Ardos were a single, rhythmic unit.

"We've kept Leon's gifts a secret to protect him. My son has informed me that he no longer wants to hide." Aaron's moist eyes looked directly into the camera. "We ask that the world allow us to live our lives in peace." He choked back a deep guttural sob, pleading passionately, "Let Leon grow up. He'll decide what to do with his life and his gifts. Perhaps then he'll reveal his true nature to us. Until that time, let's enjoy the mystery."

"We have to take a break. We'll be back in three minutes. Don't go away!"

Larry bounded from his seat and stood directly in front of Josie and Aaron, blocking the vision of his crew. "I want in. I want to help Leon."

Leon placed his hand in Larry's and squeezed.

"There's your answer!" Aaron whispered, as lights flashed above the camera.

Larry returned to his seat and listened to Mel's enthusiastic directions. "This is Larry King with the Ardo family and the most incredible story I've ever covered. General Fielding, let's hear from you. Can we let this family live in peace?"

Roy Fielding was a tug of war going nowhere. "I would like to let them be, but further investigation is required before we can determine any course of action. I have personally witnessed phenomena that could jeopardize national and even planetary security. My function is to get the facts and deliver them to the president. To get the facts will require some research and study."

"This is exactly what we are asking the world *not* to do," Snow ranted. The Ardos turned in unison and beamed at their unlikely champion. Walter Snow was boiling. "It does seem like there is no other option than to intrude upon their lives, but we *must not*! Because of our ignorance and greed, we humans have mistreated special beings." Snow's face was alive with passion. "We trounce upon enlightened masters like famished wolves until there is nothing left but bones. Let's learn from history."

The entire staff cheered as Snow's fist pounded empty air. He blinked and shrank back, surprised at his own audacity.

Fielding cut in like the commanding voice of reason he was: "Leon can be studied without impacting his life dramatically."

"People are too selfish. Besides, we have no right to impact his life at all," Snow rallied to more cheers.

"What about the things we might learn, how Leon might help the world?" Fielding countered, unruffled.

Snow was blazing. "That's exactly what I mean—we'll usurp his life to benefit ours!" Snow paused, creating tension. "Leon's contribution will naturally unfold as he grows, just as Aaron suggested. Make a test tube case out of him, and you may lose the very gifts you hope to understand and capitalize on. We've made that mistake repeatedly."

The studio was in an uproar by the time Leon stood up, exhibiting the composure of a yogi. "*After one arrives at the summit, after going through the total transformation of being, after becoming free of fear, doubt, confusion, and self-consciousness, there is yet one more step to the completion of that journey: to return to the valley below, to the everyday world.*—Ram Dass."

Snow translated: "Leon is saying that he *will* contribute to the world, when he reaches the summit. Obviously, he is not there yet." Snow looked at Leon and advised, "Give him freedom, and he'll return to us."

"I heard him say the opposite." Fielding's bristly crew cut seemed to stand up. "Leon's journey should continue under supervision." Fielding invited the camera in close with a contemplative hesitation. "I fear for his safety. Don't you think that after this," he said pointing to the rock, "Leon might need protection? I'd be concerned if —"

Fielding stopped talking the instant Leon raised his arms.

"'Grandpa,' I asked, 'tonight I must walk alone in the dark a long way to get to my tipi. Perhaps I will meet a bear. What should I do? Should I talk to the bear? Should I send it Love?'

"Grandpa leaned back and we shared a gentle space of silence together. Then he gave me this advice. 'No talk to bear. Talk to God!'" Leon bowed, announcing, "Saraswati."

"We have to cut away; we'll be right back with Tom Brook," Larry announced solemnly.

Tom Brook was preparing for the remote broadcast, aware that this was the opportunity of his life. Unfortunately, his informant had been "unavailable," and Brook didn't have anything new. Desperate, he'd acquired surveillance equipment and illegally spied on the hangar, with surprising results. His directional microphone had immediately picked up continuous screaming from inside the facility, and when several scientists came out, they were upbeat and looked drunk without being wobbly. The guards were behaving like prankster Boy Scouts. A rowdy, festive atmosphere did not fit the seriousness of the situation and Brook knew that "not fitting" usually meant one heck of a story twist!

The cameraman stood nervously, maintaining Brook's desired camera angle.

"Screw up this shot and I'll kick your ass, then fire you!" Brook threatened, pacing around the positioning mark on the ground, collecting his thoughts.

"This is Larry King back with the Ardo family, Walter Snow, and General Roy Fielding. We are now going live to Tom Brook, the CNN reporter who broke this amazing story. Tom, what do you have?"

"Larry, there are about two hundred scientists working around the clock on the alleged alien globe, the last remaining device. I have been unable to confirm specifics; however, something strange is going on at the site. Scientists and security people are behaving, well, as if they have been drinking. Word has it they leave the hangar singing and laughing; they're very boisterous. This is not behavior you'd expect from scientists and military security. There's another strange thing going on and you won't believe it—"

"We've lost the remote," Mel called out, as his fingers danced across the mixing console. "Larry, we're back to you. We lost Brook! Wait a minute." Mel commanded as he checked a connection.

Fielding clenched his jaw activating an iron dimple. *If something was wrong at the hangar I'd have been notified.* He was preparing to dispute Brook's report when Mel's voice rang over the PA, "We're having technical difficulties. Give us a minute to find the problem."

Leon's face had finality written across it and Larry knew the technical difficulties would not be resolved. It occurred to King that Fielding might be right: Leon's powers, if misguided or usurped, could prove catastrophic. *This child might require protection,* Larry thought, wanting to offer just that.

After announcing that the show was officially over, Larry invited everyone to his dressing room. Mel rushed in, reporting, "The phones are ballistic. We've never had a response like this!" He darted over to Leon and gave him a hug before running down the hall to maintenance.

The dressing room conversation was warm and upbeat, until Aaron noticed Josie's weariness and begged off. When their limo left CNN, thousands of people and press were waiting. Fortunately, D.C. police had roped off the area enabling them to pass. Once on their way, Fielding took over and ordered increased security around the Ardo estate. Josie, resting on Aaron's shoulder, expressed her gratitude. Leon took refuge in Josie's arms, though every so often he sent Fielding a loving grin. Snow drifted in and out of restless thoughts. Zelia's work was done.

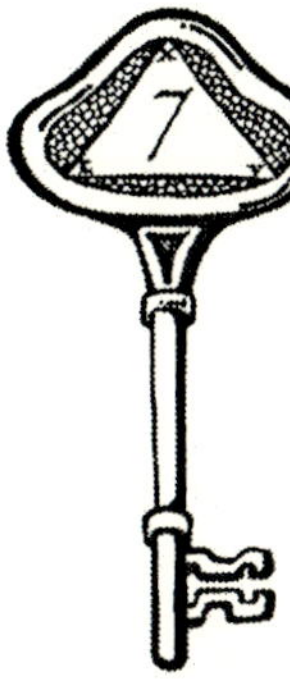

I gazed into my heart...

Fielding darted about the dome checking every square foot. Using a high-tech cellphone, he commanded his staff to secure the dirt road to the house.

Snow, Aaron, and Josie were brimming with energy. They flopped onto the couches in the great room as they reviewed the evening, praising each other amidst hilarious bouts of laughter. The joyous banter was so loud no one heard the knocking at the door until it turned to pounding. Aaron and Snow sauntered to the door arm-in-arm.

"Who's there?" Aaron questioned, trying to see through a peephole.

"Come on, come on, I told you, I want in!" Larry King pushed on the door as Aaron opened it. "Who else could get past this security, huh?" King headed to the couch like he owned the house. "Wow, this is a concrete monolithic dome, right? I hear they're indestructible."

"You know about domes?" Aaron's long face widened.

"I'm the King." Larry smiled as he took a central seat and surveyed the room. "I know a little about everything."

After talking about the challenges of constructing a circular home, the group returned to speculating about the show and its implications. Larry admitted that the Ardo family had come off very well, which brought up a potential problem. "A very positive result can spawn opposition. My crew is a perfect example. Most of them were smitten by you guys. But a few hard-liners are angry; they think the whole thing was staged to sell Aaron's books. The point is," Larry emphasized, "a similar polarization can happen in the public where a fringe segment can be hostile and proactive."

Aaron cringed. It had happened with his book *Positive Pursuits.*

Fielding rushed in. He was in a hurry to return to the compound. "Everything is secured. I've temporarily disconnected the telephones for your safety. I'll be back tomorrow. Do not leave the house; don't even go outdoors." He ignored Larry King who was grinning like a mischievous child.

As Fielding sped around the house one last time, Larry whispered to Aaron, "My producer absconded with the rock; he's having it analyzed. I'm surprised Fielding didn't grab it on the spot. Something smells fishy."

Just then Leon emerged from the kitchen with his tofu and veggie medley—flavors that would make even the most devout meat eater cheer.

Larry attempted to engage Aaron as they ate, "*Positive Pursuits* was one of the most innovative concepts ever. How many theater groups did the book, movie, and TV show produce?"

"Thousands," Aaron added.

"I was speaking to an aide at the White House, who told me the president mentions your book. You know that 'nice guy' image the president projects. It's real. He's a very good person, and I think the two of you would get along." Larry paused to dig into his meal. "Oh, the president wants to study your learning theories, something called Evolutionary Environments?"

"That's it," Snow answered for Aaron. "I run a Positive Pursuits group at my school and it's fantastic. All twenty students have experienced reduced stress, elevated moods, better relationships and rocketing creativity." Snow was excited and started to squeak as he spoke, "Joan Raymond is writing a novel, Phil Maser is composing incredible music, and Susan Lamb founded an experimental dance troupe. The icing on the cake is that every student's grade point average has increased.

"When I see these kids, my entire being brightens. I've never felt so open with a group of teens." Snow's face turned pink. "I love them," he sighed, then added thoughtfully. "Love and creativity, the 'divine duet' as

Aaron calls it; that's what Positive Pursuits is about. That's the fuel for an Evolutionary Environment."

Snow was taking advantage of this opportunity to share the depth of his respect. "I think Aaron's social reconstruction theories are unprecedented. But the real genius is how he brings his theories to life through a *theater group* which anyone can start. Improvisation is a wonderful vehicle for human exploration. You can't imagine where Aaron has taken it until you've been in a Positive Pursuits group."

He took another calming breath and looked at Aaron. "My group is ready to perform which means we can affect the entire school and beyond. Plus, two of my seniors plan to start groups in college. Every student has incorporated the wisdom of Positive Pursuits into their lives. It's alive!" Snow did a seated flamingo dance, clicking his fingers above his head.

Larry did a dance in agreement. Aaron smiled.

"You should see his new work." Josie slid over and rubbed Aaron's hand. "Short stories followed by therapeutic games—you actually become part of the story by playing the healing games with the characters. The book is aimed at families, but it has a program for schools; teachers can even customize a curriculum."

Snow got ecstatic. "I can't wait to read them!"

"I know a lot a publishers," Larry offered. "There are a few ethical types who could get behind your new work in a big way. I could set up some meetings."

"I appreciate it, Larry, but I don't want to do anything to capitalize on Leon's current situation."

"Come on, life is a package deal," Larry said, spreading his arms and exaggerating his Brooklyn accent. "Maybe Leon is meant to help get your work into the world. Isn't that how karma works?"

"Yes, but it's more complex than any of us comprehend," Aaron replied.

"I've got it!" Larry said. "I'll set up an appointment with the Secretary of Education—you're included too, Josie. I loved your ideas about redesigning the physical classrooms to support Aaron's theories."

"Maybe after things settle down," Aaron conceded.

On a roll, the consummate interviewer turned to Leon, who had been watching intently. "What do you choose to be?" he asked.

Leon's glow gave rise to a simple quote. "*I choose that which I already Am.*—Myra."

"Huh?" (King realized he'd been saying *huh* a lot since meeting Leon.)

With a sweeping gesture, Leon invited everyone to the soundproof Meditation Room, a sacred space Josie had created for her family's inner life.

Larry looked around, awed: portraits of enlightened masters lined the walls and candles illumined an array of odd figurines that glowed like living beings. Five brightly colored pillows were arranged in a circle and each person gravitated toward a specific one.

Leon facilitated in the manner of his teacher, Ommatrin of Orvonton. He used the non-breather's words throughout and, in accordance with Ommatrin's teaching style, the experience began with action, not words. Standing very straight, Leon began to breathe deeply, making the breathing pattern visible with graceful hand gestures. The group followed like orchestrated musicians, and quickly merged into a synergy of breath.

Leon reached into his pocket and pulled out the golden key made of light. He turned it toward himself, moving it closer to his body. The group was a single breath when the golden light key penetrated Leon's heart.

Larry shuddered and lost contact with the group breath for a second.

When everyone's breathing was back into sync, Leon turned the key, causing a flood of light to escape from his heart. It surrounded his body like a molten halo. Gradually, his glow diminished until it blended with the light of the candlelit room. Divinely connected, Leon spoke Ommatrin's words, "*You possess a Key of Light. Snatch it from the ethers.*"

Using the graceful hand gestures Leon had shown them, they each produced an imaginary key.

Walter Snow was overcome with excitement. *He's making the Key of Light real! This is the turning point.*

"*Do as I did,*" Leon instructed. "*Place the key within your heart and turn; feel the white light of your Soul flow out and surround you.*

They all did the movement reverently. Josie and Aaron were borrowing each other's glow, causing sublime waves of love. Larry felt awkward but experienced a surprising rush. Everyone was flushed. Ommatrin puffed.

Leon fine-tuned Ommatrin's channel, enabling the Master to speak, like a live broadcast. The boy could hear Ommatrin's soft Om sound and drifted toward it. "*The light of Love has infinite intelligence; surrender, and it will cleanse every level of your multidimensional nature now and forever.*"

Leon surrendered completely and experienced a total cessation of ordinary consciousness.

Woven light ruptured space as Zelia emerged to resume Ommatrin's transmission, allowing Leon to rest in oblivion. The fairy was visible for only an instant before she dissolved into Josie's energy field. Josie's lips began to move. "'*I gazed into my heart. There I saw Him; He was nowhere else.*'—

Rumi. *The Fourth Key of Light: Meditation's Soul Purpose."* Josie knew what was coming and smiled as the words gushed out of her. "*Techniques are not truth, simply a tool to discover truth.*—Walter Snow."

Walt nearly levitated off his pillow.

Josie continued, "*Some religions worship their meditation technique, but in fact, all meditation employs the same essential process: Awareness focuses upon an object and attempts to keep the focus. The object can be anything: viewing a candle, following your breath, chanting the name of God, or silently repeating a meaningless phrase. We have created a dazzling array of meditation objects, but the constant is focused Awareness. What is this Awareness?*"

With the warmth of a non-breather, Josie affirmed, "*This Awareness is divine; it is part of your soul! 'From the moment you came into the world of being, a ladder was placed before you that you might escape.' Meditation is the ladder because it separates the Seer from what it sees. It's your escape.*"

Josie paused. She was experiencing an enthralling level of communion with Zelia. Her entire being tingled. "*This Key is a three-part meditation system. It consists of the Key of Light exercise we just completed, the Heart of Love technique, and the Soul Purpose meditation. Close your eyes; prepare to experience it all!*" Josie intimated.

Aaron's back pain dissolved. Earth currents shot up Larry's spine. Zelia disappeared and Josie reclaimed normal consciousness. Immersed in the moment, Snow felt calm instead of his usual excitement over receiving a Key. Leon's awareness snapped back into his body, and the boy sprang to his feet.

Leon spoke Ommatrin's instructions: "*The Heart of Love breath-mantra technique is simple to do. On your next exhale, say silently, 'God's love.' On the inhale say, 'Fills my heart.' Repeat silently, 'God's love fills my heart' with each complete breath. Do it seamlessly until you feel completely relaxed. Allow it to deepen. End by forgetting about your breath and the words, and focus Awareness on simply feeling God's Love within your heart. Sit in the warmth of your heart.*" Leon paused.

He's leading us in a meditation that ignites the Keys of Light, Snow realized. *This is fantastic . . . where's my notebook . . . Oh shit, left it on the chair . . . that's a beautiful chair, the fabric would be perfect for my office. . .*

"*As thoughts race through your mind, who is aware of thinking these thoughts?*" Leon continued, his voice love-filled and blameless. "*Gently, bring Awareness back to feeling God's Love within your Heart, and thoughts will fade.*"

Larry's heart ached as images of his departed mother filled his consciousness.

"*As you feel painful emotions, who is aware of feeling these emotions?*" Leon's voice sang softly. "*What part of you experiences it? Return to feeling God's love within your heart, and emotions will dissolve like clouds.*"

Sensing a rare moment of collective inner silence, Leon provided the next step. "*Inhale and, as you do, carry God's love-light from your heart, up your spine, and into your upper brain—feel love flood the brain. On the exhale allow the love-light to drift back down to your heart and all your internal organs. Repeat the circular cleansing breathing for as long as desired. The supply of Healing Love is unlimited.*"

Every person's breath was a calm sea as Leon's voice swept over them like the wind. "*The purpose of these techniques is to prepare you for the Soul Purpose Meditation. On the next breath,*" Leon said, "*breathe God's love-light into your brain and stay there. Feel pure consciousness, absent of thought, feeling, and sensation.*" For a glimmering moment each seeker tasted Super-Consciousness—endless hope gushed like a fountain from nowhere.

Leon bathed in it, then concluded, "*Do these practices and you'll be able to dwell in your soul's brilliance every moment of your life. It is Meditation's Soul Purpose.*"

Walt and Larry were repeating silently, *God's Love fills my heart* as thoughts about work invaded. Simultaneously, their psyches split into three parts: the willful mind repeating the mantra, the uninvited thoughts that interrupted, and the divine seer that noticed it all. Larry and Walt could feel the divine Jewel and drifted toward the glassy substance.

A surge of energy rushed through the room (a trillion light-years away, Ommatrin was waving his staff wildly and singing "Om"). Leon waved his arms, orchestrating Ommatrin's currents; flashes of energy shot up their spines into still minds—duality dissolved into a blinding black void.

Time melted.

After an hour each of them was pulled back to form. Leon was still waving his arms as if he was fanning a fire. As everyone's eyes opened to a world vaguely in focus, each seeker recalled Leon's answer to Larry's question: *I choose that which I already am.* Now they knew exactly what he meant.

Leon affirmed this: "*You possess the original spark, the clear nectar of God. Today, you found it. With practice, you can dwell within the Soul even as you navigate the darkest nights.*"

He allowed these words to linger before summarizing the practice, just as Ommatrin had for him. "*Use the techniques as follows: Insert the Key of Light in your heart whenever you desire—use it to center, cleanse, and nurture yourself. Employ the Heart of Love technique and Soul Purpose meditation as follows: begin and end every day with them. Start each session with a prayer from your heart.*" Leon left the room to signify completion.

Everyone felt a pleasurable mix of the here and beyond. In what seemed an elongated perfect moment of now, everyone sat in peace. Eventually

Aaron spoke: "*The Mind of which we are unaware is aware of us.*—R.D. Laing." He reached for his pad and wrote it down.

Snow recalled a quote from an AA meeting, "*If God seems far away, who moved?*"

Laughter rattled free a quote caught in Josie's dusty attic. "This is Lao-tzu," she started, clearing her throat. "*Without going out of his door, One can know the universe. Without looking out his window, A man can perceive the heavenly Tao.*"

"Can we really know it ALL?" Walt questioned.

Aaron responded with the principal's beloved Emerson: "*Let us become silent that we may hear the whispers of the gods. There is guidance for each of us, and by lowly listening we shall hear the right word.*"

Walt countered with I Corinthian's 3:16, "*Know ye not that ye are the temple of God, and the Spirit of God dwelleth within you?*"

Aaron parried with a quote from the Golden Verses of the Pythagoreans, "*Though the good is near, men neither see nor hear it.*"

Larry King chimed in with a Hung Tzu-ch'eng gem, which amazed him because he'd never heard of Hung Tzu-ch'eng, "*The spirit of man communes with Heaven; the omnipotence of Heaven resides in man. Is the distance between Heaven and man very great?*"

Quotes kept flying faster than Aaron could write, so Walt transcribed every other one on a separate pad. "Soul fed" was how the principal described the outpouring, knowing they were channeling information in the manner of their quotable teacher, Leon. "It's what the *Second Key of Light* predicts," Snow realized. "We're accessing ego-blocked brainpower."

After another hour of quote channeling, one thing was certain: the notion of an immortal Soul being illusive but indwelling was consistent throughout time.

Later that day Aaron transcribed the quotes on his computer and gave everyone a copy. He commented on how each quote possessed a special nuance. Aaron affectionately titled the sheet, *Four Lost Souls—Found.*

The road winds out of sight...

Reporters surrounded Fielding's car. Tom Brook led the charge. Fielding opened the window, pointed his finger like a loaded pistol and growled, "I have nothing to say, especially to you."

Brook fired back. "Did you analyze the rock from the King show? Is it of alien origin?"

"Where is Leon being held?" a female reporter hollered from the back. "Can you arrange a press conference with him?"

Fielding revved his engine, then drove through the flock of media vultures toward the hangar where the alien device was housed. The guards at the gate did not look familiar, nor did the increased security staff around the building. Fielding walked cautiously toward the hangar door, opened it, and froze.

Scientists were sprawled out on the floor playing with clay, drawing with colored pens, sucking their thumbs, and enjoying milk and cookies (fresh baked by a lab technician). It looked like a kindergarten. One elderly scientist called out, "I got it!" and began doing a jig like a linebacker after a ninety-yard run. His face was bursting with insights.

I screwed up, Fielding thought, realizing he had put too much trust in his second in command. *Has the journey with Leon distorted my judgment?* He scratched his bristly head and decided he had better gain control of himself before attempting to regain control of his command.

He opened his office door. "Mr. Secretary, sir!" he snapped, stiffening into a razor sharp salute.

"Sit down," Flint Killingsworth, the Secretary of Defense, ordered.

Two guards who had been following Fielding flanked the door.

"General Fielding, we have reason to believe you are implicated in a conspiracy."

"Conspiracy, sir?" Fielding's iron face remained frozen.

"Why did you release the Ardo family?"

"I believed it was best to build trust, sir. If they were foreign agents or extraterrestrials, I wanted to give them room to reveal themselves and their network. They returned to their home only after surveillance bugs were placed, telephones tapped, the works. A hundred men secured the perimeter. Their place was sealed tighter than a prison."

"Why did you go public on Larry King without my approval?"

"Sir, exposing them to the public would—"

"General Fielding, this situation is a circus! That Ardo family should have been retained in top security, under wraps. You know the procedure!"

"They were already unwrapped, leaks were out. I believe I made the correct choices."

Killingsworth sat back. "When you sequestered the scientific staff, why did you give them access to outside phone lines? This makes it almost impossible to uncover the leak."

"Sir, reporters would have tracked down their families. I ordered my staff to call their homes to demonstrate that nothing unusual was happening. We're talking about a possible extraterrestrial encounter, and I wanted to diffuse tensions."

"Diffuse tensions," Killingsworth said with a sarcastic sneer.

"Mr. Secretary, my strategy has worked: We have the cooperation of all three Ardos and we're making progress with the device."

"The device!" Killingsworth shouted, waving a folder in Fielding's face, taunting him. "All the scientists and security people you assigned have been replaced; they're under psychiatric evaluation. To put it in psychological terms, *they went crazy*!" the Secretary of Defense roared, pointing to the researchers on the other side of the glass. "Same thing is happening to the new team out there. We're waiting for the first group's medical tests before we decide what to do with this team."

"Sir, I need a meeting with the Ardos. I may have some insight into all this."

"Insight! What do you have?"

"With all due respect, sir, I can't reveal what I know without verification. I—"

"You *can't*?" Killingsworth shouted. "With all due respect, General Fielding, you are under arrest."

One of the dazed guards came forward. "Excuse me, sir," he said respectfully, as he pulled the general's wrists back and cuffed them.

Fielding's face hardened into stone. He barely heard the rest of the Secretary's words: "You're relieved of duty. I expect a full report within twenty-four hours. Your future depends upon it!"

The guards led Fielding to the security vehicle trying to conceal the cuffs. The media surrounded them as they drove out of the compound. Tinted glass concealed the profound passion that flared on Fielding's face. It was so deep only Leon could understand its origin.

Trying to forget that the Ardos were in danger, Duffy took solace in her garden, and in Zelia. Duffy Rainbow, Saul's soul mate, was one of the few humans able to see Zelia the fairy. Josie guessed this was due to Duffy's complete innocence and her unshakable belief in the goodness of all life. Duffy was a fountain of positive energy, bubbling truth and everlasting youth.

Her buttocks were flat, her hips undefined, but her breasts bulged one foot straight out and she wore tight blouses when she wasn't bouncing about in a bikini. Such breasts were impossible to ignore. They defined her, and she knew it and used them—for good, of course. Zelia the fairy was a perfect example of Duffy's breasts being used for good.

"What's up, God stuff?" Zelia said, just before whizzing into sight.

Duffy loved the way Zelia started talking before she became visible. "Look at this garden, Zelia. It's organic! Saul planted it when I became a vegetarian." She held up a huge carrot. "Isn't it awesome! Saul is such a sweetie—oh, and you too," she said to the carrot.

"Sweet carrots, sweet Saul, Duffy is sweetest of them all," Zelia countered.

"I love you too, Zelia." Duffy bent to squeeze a cabbage which created an opening for Zelia to enter her favorite resting spot in all seven superuniverses—Duffy's cleavage.

"Oh wow, this cabbage is ready," Duffy said, picking up the largest cabbage head she had ever seen. "This is a miracle garden. Hey, that's a good name, *Saul's Miracle Garden*. Look at the size of those melons," Duffy groaned, as she stroked the honeydews.

Zelia chuckled from between warm, buoyant cushions as Duffy moved about the garden, talking to each plant like it was a beloved child. Zelia listened, overflowing with glee.

"Awesome on wheels, this tomato bed is doing better than last year when Saul was using pesticides." Duffy cupped a tomato in her small hands and proclaimed, "You like not having chemicals sprayed on you, don't you? You sweet, beautiful thing." She kissed it. Zelia snuggled into Duffy's heartbeat. "Outside of meeting you, Zelia, this ET business is the most far-out thing that's ever happened to me—not that I have anything to do with it. I love the Ardos, and it would be awesome okay if Leon was an ET, even though he's not. Anyway, I'll bet they could use a Duffy veggie meal," she said, searching the garden for ripe candidates. "I still cook meat for Saul, and I eat salmon when my brain gets fuzzy—Omega-3 oil," she babbled on to Zelia, as she picked her last green bean and sent it love through her hands.

Still explaining the benefits of fish oil, she walked to the kitchen with the harvest. A small TV was on mute, and Leon's picture flashed onto the screen. Duffy ran for the clicker.

"This is Tom Brook reporting from the Pentagon. Jane, this story gets more fantastic by the minute. I have learned from a very reliable source that General Roy Fielding has been arrested. He is accused of mishandling the Ardo incident, and possibly being in collusion with them. Why did he go on 'Larry King Live' without authorization? Why did Fielding allow the Ardo family to return home? Usually, such suspects are kept under very tight security; even reporters don't get wind of them.

"Well, the winds are blowing. In fact, there is a storm raging. General Roy Fielding, en route to incarceration, has escaped from military police. I repeat: General Roy Fielding, now officially charged with treason, is a fugitive."

"How does Brook know so much?" Duffy wondered aloud.

Zelia took off, tickling Duffy, who giggled.

Duffy continued to wash vegetables for the evening meal, but she could not stop thinking about Brook's newscast. Just as she finished cooking, Saul rumbled up in his painted hippie van. He was in good spirits: he'd sold everything from his pepper patch for top dollar. His spirits lifted even higher when Duffy served him a plate of roast with all the fixings. She sat next to him, picking at the beans on her plate.

The Sun was streaming through the skylight causing Duffy's frizzy, auburn hair to sparkle in the sunlight. Saul sighed in awe. He wondered how he'd attracted someone as beautiful and wonderful as Duffy. "Guess what I have?" he said, taunting her by waving a brown paper bag in front of her. "Close your eyes and open your mouth," Saul teased as he inserted a piece of Duffy's favorite dessert, a Mrs. Parson's carrot cookie. She bit down greedily.

"Oh wow," Duffy moaned, "these are the best yet. I never thought she could improve her recipe."

"She didn't. She baked 'em with our carrots. She wants me to supply her—everything we got. Her bakery is booming. And you were right! She loves the organic angle; it's going to take her business ballistic."

Saul handed Duffy a second bag filled with her favorite, overly expensive vitamins. He had spent every penny he'd earned. Playfully, they munched on cookies and took pills as they drifted into each other's hearts.

Suddenly, Duffy jumped up. "Did you hear that?" she gasped. "Really Saul, it sounded like the doorknob turning."

They stared at the doorknob and watched as it turned back and forth. Saul cut the lights, grabbed the cellphone and handed it to Duffy. "Go out the back and hide in the woods. If you hear a commotion call the police. Don't come back unless I call you."

His string-bean body slithered along the floor, then he slid up the front door and peered through the peephole. He couldn't see anything. He crawled to the bay window, rising slowly to the window's edge. "Oh, shit," Saul shrieked—he was eye to eye with someone on the other side. They both dropped to the ground. Despite his drugged-out mind, Saul retained an uncanny memory for faces. He dashed out the door. "Duffy, it's okay," Saul called over his shoulder. "Come in, General Fielding, sir."

Fielding was bedraggled and exhausted and doing a poor job hiding it. His steely exterior slumped over the kitchen table. "We have to help the Ardo family," he panted. "If Killingsworth gets them they could be kept in seclusion indefinitely. Leon's life would be over. We can't let it happen!"

Saul had an idea. "There's a path through some very dense brush. It's kind of an underbrush tunnel that leads to the back of the dome, ten feet from Aaron's office window."

"Zelia could help," Duffy chimed in. "Okay, this is going to sound weird," she said, sending Fielding a lovable grimace. "I know this fairy, and she could cast a spell on the guards, kinda knock them out for a while."

Fielding covered his face with his hands and groaned. But Duffy had anticipated his reaction. When she had fled the house, she'd immediately summoned Zelia. The fairy was nestled in her cleavage.

"It's like this, General. Last week, you visited your mother at St. Vincent's, and she was in awesome spirits. You had such a good time that you agreed to cook Thanksgiving dinner and invite Aunt Bessie."

"Hey, hey," Fielding halted her, snapping his fingers furiously. "How do you know that?"

"The fairy is telling me," Duffy's sweet face gleamed.

Zelia wiggled joyfully in her hiding spot before deciding to pop out. Large pointed ears emerged first, then her arms—twitching and flinging blond curls around her neon lime green face. She was wearing a hot pink mini-skirt of patched diamond shapes, attached by hotter pink suspenders. Her little fairy wings fluttered as she waved her gold wand wildly at Fielding while screaming, "Hi, my name's Zelia." The fairy continued screaming as she bombarded the general with whacks of the wand in the area of his heart.

"My Lord!" Fielding said as the green blur came into focus. He was dazed, but he was getting used to it. "Hi Zelia, my name's Roy. Pleased to meet you," he found himself saying as if he were talking to a child.

Zelia sensed the general would be able to see her, even though few humans could. She bathed him in pink fairy dust as she sang repeatedly, "I will do my part, with heart."

A radiant smile crossed Fielding's face as he realized that he would be leading two hippies and a fairy into battle. "Okay team. We'll take the underbrush tunnel and the fairy, I mean Zelia, can do reconnaissance and cast spells. It's life or death for the Ardos, so double doses on the fairy stuff, Zelia. Now if we get caught do not resist," he instructed. "Tell them I forced you on this mission." He peered into Duffy's hazel eyes and demanded, "Promise me."

She kissed him on his cheek and whispered, "I promise."

Within minutes they were crawling through the dark underbrush tunnel. As they got closer to the dome, Fielding spotted a few guards. They were marching in circles like stuck wind-up toys. He scratched his head, then gave Duffy a firm pat on the shoulder as he whispered, "Give my thanks to Zelia."

Saul pointed to the guard by Aaron's window. "Watch this," he whispered to Fielding as he urged Duffy on.

Duffy stepped out undulating for all she was worth, then she lifted her blouse.

"Oh my God," were the guard's last words before being whacked by a fairy wand.

Inside, Aaron and Josie were monitoring the news. Their problem with Flint Killingsworth was deepening and Fielding's "magical" escape had not helped. But their primary concern was that Leon appeared to be in a coma. He often looked like that when he was journeying *out-of-body* and ordinarily a few shakes would wake him, but nothing was waking him now. Nothing!

Aaron heard a rapping on the window. He turned to Josie, who pulled her gun from the dresser and cocked it. Snow and Larry were asleep in guestrooms unaware that the drama was escalating. Within minutes the rescue party was inside and everyone was awake, except for Leon. Duffy ran to Leon and placed his head on her lap and stoked it.

*****

Modeen halted transmission and the Angels trembled. The sights and sounds of the adventure were vibrating within them and they could still feel the tingle. They needed the Earth story to continue, immediately.

"Oh, it will continue," the Archangel assured them. "Now is when the action really begins." Modeen emitted serene undulating energy, the angelic equivalent of purring. "My part as Mo the gatekeeper shall expand and you must take heed," Master Modeen urged. Sweet ecstasy flowed across Modeen's infinite consciousness bringing with it Ryana, the Story Priestess. The Archangel resumed transmission, the spirals tilted, and the Angels thrashed joyously as Modeen declared, "My advice to Leon is meant for you as well. Take heed," he repeated to his dazed Angel army, "Leon's journey is your journey!"

Leon's motionless body rested, while his consciousness headed down the river unable to control the boat. As he approached the distant peak, he was forced to jump from the canoe which went crashing into the rocks. He struggled ashore where he found a rope swaying graciously and he shimmied to the mountain's top.

Mo was waiting. His eyes reflected energy and calm; his long white hair and beard blew in the wind. As always, he knew why Leon had come. "One of the hardest things to grasp on the physical plane is that *everything* is God, even ugliness," Mo said. "What humans classify as evil is just a lower vibration which God created along with the higher ones we so admire." Mo's ancient eyes radiated a youthful glow. "Everything is God's masterpiece. Everything!"

Love poured through Mo's voice. "Precious one, it is challenging to accept Earth's lower energies, particularly when they are affecting those you cherish. However, there is a purpose for lower vibrations. Trust: Every aspect of your Earth situation has God's priceless signature."

Leon responded with his characteristic trance stare.

The Master glowed as a story appeared in his infinite awareness. Mo's stories were medicine that over time released layers of truth until, at the precise moment of need, the ultimate truth appeared. Leon loved them!

"I want to tell you a story created by a three-brainer, a most delightful being." The Archangel paused as inspiration swelled.

Once, there was a child born with a heart that would not close. Feeling pain, being betrayed, even being violated fueled her compassion, not hate.

As she grew, so did the fire inside her, until it consumed her lower self, leaving but a pure passion to love and serve. So immaculate was she that just being in her selfless presence brought waves of healing ecstasy.

The child, Adina, did want one thing for herself—a pilgrimage. There was a great teacher whose path to enlightenment was love; his school was called the Temple of Love. With passion that consumed all obstacles, Adina finally set out for the quintessential temple of her dreams.

Flowers blossomed, carrying the aroma of distant memories as she neared the temple after a hike that lasted a springtime. But, when she came within sight of the holy structure, Adina collapsed. She crawled, dragging her rubbery feet, pulling herself up the steps within reach of the temple door. Slowly she opened it and was baptized by the same candle that illuminated the Master who sat as still as a stone untouched since the beginning of time.

Without taking her eyes off him, Adina struggled until she found comfort upon a pillow. Rapture turned her arms to jelly and she fell into the cushion, peering at him from her resting, tilted head.

Suddenly, her awareness peaked. She heard a whizzing sound, sensed a faint breeze, and then an agonizing pain ripped down her back. She looked up to see a disciple with a riding whip, eager to strike her again.

"What are you doing on my pillow?" he yelled, his temples throbbing. "Can't you see my initials engraved upon it?"

Dumbfounded, Adina rolled onto the next pillow and another disciple stormed into the room demanding that she move.

Adina rolled until she felt hard ground. There, her heart closed down for the very first time; she curled into a shivering ball and cried.

A gentle touch returned Adina to her heart. Someone was stroking her wounded back and pressing her spine; the caress was sublime. She looked up and there, framed in golden light, was the Master. He had tears in his eyes. He felt her confusion as he stroked her like a caring father would.

Finally, Adina spoke. "Master, I have waited a lifetime to come to the Temple of Love, and I am greeted with brutality. How can this be?"

The master answered, "Two types of people come to a place that teaches love, and they both need each other."

Adina understood, and amidst fiery faces that melted expectations, she prayed that each disciple find his heart and learn to keep it open.

"The road winds out of sight with wonder at every turn," the Master pronounced at the wedding. Who could have imagined that three years later, Adina had married the man with the whip! His anger had been burned by his fire to actualize, and when the embers had cleared, a jewel was revealed.

It boils down to heart, in The End.

Mo paused before adding, "Earth is the Temple of Love." His voice lowered in finality. "My story lives within you. There is nothing to do but watch your heart and keep it open. Be open hearted, open up, open up, open. . ."

"His eyes are opening," Duffy related as she held Leon's head between her mountainous breasts. The huge dome suddenly came aglow with light.

"Well, I'll be. He's been unconscious for hours; a minute with Duffy and he's coming to," Aaron said.

(Leon was one of the few people with no charged reaction to Duffy's chest. Snow was still sweating and he'd been looking at them for hours. People tended to obsess over Duffy until their respect for her increases beyond her bosom size.)

Not surprisingly, Duffy was the most levelheaded. "I get the feeling Leon isn't gonna be riding to the rescue like that Lone Ranger dude," she said. "We need a way to make this right."

"We can't evade the law," Fielding agreed. For the first time in his life, he was following his heart and had no plan. He expected Leon magic. Everyone was hoping for it. Saul was imagining a fairytale ending just as Leon's eyes, drenched in a distant glow, opened.

The child was luminescent as he declared, "*The Fifth Key of Light: Love's Absence Heals. You are on the physical plane to learn to keep your heart open in extreme circumstances.*

"Ask yourself: 'Why train to be a warrior of the heart?'

"The Will yearns for a single star to follow, why not choose the brightest one? (Will, like any nectar, is diluted the more it is spread out.) Humans are spread thin. They are reminded, when cast into survival situations, what a genius they become the instant Will is singularly focused on one vital task.

"For now, here is your one vital task; it is bequeathed from all the great masters. It is simple and challenging. Willfully keep the feeling of love alive within yourself. If anything causes the feeling of love to diminish, heal it. That is it! Be God-like, Soul-like, do one thing: keep your heart open. If everybody did, suffering would disappear instantly, like a quantum miracle."

Leon concluded, "*Focus on maintaining love, and anything that reduces love is revealed. Love's absence is an alarm that reveals the next blockage to be healed. Duality is mastered when Love's Absence Heals.*" Leon winked at Fielding and said, "*Everything is God's Masterpiece! Expand into it with a smile.*" The child pointed to a beautiful abstract painting of Jesus on the cross.

Duffy was quick to translate. "He's telling us to go with the flow! It doesn't matter what happens if we do the love thing. Let them make the first move," she interpreted.

As if on cue, blaring lights flooded through the windows and a bullhorn sounded. "You inside—surrender, we're coming in. I repeat—we are coming in. Show no resistance and no one will get hurt."

Snow feverishly recorded Leon's message, then hid the notebook in his coat. Larry winked at Snow and smiled.

The door swung open and an army of agents flooded the dome. They were relieved to find no opposition, but they had an unexpected hurdle—keeping cool before Duffy's blinding profile. Everyone was ushered into a security vehicle and transported to the compound where Killingsworth waited nervously.

I'm astounded by people who want to 'know' the universe...

Flint Killingsworth had to know whether the alien device was dangerous.

The first group of scientists, taken from the compound for testing, proved to be in vibrant health. Their feelings of euphoria had worn off quickly, but a profound sense of well-being remained. They were brimming with ideas and couldn't wait to return.

This glowing health report did not soothe Killingsworth's anxieties. He was outraged by the disturbing lack of progress; scientists had no explanation for the strange euphoria effect, or anything else. Exposing the Ardos and their friends to the light device was a crude test: if the Ardos knew it to be harmful, they'd balk. Dragging the scientists away wasn't easy, but Secretary of Defense Killingsworth cleared the enormous room, and positioned the Ardo gang two feet from the alien light where hidden cameras were planted.

Leon sat serenely looking at the globe, while Snow's eyes darted about taking in everything. Aaron and Josie sat holding hands, lost in the alluring light display. Larry was dazzled and leaned over to Duffy and said, "This thing shines almost as bright as you do." She smiled and kissed him. Saul became euphoric immediately.

Secretary of Defense Killingsworth wanted the Ardo contingent to remain at the compound. He returned to the Pentagon and administrated from there. The effect had been getting to him and he feared for his safety. Besides, he had to be objective to handle the new crisis.

At first the strange euphoria had only affected those very close to the globe, but it had spread to the whole compound. Now it was affecting an entire town three miles away. The townspeople called this expanding area, the "Euphoria Zone." Andy, the owner of the diner, named it the *E-Zone* for short.

Killingsworth wanted containment. He ordered a radiation-proof lead box lined with the alloy used in nuclear reactors. Reflectors were installed that would cause the light emanations to shine back on the globe. "Let's see how it likes its own medicine," Killingsworth grimaced when he heard that the containment box was ready. He sent his two best agents to perform the simple task of inserting the device into the box.

Three hours later the agents were found laughing hysterically on the floor beside the device, unable to stop; they were ushered away in straightjackets. It was surmised that the globe device, somehow, had done this to them. One scientist proposed that it was protecting itself, and attempting to confine the device actually increased its power, like the human equivalent of an adrenaline rush.

Killingsworth decided to relocate the device to an underground chamber in the desert where nuclear research had been conducted. He ordered a truck that had been used to transport nuclear weapons. A remote controlled robotic forklift was designed to slip under the device, then transport it to the truck.

A simple operation.

But when the forklift touched the device, the globe on top of the base brightened and the entire hangar began to shake. Several agents thought it was an earthquake. On the second attempt the shaking returned with greater severity. As the technicians persisted, the globe began to sizzle like a covered pot ready to explode—the shaking surpassed the danger point as blasts of light erupted. Panicked, they pulled the forklift out. The hissing and shaking stopped, and the light returned to "normal."

Everyone agreed: "The device stays where it is until someone figures out what it is!"

Killingsworth made concessions. The current scientific team would remain and select members from the first team would be invited to return. (Being in the E-Zone was a risk, but the scientists wanted to take it— and Killingsworth needed them to.)

"This is Tom Brook, reporting live from Fairview, a small town only three miles away from the compound where the Ardo contingent has been detained. Let me tell you this place is going wild. The townspeople want Leon to run for mayor of Fairview! This is the nicest place I've ever been."

"Excuse me?" Jane, the anchor, queried.

"Last night, Grandma Widellton, the town's oldest resident, made me the most delicious blueberry pie. You gotta taste this stuff. It's a story in itself."

"Tom, this is Jane, have you any more information on the Ardos?"

"Jane, the Ardos are like gods in this town. What can I say? It's Ardo-mania. You gotta love 'em!"

"Tom, are you all right?"

"I'm fantastic! Oh yeah—I hope to contact my sources anytime now, and I'll get back to you when I have more."

"Tom, wait . . ."

Several hours later, after returning home, Tom Brook realized he had made a fool of himself by going on the air stoned on the euphoria effect. He was trying to concentrate on a new plan to redeem himself but a yellow fly kept tormenting him. Those bugs were nasty biters and the last thing he needed was a welt on his face.

Tonight's story will be a mind-blower, he thought, as he drank old orange juice from the container. The reporter was going undercover which could result in losing everything—if caught. (It was assumed that no CNN journalist would impersonate an army officer to gain access to a story.) However, such stunts were how Brook had climbed "close to the top," as he put it. His plan was to infiltrate the compound dressed as a ranking officer. No one would question him if he had papers. *Easy stuff,* Brook thought, recalling capers far riskier than this. The "buzz" brought him back to reality.

He lunged at the insect. "Darn that fly!" he cursed, grabbing the fly swatter and feeling vengeful. He waited and watched. It was man against beast.

Buzz, Buzz, Buzz.

"This is the fastest friggin' fly in history," he grumbled through clinched teeth, doubling his concentration.

Buzzzzzzz.

"Ouch!" It flew right into his face. Brook swung around and swatted himself, creating a pattern of little squares on his forehead.

"Now it's war," he vowed, beginning a strange martial art breathing exercise. He expelled air like a heaving hippo while waving his swatter, Kung Fu fashion. His swinging techniques were performed with great precision.

Buzzzzzzz.

It was headed for him again. He swung furiously as the sound took residence in his ear. He freaked, slamming his ear with his hand. "Ouch! Goddamn it!"

The fly escaped and headed for the closet. Brook trailed, swinging violently. "I'm going to kill you, you son of a bitch." He saw it land on the uniform he was planning to wear and took the hint; he began dressing and thinking about the character he'd be playing.

Zelia, the yellow fly impersonator, whizzed within the ethers above Brook's head. The yellow fly performance was not just frivolous fun; she was breaking Brook down in order to cast an itty-bitty spell. She wanted him to gain entry to the compound. "Nothing like having a snoop on the payroll," Zelia sang. He was her insurance policy. Besides, Zelia found him most entertaining. "Get the big story and help the Ardos, help the Ardos," Zelia chanted, as she sprinkled green dust above his head. "Help the Ardos, help the Ardos."

Except for the yellow fly, Brook was enjoying operation E-Zone; it was so James Bond. He knew the euphoria effect must be lingering because he felt overly optimistic, and this was good since his priority was to project confidence. Attitude would get him through the gate and into the hangar where the alien device, and the story, were located.

Using Brook's shoulder like a stage, Zelia began singing a little ditty she'd written called, "What Are Fairies For?" It expressed her golden rule: Fairies create happy endings. She opened her fairy heart wide and began chanting directly into Brook's left ear, "Get the big story and be a hero. Help the Ardos, help the Ardos."

"Maybe it's the uniform," he said, when the thought of rescuing the Ardos flashed into his mind. Brook scratched his head. "Ridiculous!"

Buzzzzzzzzz!

"Not that damn fly again!"

Brook was feeling lightheaded as he drove to the compound, unaware that the euphoric effect was extending ten miles out from the center. (He would later learn that the army had attempted to evacuate the locals and that everyone had refused to leave. On the contrary, people were flocking in.)

The E-Zone was becoming a Mecca of magic seekers. Brook was impatient. Cars were stopping in the middle of the road, enabling drivers to chat through open windows. People were dancing in the street. It reminded Brook of his prime objective: Resist the euphoric effect! He gathered all his will as he finally arrived at the farthest end of the compound's huge parking lot.

He took a deep breath, straightening his shoulders, and began to walk toward the gate reminding himself, *I am Lieutenant John Kane from the Pentagon.* Brook came within speaking range of one guard and before he had the chance to present himself, the guard waved him on. Brook waved back, displaying his papers.

"Bless your heart, brother," the guard belted out, as he made a fist and tapped his heart. Several other guards were walking by arm in arm, laughing.

"That was easy, and I got blessed to boot," Brook mumbled to himself. *Maybe the euphoric effect should be the point of my story, not the Ardos. Something extraordinary is happening, and no one understands it!* He strained to maintain mental focus.

"Help the Ardos, help the Ardos," Zelia sang as she cast her spell while sprinkling her most potent powder.

Brook approached the hangar realizing he could have it all. If he helped the Ardos, he'd have an inside track on discovering the truth about the euphoric effect. *I'll be the Ardos' advocate, their mouthpiece to the world. Why report history when I can make it?* Brook was so engrossed in his thoughts, he was unaware of striding right through the hangar door.

"Wow!" he blurted out, then quickly covered his mouth.

(Inside the compound, groups were huddled in explosive communion, each wildly out of step with the others, though they were unified by a brazen openness. Intellectual boundaries were dissolving. Even fundamentally held truths about the universe were shedding brittle skins, revealing the raw flesh of revelations.)

Joyful chaos surrounded Brook as rushes of energy surged through his body. He knew he wanted to be part of what he felt, to help. *You're not a helper; you're a taker,* he reminded himself, wiping his lips with the back of his hand. He struggled to remain objective.

Dreams are jewels you snatch from the fire, Brook scribbled on his pad. He liked the phrase and thought it would be a provoking lead-in to the evening's news piece. *No it won't! It stinks!* He battled to hold his focus. Then he realized, *Dreams are jewels you snatch from the fire* would be a great first line for his novel. *What novel? You're a reporter, not a novelist—stay focused, stay focused!* "Shut up, people are looking," he murmured to himself. "Stay cool, you idiot."

Brook calmed himself by focusing. He noticed that whenever a group of scientists broke into mayhem, they would settle immediately afterward into a quiet cohesion. Like in the Hundredth Monkey phenomenon, groups near an upheaval also became more cohesive. Unity could be tasted; even people who wanted to think alone were surrounded by others thinking alone. Brook roamed aimlessly. He overheard a doctor talking to an architect about opening a preventative health clinic; the architect wanted to build it using sacred geometry. People and ideas were unifying into visions beyond everyone's expectations. Brook named these collective insights, E-Dreams; he was writing the copy feverishly when Zelia used his shoulder to launch herself toward Josie.

Across the room, all two hundred people in Aaron and Josie's lively discussion group concurred: The globe was reducing their egos, and thus creating the euphoria effect and the feeling of unity. Josie had an "aha" moment when she said, "The effect isn't foreign, the intensity is. It's the same loving, open, creative feeling one has during a Positive Pursuits group, only more."

"It's true," Aaron chimed in, "creative flow, the essential mechanism of my acting method, also reduces ego and produces the unifying euphoric effect." Bubbling with insight, he added, "Euphoria Zone would be a great name for an improv troupe. It could travel and share the E-Zone with the world."

Clearing his throat, Snow interrupted Aaron's fantasy. "It's the *First Key of Light—Undoing Exceeds Doing.*" He looked to Aaron, who gave him a thumbs up.

"Walter's right," Aaron agreed. "The light isn't doing anything to us, it's undoing us." Putting a hand on Snow's shoulder, Aaron added, "Just like Leon quoted, losing an illusion will make us wiser than finding a truth."

Speeding toward the truth, Aaron's group hit the classic impasse. Now that they had a theory about *what* was happening, the far more challenging task was to discover *how*? *How* mandated direct access to the light device, but Fielding's hands-off approach couldn't be overturned. It was, in fact, reinforced by an extraordinary development.

The alien object was growing. The change was slight, but there was no doubt that it was enlarging. Even the most aggressive researchers conceded that the evolving device must remain untouched, for now. They began calling it an "ED," short for *evolving device*, for want of a better term.

Brook was headed for the ED. People and machines were crowded into every surrounding inch; wires were in a tangled maze, much like the scientists who scampered about recording data and adjusting the electrodes attached to the human subjects being tested.

Brook lost focus. He saw Larry King receiving accolades and swerved to avoid a confrontation. Too late!

"Hey, Brook," King called out, "nice costume. Come over here; I want to talk to you."

Brook's cover was blown. In an attempt to cover his tracks, he noticed the Ardos, and threw King a question, "How come they aren't locked up?"

"Fielding let them out when they promised not to leave."

"Who let Fielding out?"

"I don't know. It just happened, like everything else around here. Fielding is running the show, coordinating research, the works. I'm doing fact-finding for him right now." King pointed to a stack of index cards in his hand. "Fielding is amazing. He's got the place humming."

King returned to surveying the progress of each group, while Brook roamed mindlessly and ended up alongside the Ardo entourage.

"How can a light dissolve an omnipresent mental function such as an ego?" Aaron said as his arms danced with his words. "People have devoted entire lifetimes to conquering their egos; they cloister themselves, purify, meditate—they even remain celibate, and with this and more, most achieve only moderate ego reduction. Separating from the personal self is the hardest thing to do! Yet, within two hours of being around the ED, BAM." Aaron's brown eyes sparkled as he peered at the glowing globe. "It's truly amazing."

Perfect, Brook thought, *they're discussing my story angle! Everything's coming together.* After listening for a while, Brook walked towards the ED and saw scientists fiddling with the wires attached to Saul and Duffy's heads. The string bean gardener could hardly believe that he, Saul Rainbow, was involved in a government-sponsored study. But Saul conceded that everything was "pretty cool" as he felt Duffy's hand searching for his.

"I'm proud of you for volunteering," Duffy said. "Dr. Rector told me you enrolled most of the subjects. That is truly amazing, dude!"

"Well it's a talent one has," Saul replied in a formal British accent, tilting his head sideways.

Duffy broke out in hysterical laughter.

Brook was standing next to Duffy and lost all focus when he saw her huge breasts heaving in her skimpy top. He regained composure the instant he heard two scientists talking about people in the adjoining town having illness remissions. When one scientist used the phrase "healing miracles," Brook knew he had to find the recipients. He left the hangar swatting the air.

The guard thought the reporter was waving at him and offered another, "Bless your heart."

"Darn these yellow flies—it's an invasion!" He laughed as he took a final swat, then disappeared behind tinted glass.

Fairies love to ride in cars.

Like the single tick of a divine clock, several days disappeared. Researchers continued to explore outlandish insights. Breakthroughs, that would normally be hoarded, went unclaimed as members surrendered to a shower of prophetic, thunderous beginnings.

General Roy Fielding was gathering it all. He was searching for a thread, a truth that would weave everything together. In his gut, he knew that when found, this truth would placate science and the government.

Fielding continued to manage security. The staff didn't care that he was an escaped felon. They knew Fielding was, by far, the best equipped for the job, and that was enough for them. Like everybody else in the hangar, Fielding was following inclinations unhampered.

(It was the same in the adjacent town, Fairview. The social order did not collapse when the euphoria effect saturated it. People pursued their normal activities, but now they were approaching them with wild enthusiasm and creativity. Laborers made their work fun by working together; storeowners lovingly created record-breaking sales. Commerce flourished within the E-Zone, along with everything else. People were working all night because they were having so much fun.)

Josie, Aaron and Walt hadn't slept since they had arrived at the compound, so Fielding insisted they use his small office. Three comfortable mattresses were carried in and the window that looked into the hangar was covered. Still, none of them could fall asleep at first. So they rested in each other's arms until they drifted off. Time liquefied, depositing them five hours downstream, entwined. Snow was the first to wake.

"What a nap! I feel great!" Snow said, with a noisy yawn.

"Me too," Josie and Aaron said in unison.

All three laughed as they headed back to the main room and a surprise.

The ED had undergone a growth spurt! The strength of its euphoric effect had intensified and was spreading. Scientists were ecstatic because they'd finally succeeded in measuring the light emanations.

They heard one scientist allege, "*When the only tool you have is a hammer, you view everything as if it's a nail!*"

Another voice rang out in a deep British accent. "*Thoughts are but dreams till their effects be tried.*—Shakespeare." This got a rousing applause.

In a sleepy-deep voice, Snow joyously contributed, "*I'm astounded by people who want to 'know' the universe when it's hard enough to find your way around Chinatown.*—Woody Allen."

Everyone in the hangar exploded into laughter. Snow was rolling on the floor holding his heaving sides until he gradually calmed into a revelation. . .*The Keys of Light—they're coming to life within the E-Zone!*

10

Imagine flipping a one-sided coin...

His gut still aching from laughter, Walter Snow remained on the floor and his eyes naturally closed. Images flooded his mind until he was paddling through a shimmering mist of water. He saw heavy rapids approaching so he took what seemed the best course, right down the center. He emerged into a wide calm and paddled peacefully toward the shore. The boat was amazingly responsive. Within seconds, Snow was standing before the crowned cliff wondering how he would get to the top.

"If I were a balloon," he sang, rubbing his belly like a magic bottle, "I could float to the top." He slowly rose off the ground past the base of the mountain, past the heart where wild flowers sprang up defiantly. Soon he was facing the large rectangular rocks that lined the crest like the spikes of a crown. He levitated above them, then drifted down on an angle to the flat mountaintop.

He turned to what he thought would be a breathtaking panorama. Instead, sprawling in every direction was his life. He was looking at his beloved grandma's home in New Hampshire, the mountain he'd climbed in Tibet and the dream house in Woodstock he couldn't afford. Even the place of his birth, Brooklyn, New York, towered amidst the golden haze. It was all taking place simultaneously.

Snow discovered that if he stared at a particular location, feelings related to it blossomed forth. He looked in the direction of Hunter College, his first teaching job. He was overcome with the pride of being a professor—and the disgrace when he was fired for teaching while intoxicated. A drenching love washed over him as the room of his first AA meeting came into focus and faded into fear of slipping into addiction. He saw himself in primal therapy screaming, "I HATE YOU," while his therapist smiled approvingly.

Then he saw the device organism—it was pure light with no polarity. Snow focused on the organism's leathery base and it began to sparkle serenely. When he looked into the globe, its swirling colors united into revelations. He took a deep breath of perfumed air and glanced up.

"I am Mo," the gatekeeper heralded, his white beard flowing in the wind.

Snow turned to see an old man swinging beneath a huge tree, and the moment their eyes met, the old man began swinging wildly until he reached the ultimate height. Momentum provided an extended ride during which Mo conversed the entire time.

"Can you imagine swinging beneath a tree if there was up but no down?"

Snow shook his head.

"Up requires down. Good requires bad. Birth requires death, and yes, death requires rebirth." With a sweep of his arm he explained: "Everything in creation is in balance with its opposite. Meditate on that." Aware of Snow's confusion, Mo suggested, "Try to imagine a one-sided coin."

Snow closed his eyes, his forehead wrinkling with effort.

"Aha! Ha ha ha," Mo laughed. "A coin must have two sides, just as up must have down and good must have bad." Pulling an ancient gold piece from his robe, Mo said, "Opposites are a single system like a two-sided coin is a single thing!"

He flung the coin into the air. "Call it," Mo dared, as it headed down like a rocket.

"Heads!" Snow blurted.

"Right," Mo affirmed! (His swing came to center just in time to catch it.) "See how exciting a two-sided world is. Imagine flipping a one-sided coin in a world where there is up but no down."

Snow's forehead widened into a flat, playful plane.

Mo looked to the heavens and declared, "*Give me one positive and one negative, and I'll have enough to build a universe*. My friend Ommada said that;

he knows that the same interplay of opposites that binds molecules keeps planets spinning in orbit. On the physical plane, duality is so all pervasive that humans fail to recognize it. So, I shall provide four tips to help you navigate God's playground, a dimension ruled by the interplay of opposites."

Oh my God. He is the source of the Keys! A shiver shot up Snow's spine. He was about to ask if this was so, when Mo provided the key piece of wisdom.

"As you encounter the darker sides of this two-sided plane, remember: Duality's purpose is to advance the soul by providing infinite possibilities, dark and light. No matter what happens, never forget that duality is a gift from God, not a punishment!" Mo repeated, "Duality is a gift!"

Angels fluttered. Dimron froze.

Mo's face brightened. "Tip number one for maximum Soul growth within a two-sided existence: *Judge less.* It's all God's masterpiece, and since it is a two-sided masterpiece, why not accept both sides? Accept that good requires bad and you've eliminated judgment and suffering." Mo sighed. "It is difficult for two-brainers—a biological polarity—to reduce judgment. The instant spiritual essence unites with the animal body polarity is born. A baby seeks pleasure and avoids pain. As a baby evolves, pleasure/pain becomes good/bad, right/wrong, and moral/immoral. When you righteously proclaim that your religious belief is better than another, remember such righteousness is rooted in primal animal pleasure-seeking, not in spirit. Judge less and love more—in any order." Mo laughed heartily. "That will begin the balancing act." He took both hands off the swing, defying gravity.

Snow caught his breath as Mo continued, "You meet someone and think, *I don't like her*; a month later, you're engaged to be married. She gets sick and you think, *this is terrible*, but she has a life-transforming healing that makes her better than before." Mo added with a twinkle, "As many times as good gives rise to bad, bad gives rise to good. They are a working system, like a two-sided coin. You don't make one side of the coin wrong and the other side right.

"It is wrong to leave a sick old man to be eaten by bears if you live in America; however, in some Eskimo cultures, it is an honor to eat the bear that has eaten your loved one. Dissimilar perspectives cause different beliefs, judgments, dreams, and religions! Here is the key to understanding the Earth plane: Almost everything you think and feel is an impression created by your experience on Earth. What you call truths are illusions created by your righteous, polarized, animal mind. They are all judgments."

"My judgments define me, not the world outside of me that I'm judging," Snow offered.

"Exactly," Mo agreed. "And that is their value!"

"Value?"

"Judgments are still-photos of your unconscious, negative patterns. You can use them to heal yourself," Mo heralded. "Ah, the perfection of this two-sided world: the malady leads to the cure!

"Willfully decrease judgments and loving presence will appear. Then you will discover God's empty eyes and know why a galaxy exploding is no more important than a leaf falling. This is even difficult for angels to grasp."

Dimron took offense; his dissension buzzed through the vast angelic field.

Snow was watching a leaf fall as Mo summed up with an assignment. "Will yourself to be aware of judgments or beliefs that are saturated with negativity. When you utter or think one, relax, trace it into yourself, breathe into it as you gently pull it out at the root. Let it go! Every day you'll feel lighter and your garden will look more beautiful." Mo winked and glistened. Snow settled into sweet contemplation.

"This is an important tip for humanity," Mo offered to a melting Snow. "Tip number two: *Avoid Extremes*. They stagnate culture, limit creativity, and separate people into conflict.

"In a two-sided dimension, extremes simply do not work." The Archangel began to swing wildly. "Imagine struggling to get a pendulum to an extreme height." He swung higher. "When you let go, the pendulum swings to the opposite side with equal force. To avoid the opposite side, you must get the pendulum to your side and keep it there. You are burdened with its weight forever."

Swinging past Snow's head, Mo cried out, "Fanatics never triumph because of this." Burning with the fire of creation, Mo added, "On Earth, there are men whose beliefs are so extreme, they'll strap bombs to themselves, and they do this in God's name. Religious extreme carries a perilous degree of judgment and danger. Extremes create opposition. That is why there are so many religious wars on your planet.

"War is a battle between extremes. Eliminate extremes, and you'll end war forever, I guarantee it."

Mo's teaching was peeking its jam-covered cheeks above the windowsill of Snow's imagination. The principal smiled childishly and said, "Hate can dissolve into forgiveness and enemies can become allies.

"Forgiveness is not necessarily a spiritual thing. This shocks holy humans who have made a religion of it." Mo zoomed past Snow's eyes.

"Behind most acts of forgiveness is a judgment: You are right and someone else is wrong. True, you are willing to forgive that wrong—but there is a more God-like way. Rather than discerning something as wrong, then forgiving it, find no fault in the first place! God does not convict you, then forgive you. Accept that everything is God's masterpiece and you are free and Soul supported!

"If extremes do not work in a world of opposites, what does?" Mo asked. Snow made no reply. "Balance! Balance works on *all* planes of existence, especially two-sided worlds."

The Master sprinkled sugar into the jam. "Tip number three: *Create Balanced Decisions.* As you reduce judgment your consciousness widens and decisions become more balanced and encompassing. For example, if you take your children to a museum where they are forced to be silent and not touch anything, afterwards, take them to the park where they can scream and roll on the grass. If you punish your child for wrongdoing, incorporate reward for right doing. By tapping the constructive interplay of opposites, you can transform an ordinary decision into an extraordinary one. Consider this account:

"Jan wanted her daughter Ana to go on a raw foods diet; the girl's severe acne was worsening because she was eating junk food with her friends. When Ana begged to go on a trip with these friends, all Jan could see was greasy food and sweets. Jan said no. Then she remembered (with a little help from an angel) tips for living in a two-sided world. She repeated them: 'Accept, Avoid Extremes, Balance.' Just saying those words triggered a balanced decision: Ana could go on the weekend providing she began the raw food diet when she returned. This idea was joyously accepted. In the end, Ana grew to love raw food and her acne disappeared. What does that say about balanced decisions?

"Tip number four: *Expand into Limitlessness.*" Mo raised his arm like Moses parting the sea and a breathtaking sunset appeared. "When you are enthralled by a sunset, you believe the Sun is setting; you forget it is also rising on the opposite side of Earth. The Sun is rising and setting somewhere on the planet at all times; however, it is natural to see what is happening where you are and make it reality.

"There is something very powerful about saying, 'Somewhere the Sun is always rising.' Acknowledge events outside your perception because almost everything is."

Snow didn't move.

"Ask yourself honestly: in an infinite world of evermore to discover, does clinging to limited beliefs seem rational? Doesn't expanding make more sense? Do you have the courage to let go of your beliefs and expand?"

Snow could feel himself clinging. He closed his eyes, traced the clinging back to fear; he relaxed, took a deep breath, then plucked it out. Energy rushed up his spine and into his brain.

Mo allowed the feeling to settle before summarizing, "To judge and limit within limitlessness is ridiculous. Expand, include, and go beyond. Rejoice in Infinity! You have forever to experience it.

"Perhaps we should balance these ideas with an experience," Mo considered as his eyes misted. "Leon always insists upon a new technique. Would you like to learn a divine meditation that supports the tips I've just shared?"

"Very much," Snow answered, his face pink with anticipation.

"It is another warm-up for the *Soul Purpose* meditation," Mo noted softly.

Snow thought about the Keys and was certain Mo was the author.

"Meditation creates balance," Mo instructed, while Snow watched the swing. "Close your eyes and observe your breath. Do nothing but experience it." Mo waited and watched. "Most likely, you've observed that your inhale is different than your exhale. Bring your breath into seamless balance by making the inhale exactly like the exhale in every way possible."

Snow did the breath technique and his mind stilled immediately, his energy field brightened. The Master instructed, "Allow breathing to continue automatically as you flow into the *Soul Purpose* meditation: Bring your attention to the brain, right at the third eye, and sit in the void—empty of thought. If thoughts persist, return to the *Balancing Breath Meditation;* then again, rise into the upper brain and rest in the void of pure consciousness."

After allowing a reasonable time, Mo looked to the heavens and affirmed, "With practice you will become the One Consciousness where there is no duality, no interplay of opposites! There, you will 'experience' the one-sided coin you cannot imagine." A light illumined Mo's eyes as he said, "God is a one-sided coin! Your Soul is a one sided coin!"

The wise old man returned with an addendum. "At moments of stress or if you are depressed, tired, or out of balance, try this magic trick. It was created especially for two-brainers."

"Cover one nostril and breathe in a few times. Cover the opposite nostril and breathe in." Mo demonstrated. "You may notice that one of the nostrils is more clogged than the other. With your thumb, close the side that is most open and breathe through the more-clogged side until it opens. Work both sides thusly until they are open and balanced. Return to the *Breath Balancing Meditation,* making the inhale and exhale seamlessly united. Doubly balanced, close your eyes and see yourself whole and happy; include anything you want to manifest into that picture as you say with conviction, 'It is done!' Affirming while in a state of balance produces magic, so if you keep the nostrils balanced throughout the day, expect miracles."

Mo looked to the sky. "Taoists understand the two-sided world; they know why less is more and more is less. Ha! We can't escape the humorous dance of opposites."

"Is this part of the Keys?" Snow asked. "Is this the next Key?"

"It can be if you want," Mo said.

"I can't choose a Key," Snow replied reverently,

"Ha! It's time you learn about Leon's way." Mo's voice was warm but firm. "The Keys are not an absolute doctrine. The Keys grew out of the moment; had events been different, different ideas would have been supplied. Cherish the Keys like a carpenter loves his tools," Mo sang. "But do not deify them, because that will ultimately result in extremes and limits. Have a contest to see who can create the next Key," Mo suggested, with a chuckle. "Enjoy being forever on the alert for wisdom."

Mo's face gave off immaculate light. "Religious and spiritual training should not be rigid hands that pull you in—rather open palms that gently usher you into the void where Truth is experienced beyond words."

Mo started swinging wildly, emitting chaotic howls that matched his defiant glow. Higher and higher he swung. "Duality has a third element," he revealed, swinging hard enough to make his first complete circle.

Snow's eyes popped open when people began shouting, "Leon is speaking . . . he's telling stories. He's talking about Buddha now; it's amazing!"

Snow's mind raced, *The Keys come in pairs! That's it! The first and second, undo and surrender, both reduce ego. The next pair is "Awareness of Awareness" and how to achieve it with the Soul Meditation. The fifth Key matched the information he had just received from Mo because both were about living in a dualistic plane.* Snow realized that the name of each Key was exactly three words long. *Why?*

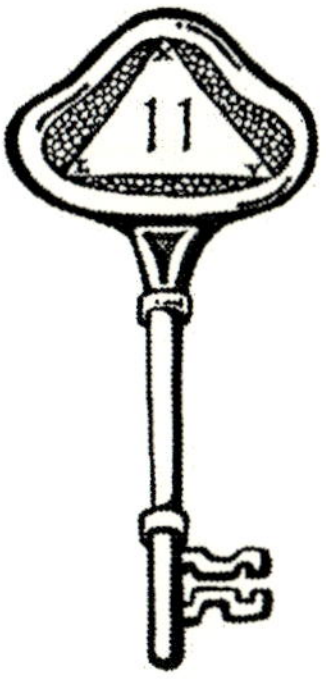

Out beyond ideas...

Tom Brook gazed through the trees at a beautiful waterfall. The remote truck was late. He called CNN control and confirmed that the crew was on its way. It was decided that if they didn't arrive within ten minutes a timeslot would be created at the top of the following hour. It wasn't as good but it would do. He was on the phone with operations when the crew arrived.

The cameraman stormed out of the van trembling. "I'm sorry, Mr. Brook. The traffic. . .people are stopping in the middle of the road. It's—"

"It's okay." Brook smiled. "We can make it." He raised his voice so the crew inside the truck could hear. "Let's pull together."

"Yes, sir." The cameraman snapped to attention, adding a funny hand gesture mimicking Brook's perfect camera angle. The reporter smiled.

The E-Zone was continuing to expand and the crew was giddy from the effect. Realizing this, Brook scurried between helping them and coaching the guest waiting in the car. They were ready with two minutes to spare. Brook walked up to the camera, positioning himself for the perfect angle. He took a deep, fulfilling breath. "Jane, this is a humble and amazed Tom Brook reporting from the edge of the E-Zone."

Evening's glow cast a halo around him. "*Miracle* is the word used to describe this astonishing development." Brook's voice was soft, vulnerable. "People in the E-Zone are being healed of life-threatening diseases. I personally spoke to three terminally ill patients who've had complete remissions. "I have with me Doctor Nathan Rector, administrator of Archmont Hospital, the only hospital in the Euphoria Zone. Dr. Rector, what's changed since Archmont came under the influence of the E-effect?"

"There's no scientific way to explain it. All my terminal patients have had complete remissions. Over thirty attending physicians report similar incidents. The remission count is over a hundred people."

"How common is this?"

"Complete remissions, in such advanced cases, are extremely rare. I've seen two in my forty years. What's happening is unimaginable."

"Dr. Rector, is anything else unusual happening?"

"Oh my, yes! For the first time in Archmont's ninety-year history our emergency room is empty. Even minor accidents have ceased!" The doctor's face was alive with awe. "People are less prone to accidents in the Zone." He snapped his fingers and spoke in rap rhythm, "I say, people are less prone to accidents in the Zone. I say, people are less prone—"

"Doctor, you mentioned earlier that the word *miracle* best describes what is happening. Could you elaborate?"

Dr. Rector considered. "The sheer magnitude of these events implies a supernatural force." The setting Sun was a playful red ball behind the doctor's head. "The best explanation we have is that these healings are the act of a loving God, a miracle."

"Dr. Rector, are you doing anything on the scientific front about this amazing phenomena?"

"We've sent a research team to the compound. The government has over three hundred medical researchers there, with more coming. We hope that together we can understand this extraordinary occurrence. We pray these healing miracles will continue, and hopefully deepen."

"Deepen?"

Magic lit the doctor's eyes. "The euphoria effect does more than heal; it promotes longevity. It elicits an anti-aging effect and possibly age reversal."

Brook shivered. He knew he had the story of the century. "Doctor, can you elaborate on this anti-uh-age reversal effect?"

"Like the miracle remissions, it's a mystery. I don't know how people are being healed or how aging is being reversed, but it's happening!"

"You're saying we may have discovered the fountain of youth?"

"Based upon what I've seen, we're bathing in it as we speak. Anything is possible in the E-Zone." Doctor Rector began snapping his fingers and chanting sweetly, "Anything is possible in the Zone, anything is possible in the Zone."

The camera zoomed in on Brook, who repeated, "Anything is possible in the E-Zone! But one thing is certain! Something beyond human comprehension is going on. Is it a divine miracle or a message from an extraterrestrial culture—perhaps both! Whatever it is, CNN will be here to report it. This is Tom Brook—"

"Tom," Jane interceded, "Tom, are you there?"

"Yes, Jane."

"Tom, has anything definitive been learned about the alien device?"

"That's the question of the day, Jane. So much is happening at the compound; it's literally overwhelming. There are over forty research groups, some with over two hundred members. Research is just beginning, but it won't take long to get answers with General Roy Fielding in charge! I'll be following the Fielding story closely and when anything happens in the E-Zone—and it will—I'll be there."

Brook yearned to be back in the compound as he paused for his closing remark. "No one knows what's happening. But something unbelievable is occurring, and by all definitions it is, indeed, miraculous."

"Tom, that was a 'miraculous' report," Jane cut in. "We look forward to your story tomorrow. That was our own Tom Brook from the edge of the E-Zone."

They knew they had just filmed a defining moment. Brook found himself dancing with Igor the cameraman, while Dr. Rector accompanied them with rap.

"Did you see that closing shot?" Igor bellowed. "The Sun was setting behind your head, Mr. Brook; you looked like an angel from heaven. It was," everyone declared together, "Miraculous!"

"Alien device—divine miracle?" questioned the man peering into his TV screen as he watched Brook's CNN report. As the segment ended, he thrust up his pen in a movement like disemboweling prey, then scribbled a few notes before falling back into his torn, vinyl recliner.

Boyd "the Bird" Venton had made a career of hate mongering, culminating in Rights for Whites, a hate group with millions of members worldwide. It had grown because of his media stunts. On the previous Martin Luther King Day, a hundred Klan members had removed their hoods and revealed their identities while chanting, "I believe in Rights for Whites." Though Venton was a gifted media hog, the press had gotten tired of his dirt and stopped covering him. Out of the spotlight, he had gone searching for a way to slither back in, never dreaming the E-Zone would provide it.

The Powers That Be were monitoring sales figures in the Euphoria Zone. Cigarettes, pharmaceutical drugs, illegal drugs, and alcohol sales had stalled. Junk food and meat sales were zero. The gun shop was empty, even the owner didn't want to be there. Except for people watching Tom Brook's reports, television viewing was minimal. The Powers That Be didn't need an accountant to project what would happen if the E-Zone continued to expand. Venton knew they had no choice. The organism had to be destroyed!

An intermediary had offered Venton the job, because Boyd provided perfect camouflage: If he succeeded, it would appear that racist fanatics had destroyed the E-Zone. The Powers knew that *instant* terrorism with Madison Avenue flare was Boyd Venton's specialty, and they'd counted on that when they had handed him ten million dollars in cash.

Venton rocked in his recliner, considering his plan. He would assemble a fifty-man assault team. From what he'd heard, people in the E-Zone were incapable of violence: to infiltrate and destroy would be easy. But first he would create a media campaign depicting the E-Zone as an evil threat to mankind. With media saturation he could make his military operation look like a grassroots uprising, exactly what the Powers That Be wanted.

Venton's first action would be to enlist Dick Falco, his VP at Rights for Whites and the meanest bastard he knew. Falco, a mercenary soldier, would be the perfect man to assemble a small army of terrorists and keep it underground.

It was set! While his underground army was being assembled, the Bird would soar above ground polarizing public opinion. He would allocate two million dollars for mailings and press releases, and beef up his staff at Rights for Whites to do the job.

Eagerly, he contemplated his standard formula: brainwash with a snappy slogan that decimates the enemy. He had to make the E-Zone appear evil. He needed a hook, a gimmick—one concept to unify every flier, e-mail, and press release. "Continuity facilitates trust and mobilization," he affirmed.

Inspired by that, he wrote: *The E-Zone will destroy you like any devilish drug!* The phrase "devilish drug" was powerful; it contested the news about healing miracles. *Addicts have to believe their drug is good! They defend it more fervently than they defend their God.* His mind wandered: *The E in E-Zone means—The End!* It sounded good. He sketched it out and studied it from a distance. It looked as good as it sounded.

A large segment of the mainstream was consumed by predictions of an apocalypse. He could tie his anti-E-Zone campaign into this widespread fear and claim that the E-Zone is the *end* that so many have prophesized.

Exhilarated, he wrote, *The E-Zone is the apple in the Garden of Eden! God told us once, "Do not eat of it." But we did! If you were Adam and could have grabbed the apple from Eve's hand before she took a bite, would you have done it? The answer is yes! Yes, you would! This is your chance. Take the apple from Eve!* He imagined thousands of voices chanting, "*Take the apple from Eve!*" (His market was men, and he knew this angle would pull big.)

Venton was very skilled at building a foundation for hate by weaving extremes. He pulled out a non-filtered Camel, then flicked his lighter; he wanted to see how long he could keep his hand under the flame. Boyd smelled flesh before withdrawing his singed palm and lighting his cigarette. *Extreme situations create extreme reactions*, Venton thought, knowing he would be the extreme reaction.

He returned to writing. *Take the apple from Eve! This light, this alien enslaver, this devilish drug is hypnotizing people, altering personalities, and changing basic human nature. Who knows what else it's doing to us? You've seen the news clips from inside the zone. Imagine our armed forces under the E-Zone influence. We would be incapable of defending ourselves. We'd be in fairyland. It would be our End!*

Zelia squelched a cry—Boyd felt a sharp pain above his eye.

Blinking his beady, bird eyes, Venton fell into a deep concentration and after a second creative surge, he had the entire campaign perfected. *The E in E-Zone means—The End!* would headline two million newsletters, e-mails, and press releases by the end of the day. "Less is more," he muttered, unaware that the Powers That Be were activating hate groups all around the world, and he was the trigger.

Certain that Tom Brook would devour his story, bone and all, Boyd Venton set out to find him. He had a hunch Brook was at the compound and drove towards it cautiously. Venton sat motionless studying the activity at the gate. No one was being stopped or searched for weapons. He had wondered how Tom Brook was getting his information and now guessed that the reporter simply walked into the compound, just as he was planning to do. *Brook and I are cut from the same mold*, Venton thought. He forced a scowl, hoping to erase the lightheaded feeling.

It was no accident that he was wearing his worst polyester suit and resembled the three scientist geeks walking toward the gate. Boyd "the

Bird" glided next to them and walked right into the compound. *This has to be a trap,* Venton thought as he entered the hangar. His buttocks clenched like a man on a tight rope; his beady eyes darted like a trapped hawk. "Bingo," Boyd whispered the moment he saw Brook standing by the device.

Though Brook had been coming to the hangar every day, he was dumbfounded as he stared at the organism that had now grown to the size of a small house. He also noticed that the mood in the hangar had deepened—there was more introspection. Brook saw an almost divine glow upon the scientists' faces.

Venton scanned the room capturing every detail with his photographic memory as he moved toward Brook. He tugged the reporter's sleeve and said, "Brook, it's your good friend Boyd with a story you can't refuse." Boyd winked sarcastically. "By the way, good disguise, fooled me for oh—two, three seconds!"

"You too, Boyd. By the way, you look white as a ghost. How long you been in the Zone?"

"Long enough." His pellet eyes glanced at his wristwatch.

"Give it another hour and you'll feel better, I guarantee it—and boy oh Boyd, you sure could use it," Brook smirked.

"I won't be staying. I came to see you about a big story that's brewing. Want it or not?" Boyd made for the door.

"Wait, wait, I want it. I'm playing with your head, Boydie Boy."

Boyd got right to the point. "There's a growing anti E-Zone sentiment in America, and I'm their spokesman."

Brook knew Venton was a fanatic, but he was a credible source in this context. The reporter shuddered and asked, "What's your story?"

"This light thing," Venton snarled, turning to it in disgust, "is a drug and it's devouring our culture. Lots of people think it has to be terminated! You want details, meet me with your remote crew." Boyd handed him the directions and time, knowing Brook was hooked. Boyd's forehead was mellowing. "I'm getting outa here while I can; this thing ain't right." He turned to leave, only to be met by an iron chest.

"Boyd Venton," General Fielding growled, "you know it's illegal to be in here." Three guards surrounded Venton. "I'll have to detain you for questioning. You might be in the Zone for weeks." Fielding winked at Brook, who squirmed. The general's open-door policy was an ingenious trap, and it was working!

Walter Snow saw the arrest and chuckled. *Polarity in action,* he thought as he began to write. *Sixth Key of Light: Up Without Down? "Out beyond ideas of wrongdoing and right doing there is a field. I'll meet you there."—Rumi.*

God's playground, the physical plane, is a two-sided dimension. Accept both sides by judging less, avoiding extremes, making balanced decisions, and expanding beyond self-imposed limits. Expand into limitless possibilities, rather than bear the weight of one side. ALL these actions reduce your lower ego mind which bring you closer to God, Soul, and Truth. Accept both sides in a two-sided world and you are Free! The path is simple but challenging. Judge less—Love more (in any order). If life becomes challenging, ask yourself, what fun would it be to flip a one-sided coin in a world where there's up but no down?

Snow felt the presence of great Souls and heard their voices. His hand danced across the page as he spoke their words. "*To set up what you like against what you dislike - this is the disease of the mind.*—Seng-t'san.

"*There is nothing either good or bad, but thinking makes it so.*—Shakespeare.

"*Thou canst not stir a flower without troubling a star.*—Francis Thompson."

Mo smiled radiantly and began swinging on angles never swung.

12

Scientists are people who...

The ED was now the size of a two-story house and its gray skin was becoming increasingly translucent. Scientists agreed—the ED's skin was stretching, indicating that, like any organism, there was a limit to its size. Surrounding the expanding ED were scientists and equipment. This ring of science (as it became known) was surrounded by another ring of people who stood mesmerized by the globe's light emissions. As the organism increased in size, so did its brilliance.

Occasionally the ED produced intense bolts of gold light, and after the "oohs" and "ahs" died down, those standing the closest experienced incredible insights. One scientist had colleagues note the time and degree of their breakthroughs which he compared with the time and degree of the light emanations. The results were uncontestable. The bolts had a magical effect upon the brain, particularly on the right side that regulates creativity.

Ironically, as brain research began, it looked like the ED was growing a brain! Where the globe met the gray base, hidden by the rolling colors, was a ridged membrane. The lights appeared to originate from it, but the colors were so bright the so-called brain was hard to observe.

What was easy to quantify was the ED's physical growth. This led to the only real fact, supported by precise equations: the larger the organism grew, the larger its zone of influence became. By now, the euphoria extended a hundred miles from the center and it was moving about a mile an hour. Time, distance, size, and intensity variables were charted. But these projections had nothing to do with the real mystery. It seemed an insurmountable leap from *what* was happening to *how*.

Many scientists spent time seeking intuitive answers. Like mystics gazing at candles, they sat before the ED in open-eyed contemplation. Some meditated while touching the soft leathery surface hoping contact might provoke revelation. Some stroked it lovingly. There was a small group that humbled themselves in prayer, pledging devotion and asking for a sign.

The ED seemed to be tranquilized by all forms of affection and communion. One of the original scientists, remembering the organism's violent reaction when agents tried to move it, deduced that it must possess a range of emotions. He performed a simple experiment and the results were conclusive: The more hate projected at the organism, the brighter the globe shone; the more love projected at it, the less it shone. This discovery spread through the compound. It was a crack in logic that might solve the mystery.

The discovery caused blissful optimism as the afternoon progressed and Fielding's daily meeting approached. At six sharp, all the groups ripped themselves away from research and headed for the area by the exit known affectionately as Fielding-Zone or F-Zone.

The general, uncharacteristically late by thirty seconds, bounded onto the makeshift podium. He seemed more in control than anyone else and wasted no time. "Any significant discoveries?" he asked, fingers snapping.

He heard a shy cough from the back, followed by a chuckle that spread across the room.

"It's me again, Albert, and I'm no *Einstein*, but I have a theory that explains everything in rhyme," he reported in rap. (Lots of people were talking in rap—rhyming and rhythm seemed to balance the brain while making a point memorable.)

After enthusiastic applause, Albert Feinstein, "not quite an Einstein" stepped up to the platform. He marveled at the ease he felt. "Most of us believe the organism is alive and conscious. I'm convinced it has a four-hemispherical brain, and each hemisphere has unique functions." Albert

Feinstein's face glowed with wonder as he speculated, "Imagine what its consciousness might be like with four brains, each over ten feet in size, each working at full capacity." Albert pulled his prized Cross pen from his ink-stained shirt pocket and made three little dots in mid air. "I want to lay out a three-part hypothesis, as concisely as possible."

Fielding loved the orderly nature of scientists and listened intently.

"The foundation of my theory is this: The ED feeds on lower vibrations, of which our ego is a part. I repeat—The organism eats lower vibrations; its food is literally our anger, fear, hate, and anxiety."

Faces brightened.

"We assumed the lights were reducing our egos, and thus producing the euphoria. This is not true. The organism's light is nothing more than the human equivalent of feces. When confronted with negativity to consume, it shines brighter. The more it eats, the more it poops."

Laughter turned into buzzing conversation. Excitedly, Fielding turned to the scientist sitting next to him and said, "You have to respect a guy who gets 'poop' into the first minute of a major scientific theory."

"That is why, that is why," Albert kept repeating, trying to be heard above the buzz. "That is why our emphasis on finding the healing property within the light has yielded nothing. We've been looking in the wrong place. The healing agent, the 'how,' is something on a much higher wavelength or possibly on a different dimension altogether."

A cheer rang out from six groups, including the Ardo contingent. One group had an immediate insight; their leader called out, "I think we know where to look!"

"I think we know *how* to look," another group leader declared.

"Let's take a break," Fielding encouraged. He knew the scientist had struck gold, and this was the general's way of allowing creativity to synthesize while maintaining order.

Albert watched the room whirl with excitement. He was having the peak experience of his bashful life and he allowed himself to wallow in it. He placed his pen back in his pocket, creating yet another ink line next to his heart.

Fielding pranced over. "Maybe you should drop the *F*, Mr. Einstein. Good work, son." Fielding squeezed Albert's bony shoulders as he commanded his troops, "Attention! Your attention, please! I believe that Feinstein the Einstein has part two of his theory." The room silenced quickly, except for a few lingering exclamations of: "Oh, wow!"

Albert resumed. "Realizing that the organism is doing something beyond our present awareness, we can assume it is connecting to an aspect of 'us' that's also beyond our awareness." He was about to become technical but changed course when he saw Saul Rainbow. "Science has not adequately studied the energy field that surrounds the human body and all living things, including plants."

One of the botanists present couldn't contain herself. "It's an Eden outside! Dead plants are coming to life. I found several undocumented species. It's unbelievable."

"I think I know why," Albert volunteered.

The audience leaned forward.

"We believe the human body creates an energy field. Right?" Albert looked around. "Right?" Heads began to nod affirmation.

"Wrong! It's the exact opposite! The energy field is creating your body!" The crowd was riotous. "Your aura is not just creating your body, it's housing your mind, emotions, and your Soul." Amidst the uproar, he acknowledged, "Again, we scientists got fixated by one side of the coin!"

"Right on!" Snow confirmed.

Josie whispered to Aaron, "Honey, wasn't that the premise of a story you wrote? *Emily's Aura*, that's it."

Aaron planted a kiss on her high cheekbone and whispered into her ear, "Fantasy becomes reality!"

"If it is true that the field around us creates us," Albert continued, "then by influencing the field, you influence the body, mind, and emotions that make us up. Physical illness, mental illness, everything has its vibrational counterpart in the energy field."

The crowd applauded, then settled into silence quickly.

"The organism is consuming the lower vibrations in our fields. I've met healers who claim that maladies appear as debris in the aura, and that they can dissolve them with the appropriate vibrational remedy. They further state that they can strengthen the energy field and thus strengthen the entire constitution of the body, mind, and spirit. And that is exactly what the ED is doing!"

Albert produced a pair of rattles and shook them. "Vibrations," he proclaimed, and began dancing and rattling like a Native American Indian. "Heeya ho, heeya ho," he chanted.

The crowd was captivated by his unexpected antics. Fielding tapped his foot in time.

"When I was a kid, a typical science nerd," Albert confessed, still shaking the rattles, "I thought the Indian medicine man was an idiot. Remember the old Western movies where the medicine man dances around the dying chief, shaking a rattle and singing?" He mimicked the medical practice as he chanted, "Heeya ho," and got a thunderous laugh.

"I was wrong," Albert confessed above the laughter. "This medicine man was a shaman; he could see energy fields! He was using the rattle to dislodge debris from the chief's aura. Simultaneously, he danced and chanted to the Gods. Plus, he gave medicinal herbs to address the problem on the grosser physical plane. This *idiot*, as I thought, was actually providing physical, spiritual, and vibrational treatment concurrently. His approach was far more advanced than our myopic one-dimensional medical practices."

Albert paused, then spoke deliberately. "Saul Rainbow came to me the other day and said, 'Scientists are people who take 2000 years to discover what folks back then already knew.'"

Wild applause broke out from the audience.

"He's right!" Albert agreed, shooting Saul a two-fingered peace sign. "I wish my doctor waved a rattle instead of a prescription pad."

Laughter and more applause ensued. A group of doctors did a Native American dance together.

When Albert put the rattles down and announced, "Part three," the room stilled. "Albert Einstein, not quite a Feinstein," he began to another uproarious cheer, "said roughly: The more I study matter, the more it looks like a thought.

"The notion that the gross material world has its origin in non-material essence is not a new idea. We've been told all our lives that we are of spirit. Enlightened masters claim to have direct experience of this non-material essence. Many of you, because of the E-Zone effect, are beginning to experience such direct-knowing."

The crowd nodded confirmation. Aaron pulled Josie close as he pictured Leon's angelic eyes.

"If we can prove that the aura creates the body, then we have proven the existence of non-material essence. The problem is, we can't prove it—unless we get help from our four-brained wonder." A rainbow streak of light shot straight up from the ED. "I think it said 'yes'," Albert interpreted to unrestrained cheers.

Slowly the room hushed and every Soul "knew": The ED was a living super-being. The group entered a deeper sense of wonder.

"Your Soul is the substance that holds the energy field together. Death occurs when the physical body can no longer support its vibrational maker, and the Soul-enmeshed aura withdraws. Since this imperishable, non-material essence has no physical substance, it must ascend to a dimension that is also non-material and imperishable. We may be able to prove the existence of a Soul and an afterlife," Albert claimed, gazing reverently at the organism. "It's our link to it All!"

The audience was breathless as Albert continued, "I believe the organism uses two of its four-brain hemispheres for spiritual explorations. I presume it dwells in multidimensions simultaneously. In fact, I believe that billions of dimensions exist in this room right now, and it can experience them all.

"We concede there are other dimensions because we experience a few of them: there is the physical, what we see; there is the atomic, and there is the subatomic. What else? It knows! It knows the truths our lost humanity so desperately seeks. And it's possible we can know!" Albert paused then said solemnly, "I'm close to communicating with the organism, directly."

The room was still.

He looked at the ED lovingly. "Through it, we can prove the existence of God!"

People gasped. Fielding's eyes closed as his head dropped forward. Everyone followed his lead. No thoughts interfered—only the stillness of One Consciousness reigned. When everyone's eyes opened simultaneously, they saw Albert raise his arms like a giant seizing a bolt from the sky. "The ED is our link to the unknowable—it can fulfill our impossible dreams, " Albert heralded as he stepped off the podium amidst wild applause.

Saul and Duffy were standing right beside the stage; Albert began to giggle when Duffy's breasts obstructed his path.

"Hey man," Saul said, rubbing the scientist's bony back. "You need anything— people, materials—you come to One-Stop Saul. Okay?" Never in Albert's wildest dreams could he have imagined that this tie-dyed hippie would become his devoted confidant.

As people cheered, Zelia emerged from her hiding place in Duffy's cleavage. She was happy for humankind, but unraveled; if people understood energy fields, they would understand how fairy dust worked. It could destroy the mystique. She wiggled off that unpleasantness as she flew to her next target, the tip of Albert Feinstein's large nose.

Amidst the clamor and non-stop clapping, Albert returned to the podium and picked up the rattles. "Heeya ho, heeya ho, . . ."

Softly, others joined him until the entire room dissolved into the simple sound. "Heeya ho, heeya ho, . . ."

While he was scratching a strange tickle on his nose, Albert noticed that the ED was glowing differently. For the first time, a blue colored light was coming from hemisphere three; he could actually feel the rich hues touching his skin. Invisible fingers of light began massaging everyone's muscles. People moaned as they chanted, "Heeya ho!" Albert watched the audience begin to move, until two thousand souls united in a mysterious, swaying resonance.

The ED continued to produce waves of colors that now penetrated people's connective tissue. Physical sensation was peaking!

Spontaneously, Duffy began to move her arms gracefully above her head like impulsive snakes. The ED responded with vibrant bursts of color, and everyone felt a buoyant sensation, as if gravity were lessened. Josie and Aaron began dancing wildly towards Albert. The scientist pointed to Fielding, who was swiveling his hips while making impressionistic salutes with both arms. Joy rushed through Josie, triggering a wild shriek. Like a whistle starting a game, her shriek caused mayhem.

Free form movement broke out. Cartwheels and flips were occurring everywhere. Pairs formed spontaneously, and the energy in the room quadrupled into a medley of dance, physical comedy, characters, skits—whatever a thousand playful geniuses could produce unhampered. Pairs flowered into groups of twelve or more. The movement madness surged into eight large groups that merged to become the whole group again.

The ED marked the event with erratic pulses of light. Voices sang, "Heeya ho, . . ." The chanting grew louder and louder as makeshift drums and rattles accompanied the shrieks. The ED's lights continued flashing. "Heeya ho, heeya ho, . . ." Louder and brighter it became like one drum pounding thunderously on and on, until an array of light shot around the room, finding its mark in every heart.

Everyone froze, holding whatever pose they happened to be in. The light also halted in perfect accord. Fielding was frozen in a passionate salute aware that the mysterious, magical ED had baptized them all.

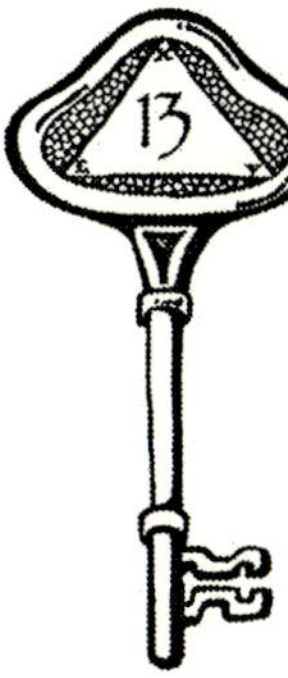

Take the apple from Eve...

Tom Brook cruised down the highway. It was surprisingly quiet. Trees, rich with new growth, swung playfully, causing old leaves to cascade in graceful spirals. Brook's heart was pounding. He was headed for the story of a lifetime, and he wanted to turn around.

The day before, he had interviewed Boyd Venton who had accidentally mentioned the Powers That Be. Brook had known a friend from journalism school, Max Palter, a reporter daredevil who had been doing a story on the Powers That Be. Max claimed that five men of incomprehensible wealth were "in control" of world affairs. This control was all consuming and amounted to a single, worldwide government. Even the United States was its puppet. Weeks before publication, Max had died in a car accident along with his story.

Brook shivered as he slowed to the speed limit. He had no illusions. The Powers That Be had vast avenues for destruction, and if they wanted the E-Zone destroyed, they would not rest until it was. *They've never encountered anything like the organism*, Brook thought, trying to ignite some hope.

He began daydreaming about Dina, the waitress he had met at Andy's diner that morning. She had started a conversation about the effect of media on culture and had given him her undivided attention when he responded. He had done the same and was rewarded by her sparkling insights. Asking for her telephone number had been easier than asking for the second cup of coffee. He recalled that after breakfast, people were driving more courteously. Townspeople seemed to be happy and present, engaged in the moment. The original E-Zone wildness had been replaced by a serene focus.

As Brook continued driving toward the outer edge of the E-Zone, the pace began to pick up. Cars were stopped, people were screaming out of their windows and dancing in the streets. It felt like the first crazy days at the compound. Then Brook realized the obvious. The E-Zone effect was an evolving phenomenon. *Who knows where we might end up in weeks, let alone years? What about lifetimes?* Brook's imagination went Technicolor.

What if the organism is an intergalactic vacuum cleaner sent by ETs to save us from ourselves? What if this cosmic cleanser is not alone? Cloaked spaceships could be hovering above Earth, ready to protect the organism. The organism could be in constant communication with them. Even the Powers That Be wouldn't have a chance. It seemed like a great science fiction story and Brook saw himself writing the screenplay.

Earth is completely encompassed by the E-Zone effect and becomes the Eden of everyone's dreams. But then, extraterrestrial warriors discover us and, thinking we are easy prey, they attack. The newly-empowered UN is in control of the world's army. It wages a great battle and loses. The conquerors enslave the masses and all the beauty of the E-Zone is gone.

A rebel leader emerges (Brook cast himself in that part) *and seeks to rescue Earth by organizing the masses. Just as this revolt is about to fail, organisms like the one at the compound materialize everywhere. Their negativity-devouring capacity obliterates the invaders who escape, swearing never to return. The E-Zone is back! The movie ends with one of the organisms spelling four words out in light: "Love is the force."*

With tears in his eyes, Brook imagined the titles dancing down the screen as he and the heroine (played by the waitress) walk into the sunset, her lustrous blond hair glistening in the warm light of a new day.

As he drove out of the Zone, Brook realized that the euphoria effect, without the wildness, was heaven on Earth. He noticed that trees were hanging like skeletons in the stillness. A gray cast overhead seemed to be pushing down the sky, causing Brook to feel suffocated. The thought of returning to his old "out of zone" ways made him sick.

He knew an invincible force was converging upon the Zone to destroy it. Dark and light might collide before his eyes, creating the story of all time. All he could think about was saving the organism.

A horn blared behind him and a threatening fist shook from the window. "Move it, buddy," the stranger shouted; his intensity was like a blow to the head. Brook couldn't understand why there was so much traffic. It didn't take him long to discover that anti-zoners had surrounded the Euphoria Zone and were limiting entry.

Brook found their hub, a small roadside town with lots of motels. The dissidents recognized him, and within an hour Brook was doing preliminary interviews with anti-zone leaders. They were obviously financed by the Powers That Be and had a unified message, straight from Boyd Venton's newsletter. Brook pushed for new information but only got variations of Venton's platform: "The E-Zone is a killer drug and must be destroyed!"

When he called CNN with his remote location, Brook's awakened self was crying, *Return to the E-Zone.* He chose one anti-zone leader for the live broadcast; he didn't want to give all of them exposure. He had just finished prompting his guest when the truck arrived and Igor vaulted out, giving Brook the now patented, *I know the right angle* move. Brook faked a chuckle, then told him where to set up.

"Feeling a little down?" Igor offered sympathetically.

"Wait till you hear tonight's story," Brook said, indicating he would say no more.

Igor was getting an establishment shot down motel row. A dark cloud cooperated as he filmed the motels where several large meetings were emptying into the streets. The shot looked and felt like an evil carnival had come to town.

Brook questioned whether going live on Larry King from this location was wise, but King had insisted. As the time approached, Brook's weighty ego re-appeared, bringing with it fear and anger. The euphoric effect was almost gone.

"Lights, camera, action," Igor commanded.

Brook listened through the earphone as the show started. "Ladies and gentlemen, this is Larry King and tonight's show is about the story of the century, the Euphoria Zone. We have Tom Brook, the man who broke this story. He has a special report. Let's go right to Tom."

"Hello, Larry, this is Tom Brook with a heavy heart. Around the perimeter of the E- Zone is a growing army of people calling themselves anti-zoners. Various fringe hate groups have set-up headquarters in this small town where they're recruiting and organizing dissidents." Igor was cued to show his set-up shot as Brook said, "You can see down Main Street several meetings are breaking up. In ten minutes, these streets will be filled with people who want the organism destroyed at any cost. We have with us one of the organizers of the anti-zone movement, Mr. Dick Falco, vice president of Right for Whites. The same group founded by Boyd Venton, who, rumor has it, is being detained in the Zone.

"Mr. Falco, we've heard your argument that the E-Zone is an evil drug. Don't you think you should experience it before you condemn it?"

"I don't have to try heroin to know it is bad," Dick Falco countered, shooting Brook a menacing look. "Every drug peddler sounds like you, 'Try it. It won't hurt you.'" He made a fist and shook it at the camera. "We are not going to try it. We're going to stop it!"

Falco was more radical than he had been in the pre-interview and Brook realized he'd been duped. "Mr. Falco, how do you plan to stop it?"

"First priority is to stop the spreading. People have to understand that we *cannot* allow some unknown life-form to control our minds and bodies without our consent. If this E-Zone effect continues to expand, it will mean the End! As for stopping it, we hope that public pressure will cause our government to intervene. We know the president is keeping a low profile, but soon he'll have to take action." (At that moment the president of the United States was approaching the compound by helicopter.) "We are here because this could be Earth's defining moment, and we want to cast our vote. Keep out! Stamp Out! The *E* in E-Zone means the End."

Brook cringed.

King was thinking about the organism and yearning to return to it. "Mr. Falco, this is Larry King. Reports indicate the spreading is slowing significantly. Would you be satisfied if the government could contain the E-Zone to about its present size?"

"Larry, as far as containing it, I don't think they can. We want the government to stop this thing completely! America can't risk the possible fallout. These next few weeks are critical."

That's a specific time period. Falco slipped, Brook thought. He wanted Dick to divulge more. "Mr. Falco, Boyd Venton told me about a plan to attack the compound. Do you think it is still feasible?"

"I don't know what you're talking about," Falco spit back. The watching world could feel the tension.

Brook retorted immediately, "How do you reconcile the destruction of a living thing that is healing diseases and saving American lives?"

"There is no substantiation to any of that, and if there were, remember, the devil wears disguises. We have a chance to take the apple from Eve, and this time we will do it. We can't risk the negative, long-range effects of this thing. No one knows what it's doing to us; we're playing with the devil's fire."

Brook saw a fight break out a hundred yards behind them and watched as it spread into a riot. Igor filmed as Falco bolted with Brook at his heels. Bodies were flying and Dick Falco, after several wild punches and equally wild profanities, began pulling people apart. Brook watched and realized Falco was nothing more than a vicious henchman leading a pack of wolves.

Igor motioned to Brook to begin a new commentary. Just as a body fell between them, Igor let Brook know that he was shooting the perfect angle.

The reporter laughed and amid washes of love he realized that the E-Zone was alive within him. "This is Tom Brook reporting amidst the chaos."

14

This might be the Second Coming...

Leon had gone to the ED's north side and was sitting with his back against its leathery base. Those with third-eye sight noticed a subtle change; the organism seemed to be leaning toward the child, like a tree growing toward the Sun. Though the ED towered sixty feet, it did not overpower Leon. Albert Feinstein wondered if the "opposite factor" prevailed, which would mean that Leon was fortifying the organism, not the reverse! Word of Feinstein's latest idea spread faster than flapping fairy wings.

Astounded by his portrayal of Buddha, people continued to gather around Leon, expecting to hear revelations. Even Albert Feinstein and his team made the hundred-yard pilgrimage. Leon was about to begin his dramatization on the life of Jesus of Nazareth when the president entered with Fielding and a dazed sergeant from security. Only the sergeant saw the president turn pale as he beheld Leon and the organism.

Fielding looked concerned. "Mr. President, I—"

"Roy, will you stop calling me that," the president insisted as he stared at the ED.

"Okay, Sam," Fielding conceded. "I've been reporting to you and not to Flint Killingsworth because he can't grasp the miracle."

"This is the most unbelievable thing I've ever seen," the president said, squinting. "Look at the colors around Leon; he's connected to that thing, isn't he?"

"You can see the connection?"

"If I look sideways," the president answered.

"Fantastic, Sam. Only a small percentage of people can. We're discovering that third-eye sight is linked to other hidden powers. Probably why you're the best damn president this country has ever had!"

"Enough, Roy," the president said affectionately. "You know, I regret you didn't accept Killingsworth's post. I know Sylvia's passing shook you, but half of you would have been enough."

"Thanks. If I had known you were going to appoint Flint, I would have taken it. I know you did it because you needed the conservatives to get your agenda accomplished." The general's mind flashed to the moment the objects had disappeared and he'd allowed Leon and Aaron to return home. "Killingsworth hurts people. He scares me, and you know I don't scare easily."

The president shook his head. "About your arrest, we'll get a retraction out." The president poked the general's iron arm and noted, "Your escape didn't make us look very good. You'll have to tell me how you did it." He leaned in and winked. "Flint was getting a lot of heat for your arrest. After your escape, he stormed into the Oval Office feeling vindicated. I told him I'd sooner believe myself a Russian spy than you a traitor."

"Don't bet on it," Fielding said, as his lips rolled into a rare sarcastic grin.

The president smiled, squinting. He could see Leon's aura bleeping between one dimension and another as the organism did the same. Suddenly an arc of light connecting Leon and the ED became visible. Everyone present gawked as the two auras melted into each other, creating delicate sparks at eight points—what some call chakras. Leon and the organism appeared to be an energetic whole.

"He's in communication with the organism. Somehow we have to get through to the boy," the president said to Fielding, just as the energy field around Leon's face started to pulse.

General Fielding grabbed the president's arm securely.

The child's cheeks were bulging like dough bubbling in a pot; it looked like his head might explode as it reshaped itself. It was terrifying to look at. Then the light around Leon's body began flashing, frightening the crowd. Confusion ensued. People groped in the blinking madness unable to see anything. But when the brightness finally subsided, everyone opened their eyes to a miracle: Sitting before them was an exact physical representation of Jesus Christ at the age of fourteen. Gasps and groans rolled across the audience.

Albert Feinstein scribbled faster than his heartbeat. *Changes in an energy field can cause immediate alterations of matter. Energy-field manipulation could render surgery obsolete! Matter can be rejuvenated! Death can be eliminated!!!!*

"I am Jesus," Leon said serenely. The sound of his voice was surreal, as if he were speaking directly into each person's ear. Those present could almost feel the moisture of his breath, and it took a moment for this strange intimacy to become pleasing.

Leon, as Jesus, began with a revelation: "You may wish to rewrite your calendars because my actual date of birth was August 21, 7 B.C.!" Jesus scanned the audience as he said, "Humans erect huge informational structures which they confuse with truth. Truth transcends mind; it is found in silence where the Light of One Consciousness shines. Finding the Light of your Soul, finding God is the divine sport of life on the physical plane."

Snow realized that Jesus' first statement summarized the essence of the keys. He turned to a blank page and wrote—*the Seventh Key of Light.* His pen hung over the page.

Jesus sat very still. A look of compassion spread across his youthful face before he said, "Blaming yourself for my death is as foolish as blaming a cat for killing a mouse. Accept your animal nature. Then, transcend it by uniting with the Divine. Rejoice in the dance of dark and light, and you too will be able to hang from a stake while loving those who drive the nails into you."

People cringed.

"I celebrate your evolution into divinity with stories about my life and times." Jesus paused.

The president's eyes were glued to the ED, certain that this miracle was a turning point for planet Earth. *There are times when a leader must turn all his attention onto a "single" event. War is such an event: why not a miracle? I need to be here,* he thought, though he knew some people would not agree. He solved his internal battle by surrendering to the story, sensing that the answer to his dilemma was contained within it. The president squinted as the teen-age Jesus began glowing like a shining sun. The ED's lights were like wispy clouds in the background.

"At the time of my birth," Jesus offered, "humankind was undergoing a spiritual awakening. It was a perfect time to reveal God's love.

"Several centuries prior to my Earth incarnation, Greek culture spread and the Jews made effective use of the culture and the language, using them to grow a religion throughout the East and West.

"A degree of religious tolerance existed along with a fertile cultural mix." Jesus gleamed. "For example, the Apostle Paul was a Hebrew Jew, an open believer in the Jewish Messiah in the Greek language, and a Roman citizen.

"The Romans reigned over a unified world. For the first time, good roads connected major centers and waterways were free from pirates; this enabled an unrivaled era of commerce. The Jews occupied a geographic location perfect for capitalizing on their mercantile inclinations, and they dispersed, resulting in hundreds of religious communities scattered hither and yon throughout the Roman world. These cultural centers were the stepping stones on which my gospel spread to the uttermost parts of the civilized world. During my so-called lost years, I traveled to Europe, the Far East, and the Orient as the tutor for a wealthy merchant's son."

Jesus paused; the president felt the boy's eyes searching and was certain they were searching for him. "Another factor in the timing of my birth was the state of humanity," Jesus explained. "There was a small, thriving upper class, no middle class, and a massive lower class. Most people were impoverished, and many were slaves or had once been slaves. The prevailing spiritual philosophies appealed to the educated class, not to the mass of struggling humanity. The multitudes needed a faith that was relevant to them. And what could be more relevant than the truth: a loving God."

The president's eyes brightened.

Duffy gave Albert a big hug, which officially began a cherished friendship. Saul fell into both their arms.

Jesus' face was love-lit as he set the stage for a string of revelations. "Besides choosing my birth date, I chose my parents and their culture. Jewish men were family oriented during a time when most men were absent from child rearing. Many men treated women harshly."

Looking at Josie with love beaming from his eyes, Jesus advised, "Quelling the evolution of women, or any segment of a culture, retards evolution of the whole! Restricting women is a form of mass self-destruction. Humankind will take a leap when men and women lead the way equally!"

Josie threw Leon a kiss, which to her surprise was acknowledged by a subtle nod. Her heart opened even more.

After announcing he would share little known facts about his beloved parents, Jesus became silent. Zelia was sprinkling dust around Josie's heart, just when the fairy received an urgent alert. Zelia went inter-dimensional in a flash.

Leon waited for her green glow to dissipate before continuing. "My mother, Mary, daughter of Hanna and Joachim, was a bright, evolving being. My father loved her qualities dearly, and such admiration was rare."

"How does he know all this?" the president asked softly.

"His consciousness travels," Fielding whispered back. "He can make direct contact with anyone, past, present, and maybe future. He's tapping into Jesus right now!" The president wiped his brow as he watched.

Although throngs of people were watching Jesus, it felt like a single eye looking. Several seers gasped as they watched the audience, Leon and the organism became one huge energy field.

(Outside the E-Zone, crowds were becoming increasingly agitated. Slogans echoed through back streets and dingy bars: "Stop the organism before it stops you! The E in E-Zone means the End!")

Energies stirred within distant dimensions as a lone fairy soared between dark and light. Forces were gathering on both sides.

Jesus, radiating like a morning star, cast his gaze upon Aaron. "Joseph was employed by Mary's father to help build an addition to his house. It was during the noontime meal, when Mary brought Joseph a cup of water, that their courtship began. Her sunny disposition instantly captivated him.

"My father and mother were opposite in many ways," Jesus said reflectively, "another reason I chose to incarnate into their family.

"Father talked little and thought much. He was mild-mannered, extremely conscientious and devoutly faithful to Jewish practice. Though passionate, he was colored by bouts of depression and spiritual discouragement, usually triggered by financial concerns. Admittedly, his good cheer increased when he became a prosperous contractor. From Joseph I secured strict training in Jewish ceremony and the Hebrew scriptures." Jesus' face softened. "With his serious nature came an unusual gentleness and sympathetic understanding of human nature." Jesus cast a glow toward Aaron, who was weeping unabashedly in Josie's arms.

"Mary's sunny disposition was delicately spiced with intense feelings and a consuming intelligence. She was a gifted teacher and mother, as well as a superior homemaker and weaver. From her, I inherited my righteous indignation and fiery spirit.

"I was like my father, meditative and worshipful, characterized by apparent sadness; but most of the time I was like Mary, optimistic and determined.

"It is ironic. Had Joseph lived, he would have become a believer in my divine mission. Mary, who was greatly influenced by friends and relatives, wavered. It is a fact that Joseph's family became believers, but few of Mary's people did until after I departed from this world."

Outside the E-Zone mindless hordes believing world extinction was eminent, chanted: "Kill the organism. Kill the organism." One hate group was headed for the town's largest church where Brook was waiting. When the church doors opened, Brook moved in. Igor followed, deftly balancing the heavy camera.

"Father, what do you think of the impending E-Zone effect?" Brook asked. Parishioners gathered close to the reporter.

Hoping for television exposure, the hate-mongers approached. "Kill the organism before it kills us. Kill the organism . . . ."

Their chanting competed with Brook's voice. Igor continued filming, even after Brook told him to stop. "You people have no idea what the organism can do for this world!" Brook bellowed at the chanting mob. "In a few days the E-Zone effect will be here. Give it a chance; it's harmless. It's loving and kind." Brook was trembling.

A drunken agitator threw a beer bottle that hit Brook over his left eye, causing a deep gash. Brook wiped the blood from his brow and held it out to the priest and his congregation. "This is how love is answered! Sound familiar?"

Falco emerged from the mob egging them on with a raised fist. "Kill the organism. Kill the organism. Kill it now . . . ."

Igor was at the perfect angle to film the parishioners creating a barrier, enabling Brook and the priest to take refuge inside the church. Igor stayed and filmed a brief but vicious brawl which finally resulted in Falco halting his troops.

"Don't waste yourself on these losers, save it for the real enemy," Falco asserted. "It's time!"

Igor called to Brook, "Quick! Get out here. They're on the move!"

Brook knew the Powers That Be had mobilized hundreds of hate groups. At any moment they could ignite into one boiling rage. He knew he had to warn Fielding.

Brook called Fielding who told the president.

Now I have a miracle and a war to attend to, the president thought.

15

These wise men had no star of Bethlehem to guide them...

Fielding assigned a rotating army to secure the compound; no soldier would stay in the zone for more than two hours. One thousand troops were ordered to secure the outer zone, with an equal amount on call.

Snow found his way to Aaron and Josie and sat in communion. Josie's radiance contrasted Aaron's drooping face. Snow tried to imagine what Aaron might be feeling as they watched Leon increasingly settle into the persona of Jesus of Nazareth.

Jesus spoke as if chatting to friends; "My parents lived in a one-room, flat-roofed, stone structure with an adjoining building for animals. Their furniture consisted of a low, stone table, a loom, a lamp stand, several stools, and two mats for sleeping on the stone floor.

"In the back yard was a shelter that contained an oven and grain mill. The mill required two people to operate it, and when I was small I often fed the grain while Mary turned the grinder. Mother and I would discuss all manner of things as we worked. These were some of my happiest moments on Earth.

"Mary did not have to go to Bethlehem for the census. Because she was pregnant, Joseph insisted she remain. But Mother, fearful of being alone so close to delivery, and having an adventurous spirit, demanded she accompany him. As usual, she won.

"They were a poor couple. Building and furnishing their home had been a financial drain on Joseph, particularly since his father had recently been disabled and required financial support.

"On August 18, 7 B.C., with nothing to spare and much concern, Father and Mother set out for Bethlehem. Having only one mule, Mary rode with the provisions while Joseph walked. It is true they stayed in a barn, but it was clean and prepared for guests by the innkeeper. Still, Mary was restless so neither of them slept well. By daybreak Mother was in labor and by noon, with the help of women travelers, I was born. Mary wrapped me in a cloth brought for just that purpose and placed me in a nearby manger.

"The next day Joseph enrolled in the census; the Powers That Be were numbering every citizen for taxation purposes. It was good fortune that Joseph met a man staying at the inn who agreed to exchange quarters. That afternoon we moved inside and stayed for almost three weeks. On the eighth day, in accordance with Jewish practice, I was circumcised and named Joshua (Jesus)."

Roy Fielding had bristled when Jesus mentioned, "the Powers That Be." He pulled himself away unnoticed. He could sense danger even amidst the E-Zone's effect.

A bashful smile consumed Jesus' face igniting his flaming blue eyes as he said, "Now I must clarify a myth; though a beautiful story, it is not the complete truth.

"The myth began when a religious teacher dreamed that 'the Messiah' was to be born among the Jews. He told three priests from Mesopotamia who went on a fruitless search for the infant Master. They were about to return to Ur when they met Zacharias, who shared his belief that Jesus was the object of their quest. Zacharias sent them to Bethlehem where they found me, and indeed, they left gifts with Mary. I was almost three weeks old at the time.

"These wise men had no star of Bethlehem to guide them. This legend originated from a cosmic happening. I was born on August 21, 7 B.C.—on May 29, 7 B.C. there had occurred a rare conjunction of Jupiter and Saturn in the constellation of Pisces. It is a remarkable astronomic fact that similar conjunctions occurred on September 29th and December 5th in that same year. From this stellar oddity, the enchanting myth was created a generation later by well-meaning zealots.

"Before printing presses, knowledge was transmitted by word of mouth, giving rise to imaginative embellishments. People from all cultures love to spin tales about their spiritual and political leaders, so it was easy for mistruth to become tradition and eventually fact. Knowing this can save humankind lifetimes," Jesus claimed, as the light around him brightened. "Do not take any scripture literally. Rather, search for the hidden truths within the stories."

The president knew he had to preserve the ED at any cost. His gut and his heart agreed that the only danger the organism posed was the mess humans might make in response to it.

The ED's lights softened as did Jesus who was giving a specific account of his infancy. Everybody present knew Leon "was" Joshua, son of Mary and Joseph.

A member of the devout group murmured, "This might be the Second Coming."

"Maybe the First," her group leader said with a serious chuckle.

General Roy Fielding rumbled along in his jeep.

Brook paced nervously as he considered the interview he was about to do. The reporter's vision blurred as his eyes drifted to the top of a tree where an idea waited. His screenplay, now called *E-Zone Alert*, would be based upon actual events. General Fielding would be a major character, plus the movie's promotional hook. Brook pictured the movie trailer and in his announcer's voice he projected, "General Fielding's Secret Revealed."

The reporter thought back to the moment when Fielding had approached him with the deal. He couldn't have written a better script than reality had played out. It was Fielding who'd leaked Aaron's arrest, the disappearance of the objects, even the news of his own arrest and escape. Fielding had been Brook's secret source! The general's motives had been simple. If Flint Killingsworth had gotten the Ardos and the organism, they would have been exploited and never heard of again. Fielding couldn't allow it, so he'd used the media to expose the story, which had halted Killingsworth.

Fielding had gotten justice and Brook had gotten a ticket to stardom. It had been a perfect deal, providing both men with what was most important to them.

It's ironic, Brook thought, as he kicked a rock. *All I ever wanted was fame, and now it doesn't matter. Saving the organism and returning home to the E-Zone is what's important.* Brook shivered, fantasizing about sacrificing his life toward that end—a twist to his screenplay.

He kicked another rock, but it didn't feel like his foot sent the stone tumbling. Everything felt different. He closed his fists and squeezed hard, causing a physical tingle from the E-effect and a slight rush. Images of the waitress were dancing across his mind when he saw a light in the distance and assumed it was Fielding, on time as always. His mouth was dry. He felt orphaned and needed to be with "Roy the Rock," as he affectionately thought of the general.

The CNN truck rolled up. Igor hopped out, handing a jug of water to Brook while doing his "I got the right angle" move. Before Brook could take a slug, Fielding pulled up and stepped out, scratching his neck nervously. "Damn flies."

Brook ran over to him.

"I've lost my edge," Fielding admitted, fidgeting with his starched collar. "Tom, the outer zone is ready to ignite. There are more dissidents than we'd anticipated; they're organized, and have weapons. Our intelligence has come up with nothing. We're in the dark and it's all my fault." The general's eyes dropped in shame. "The E-effect got to me; I reacted too slowly."

Fielding pointed to Igor setting up his camera. "I don't have time for this."

"I'm ready, let's do it right now," Igor coaxed.

Brook offered a supportive pat. "Roy, anti-zoners are monitoring my reports. Speak to them. Send them a message. At least we'll be able to say we tried to negotiate." Fielding moved toward the camera. The lights went on. Brook turned on his earphone.

"This is Larry King. We're going live somewhere at the edge of the E-Zone. Our own Tom Brook is there with General Roy Fielding. Tom."

"Yes, Larry, this is Tom Brook just outside the E-Zone where a line has been drawn. The armed forces have arrived, creating a barrier between the E-Zone and a growing army of radicals hell-bent on destroying it. Two worlds are ready to collide, and General Roy Fielding is attempting to avert the collision."

Brook turned. "General Fielding, does the organism pose a threat, and what is its present disposition?"

"We have very good news. Its growth has peaked, which means the Zone, or euphoria effect, will not expand much more. It is confined! I repeat: It's not going to consume the country like the anti-zoners claim. Under control, we can study its enormous benefits without national concern." Fielding's eyes bore into Igor's camera lens. His voice became stronger. "I urge all citizens to stay away from the E-Zone. Those who have gathered in the outer zone must disband before any lives are lost. We value your opinions and want to negotiate." Fielding paused, then said, "I officially invite anti-zone leaders to meet with the president of the United States to work out a proposal. Until then, I pledge to every American that there is nothing to fear. The organism poses no threat, nor is it a prelude to an apocalypse. The apocalypse is being created by those threatening the miracle of our age." Fielding regretted his antagonizing statement and stopped.

"General Fielding, who is behind this violent uprising?"

"America, know the truth! Certain power brokers, the Powers That Be, want the E-Zone destroyed because it threatens their financial interests. This is not a grassroots uprising; it's financed terrorism. People involved in this uprising, go home, disband. The Powers That Be have manipulated you with money and misinformation. Don't destroy a vital living thing. Do not end what is perhaps our first encounter with a benevolent extraterrestrial."

"You're saying this organism could be an ET?" Larry chimed in.

"I'm saying it has to be from somewhere, and it sure ain't from these parts!"

Larry laughed heartily.

Fielding softened, "People of America, pray for the organism and the soldiers defending it. As for you powers financing this madness, when I'm finished winning this battle, I'm coming after you." Fielding shook his hand at the camera, then turned toward his jeep.

An explosion startled him to attention. Fielding lunged for his walkie-talkie. Igor zoomed into a close-up of Fielding's face, just as it turned white. "What! I don't believe it! Are you seeing it with your own eyes?" Fielding threw down the phone, crying out in alarm. "Anti-zoners have blown up a school." He broke down, sobbing uncontrollably. "Thousands of children are dead!" Two more explosions were heard as he sped off.

Igor's instincts were perfect; he captured Fielding driving away as distant smoke clouds formed into billowing, black veils. The cameraman turned to Brook and said, "The line has been crossed. It's in God's hands now."

Back at the compound, people hadn't eaten or slept. Some felt fresh pangs of sadness as Jesus began the description of his final hours with an unlikely analogy: "Evolution is a stalking cat. It creeps patiently for a long time, then leaps upon its prey. Earth's humanity has been creeping slowly since my ascension; basic human nature has not changed in two thousand years. For example, my death was created by fear, anger, greed, and lust for power," Jesus said with no judgment in his voice. "The same energies rule Earth now, with the exception that media feeds it directly to us and our children in massive daily doses."

Aaron fell into Josie's arms. (Transforming the media had been his life's passion. Positive Pursuits TV was intended to be the springboard, but it brought a vicious conservative backlash. Aaron had been tormented with hate mail and threats, which had caused him to withdraw, becoming a hermit lost within his immense, creative inner life. So lost that even the E-effect couldn't completely wrench him free.) His mind drifted to a line in one of his short stories spoken by a politician: *I love humanity! It's people I can't stand.*

Snow felt an urge to put his hand on Aaron's overheated heart; Josie covered Snow's hand with hers.

"Some people evolve faster than others," Jesus said, looking right at Josie, Aaron, and Snow. "When enough cross the line, your entire world will leap together. Remember, evolution crawls, then leaps."

Jesus paused. "On that fateful day, I crawled through the streets. I hadn't eaten or drunk since the Last Supper at the home of Elijah Mark. The weight of the stake was too much to bear, even for me. As I struggled, many grief-stricken Jewish women gathered around me offering kindness and comfort. I was greatly concerned for them, for it was illegal to show affection to one being crucified.

"Shortly after passing through the city gate, I fell beneath the weight of my burden. The soldiers raged and began kicking me, but I could not lift the beam, short of performing a miracle, which I would not do. The captain ordered the soldiers to desist before commanding a passerby, one Simon of Cyrene, to carry my burden the rest of the way to Golgotha.

"Simon was on his way to the temple but never made it. He stayed with me until the end and, indeed, never left; he became a valiant believer in the heavenly Kingdom.

"It was shortly after nine o'clock when the death procession arrived at Golgotha, and the Romans began nailing me to the stake."

"Oh my God! No! No!" Fielding wailed, pounding the hood of his jeep and lacerating his hand. He'd misjudged Falco.

Voices wailed as a parade of soldiers emerged from the rubble, carrying bodies. Mothers clutched each other, some so shocked they couldn't move;

others pounded the ground. One mother beat herself about the head until she went unconscious in a pool of her own blood.

A helicopter used the ball field to bring in medics and supplies, but there weren't any lives to save; instead, they turned their attention to the parents.

Igor captured the scene from the truck roof: He panned grieving faces, then shot to the ten-deep line of small, disfigured bodies lying on the grass. (His sobs became part of the televised message. It would become one of the most influential moments ever captured by the media.)

A few blocks away the streets were gorged with anti-zoners. Fielding was about to send more troops to "put them down". He was brought back to sensibility when Brook arrived.

Brook wasted no time; he was a soldier reporting to his commander. "Sir, I received a message from Falco informing me that seven other sites have explosive charges planted. They're threatening to ignite one every twelve hours until the organism is destroyed."

"Go live!" Fielding commanded. "Warn the community! Tell them to evacuate all public buildings and go home. Home is the only safe place. CNN has to keep this going nonstop. You got that? I'll contact local authorities and get the military out with megaphones."

Fielding called the president. In one ear, the leader heard the general's news accompanied by wails and cries—in the other he heard Jesus describing the procedure employed to affix him to the cross:

"First, the soldiers bound my arms to the crossbeams with cord. This enabled them to nail my hands to the wood. Then they bound my feet, using only one nail to penetrate both."

"There's not enough time to deploy more troops; make the best use of what we have," the president ordered. "Remember, protecting the organism has to be our first priority. I want you back here ASAP. I'm pulling Venton out of security. I'm going to cut off his balls if he doesn't give us some information. If I get something, I'll call back."

"Yes, sir," Fielding replied with a brittle snap.

Falco would single-handedly destroy the organism! That was the plan.

While his guerillas were distracting troops at the edge of the zone, he was creeping through underbrush beside the compound gate. He was dressed like a soldier and carried a machine gun and high-powered grenades strapped to his belt. A mantra played in his head— *The E in E-Zone means the End.*

Believing he was saving the world, Falco was eager to die for this unprecedented place in history. As he crawled within a hundred yards of the gate, another distant explosion rocked the ground. *Must be Archmont Hospital. That'll keep Fielding huffing.*

Moments later, the president's phone range again. "Oh my God!" the leader said so loud even Jesus took notice.

Brook was finishing his live alert, which CNN agreed to repeat, preempting all programming. "People, this is a war zone; you can hear the cries, see the blood. Most of the bodies retrieved from the explosion are burned beyond recognition. The anti-zone movement claims to have more bombs planted, all in public places. Leave all public buildings. Return to your homes. I repeat: You must leave all public buildings and return home!"

Igor's hand was still trembling when he realized he was shooting Brook at the wrong angle. He saw the reporter cringe and cry out, "Dina." Brook bolted from his mark; Igor turned and filmed him engulfing the waitress he'd met just days before.

"He's dead. My boy is dead. Did I tell you his name was Tommy? Of course not! I never told you about him! Did I? Did I?" She pounded her head with her fists. "I thought you'd run if you knew I had a child. He was a beautiful boy. My baby is gone. He's gone," Dina cried hysterically.

Igor kept filming. He wanted to capture Dina's grief and Brook's inflamed compassion. As he zoomed in, he mumbled under his breath, "This kind of love you only find on a battlefield." His whisper was heard around the world.

Zelia heard it too. She was hovering within Brook's energy field, beside his heart, when she felt the moment Brook knew Dina was his soul mate. A raucous commotion jolted Zelia and Brook back to the blood-drenched reality surrounding them.

Thousands of townspeople were gathering around the school.

Only two blocks away, anti-zoners were chanting.

"Let's get those murdering bastards," a father at the school ranted as he charged, carrying his lifeless daughter. A hundred armed men followed him. As they advanced they heard a deafening howl—they turned and saw a mother discovering the remains of her three sons in the rubble. The oldest son covered the two younger twins; she couldn't tell where one began or ended.

The men charged. Within a block of the anti-zoners, the man carrying his daughter was screaming obscenities and wailing wildly. Brook ordered

Igor to film. The cameraman wanted to wield a gun, not a camera, but obeyed. Igor jogged alongside the mob, camera rolling, while Brook ran to the front and put his arm around the man leading the way.

Jesus' face possessed the density of human nature. "The upright timber had a peg inserted at groin level, a saddle to support my body weight. In your renditions of me on the cross, I am depicted in God-like grandeur rising high above the ground. In fact, the cross was three feet off the ground, enabling me to see the eyes and hear the words of those who mocked me. And they, too, could hear what I had to say during my lingering death.

"The moment I was hoisted upright, I saw Mother with Ruth and Jude. John had accompanied them and was the only apostle to attend. I smiled at them. They understood what no words could convey. I never spoke to them thereafter."

Jesus looked at Snow, indicating "now." Snow's pen was poised above his notebook.

"My crucifixion seems unjust, but it was not. Injustice is impossible when cause and effect govern all of creation. Dear ones, universal law is derived from a circular universe, which guarantees that justice always prevails.

"A baby is born and suffers agonizing pain for two days, then dies. How can this be just? Cause and effect, karma, does not operate sequentially. Instead, the strongest, rather than the most recent patterns play out." Jesus' face was illuminated by wonder. "Your indwelling soul has millions of past incarnations affecting this brief encounter on Earth. Every moment scores of karmic strands converge from infinite dimensions to create balance; it is unfathomable to the mind but always perfect and just. Injustice is an illusion—it's impossible."

Snow captured every word and wrote: The *Seventh Key of Light: Injustice is Impossible.*

A mysterious glow permeated Jesus' eyes. "My last conscious memory was of reciting the Hebrew scriptures. I was too weak to utter the words, but my lips moved. Upon my last breath, who do you think risked their lives at the foot of my cross? It was John Zebedee, my brother and sister, Jude and Ruth, my childhood friend Rebecca, and of course, dear Mary Magdalene.

"Because it was both preparation day for Passover and the Sabbath, pious Jews petitioned Pilate to expedite the crucifixions. Forthwith three soldiers were sent.

"My voice rang out just before three o'clock. 'It is finished! Father, into your hands I commend my spirit.' Thus spoken, I bowed my head and gave myself to God. The Roman centurion who witnessed this became an instant believer."

Jesus radiated divine compassion, then issued a familiar wink. Both Josie and Aaron knew that Leon's personal signature was merging with the Christ. Josie bit her nails but smiled serenely at her beloved son.

"The soldiers commanded to expedite my death were surprised. It had been only six hours, and the ordeal was designed to last much longer. Still, they broke my legs, pierced my left side, and took me off the cross. I watched from above, surrounded by glorious celestial hosts."

Upon those words, Jesus allowed his face to relax and a startling transformation ensued, resulting in the ever-serene Leon stare.

Aaron and Josie ran to their son.

Death is a dream come true...

"People, people," the president shouted over the crowd, "we're under siege." Tears rolled down the president's cheeks. "There are riots in the outer-zone. General Fielding reports that lots of innocent folks are dying out there. The anti-zoners will stop at nothing to destroy the organism." He looked at the ED's glowing light and softened. "We're doing everything in our power to stop the insurgents. We're on high alert!"

Saul was the first to get up and place his body in front of the ED. Duffy ran over and draped her body in front of his. Albert Feinstein followed.

Josie and Aaron sat motionless beside Leon. A piece of gray fleshy membrane from the organism had attached to the child's right arm. Aaron dropped to his knees and held the boy. "I love you, son," he wailed, as Josie wept new tears. Only they heard Leon say, "I love you too, Father." Aaron collapsed into Leon's lap and pulled Josie with him. Minutes later, the child went comatose as if he were lending his energy to the organism which began to emanate blinding flashes. Everybody in the room turned away from the light explosions.

The president grabbed Venton and began shaking him by the throat, demanding, "What is their plan?"

"I'm not sure," Venton sputtered. "I planned to infiltrate the compound with a small troop of about fifty men. He might do the same. I never intended to harm innocent people. Falco is crazy. He'll do anything. I'm sorry. I'm so sorry."

The president ordered every available soldier to surround the building, stationing them four-deep by the door. But Falco was already inside, in uniform, standing in a line of soldiers like a sardine stuffed in a can. He considered his move. *I'm too far away to launch a grenade. I'll only get one shot before I'm a pork chop.* He squinted. The light from the organism was blinding.

Suddenly, the organism emitted a huge bolt of green light from its crown, which sent a shower of sparks spiraling down. Falco knew he had to make his move now.

A few miles away, the father who started the uprising held a pistol in his right hand and his daughter's limp body in his left. Fifty yards down the street an anti-zone leader hollered at him, "Disperse or we'll shoot." The father aimed and fired. The anti-zoner dropped like a weight. The father placed his child's Raggedy Ann body on the ground, then fired into the mob, dropping five confused anti-zoners before being hit through the heart. Brook crawled to him through the raging gunfire. Struggling to remain conscious, the father pulled a clip from his vest and loaded the gun. He slid it to Brook and said with his last breath, "Kill the bastards."

Zelia wanted to return to the compound, but her efforts in the field were saving lives.

When the second bolt of light shot out from the ED, there was a slight easing of tension in the outer-zone.

Aaron and Josie ignored the light as they stared at each other in fear. The organism's membrane of skin had consumed Leon's right arm and was now gripping his shoulder. Josie stifled a sob and began smoothing Leon's fine hair back from his forehead.

Falco prepared to strike. *It should be easy. No one is expecting this,* Falco thought. He gave his grenade a loving squeeze and stepped out expecting a fiery end. He took a deep breath and pulled the grenade pin with his teeth.

"It's him!" Boyd Venton shouted, pushing the president out of harms way as he charged Falco, who fired two bullets that ripped through Venton's chest.

"Mr. Venton? Oh God, no!" Falco stumbled back, confused. His adrenaline gushed. The first grenade slipped from his hand. He ran toward the organism.

Blood streaming from his chest, Venton jumped onto the rolling grenade. The explosion killed fourteen soldiers and the president of the United States.

Falco fired his machine gun as he searched for the second grenade. Albert was the first to drop, suffering a severe stomach wound. Duffy was next, the bullets piercing her throat and left ventricle. Falco raised the grenade to his mouth. Saul charged just as a flurry of bullets ripped through Falco's back. A soldier secured the grenade.

Saul crawled to Duffy and collapsed on top of her. "God, if you must take her, take her in your arms," he bellowed. Albert's bloody hand found its way over Duffy's eyes. He was attempting to embrace her, then fell back. Saul touched Albert's clammy face and cried.

Those who couldn't get close to Saul held onto the back of the person in front of them, creating a chain of sympathy. So many people had grown to love Duffy, and they could feel her "awesome" presence.

Duffy's aura hovered, as Zelia floated within it. The fairy was orienting the brilliant Rainbow, whose old soul was shining, revealing a string of ancient faces. Zelia explained to Duffy's essence, "Death is a dream come true, and for an instant, you can see all of you."

A soldier was cradling Albert's head while others attended to his wounds. "She is more beautiful than ever," Albert whispered to Saul with his last breath of life. Saul wrapped his arms around Duffy and Albert, crying strong, hard sobs.

The ED began to rumble as Leon's voice resounded, "Help ED with love. You have an infinite Heart. Help with love." Leon's lingering words were the perfect blend of heaven and Earth, and the familiar look of finality on his face indicated that he would say no more.

"Think loving thoughts," Aaron avowed, diving into the boy's lifeless arms.

The organism began to vibrate like an active volcano. People stepped back. Josie found her courage and cried out to them, "Don't be afraid! Feel love! Think of someone you love. Hold that image in your mind and allow the feeling of love to flow from you."

Like almighty artists, two thousand Souls painted pictures in their minds with pets, parents, children, and lovers at the center. Faces began to glow, hearts widened until a collective energy swept them to higher levels of love.

The ED struggled to contain what was building inside of it. Its already strained skin began to glow. People urged Saul to move, but the string bean would not budge from his sobbing puddle of tears and blood.

"We're killing it!" Aaron shouted. "It's attempting to absorb the negativity here and in the outer-zone, and it's just too much. It needs our love!"

People fell into each other's arms.

Aaron screamed to Josie, "I'm detaching Leon, the organism is going to blow-up."

Josie threw Aaron a loving kiss of encouragement. She had resigned herself to accept whatever fate had in store. Snow was beside her, and she gently moved into his arms for support.

Gripping Leon from the back, Aaron gently tugged. He could feel the organism's heat and the give of its flesh, but he couldn't detach his son. Leon appeared to be in a blissful, opened-eyed coma. Aaron felt the warmth of his breath.

The organism rumbled louder but Aaron would not leave. He was covering Leon like a blanket. He didn't see the ED stretch another ten feet, but he felt the skin getting thinner. The boy was more deeply enmeshed. Layers of skin had now gripped Leon's back, like plastic wrap under heat, pulling him in tighter.

Suddenly the organism's rumbling turned into rapid shaking. An ear-piercing sound filled the air as millions of particles of light erupted from the ED, fanning out for miles before falling like rain.

Igor tilted his camera up to capture what seemed like a trillion fireflies dropping from the sky. They fell on the uplifted faces of the grieving parents. People started to drop their guns as they chased the light particles, trying to catch them in their hands. Time collapsed as the light particles touched skin, enabling its sticky consistency to spread like cream. One anti-zoner began to laugh, even though he was holding his brother's dead body. A severely injured father began an aching chuckle from his bloody pool. The laughter was contagious.

Brook searched for Dina. He found her sitting on the grass with her son draped across her lap as she half-heartedly directed the light particles onto him. Brook crouched down and held them.

The ED began pounding like a giant drum.

"It's the organism's heartbeat!" Aaron screamed. "We're breaking its heart." Entwined with Leon and the organism, Aaron was lunging back and forth with every beat. He managed to find a space between Leon and the organism's flesh and slipped his hand in between. With increasingly intense thumps, Aaron pushed his arm in further, getting a firm grip around Leon's back.

"I want to help Aaron," Snow whispered to Josie, "but something's telling me to let him be. Forgive me for saying this, but I think Leon belongs there."

Josie listened in a daze, watching Zelia hover above Aaron. The fairy was sprinkling special dust.

When the organism's throbbing approached life-threatening intensity, Saul decided to move Duffy, carefully laying her between the president and Albert. He knelt in prayer.

"Aaron," Josie cried, "Leon belongs there. It's his destiny but I don't think it's yours. I need you, Aaron," she pleaded, reaching out her arms to him.

A convulsive thump nearly dislodged his grip. Aaron pulled his hand loose and reluctantly stood up. His gaze stayed glued to Leon, who was nearly encased on all sides by the ED. Leon's expression was of undiluted bliss—euphoric.

Snow closed his eyes. He recalled one of Mo's rules for living in a two-sided world as a smile spread across his face: *Avoid clinging to limited knowing.* An explosion from the organism sent them stumbling back. *Even amidst all this, my mind is still clinging,* Snow thought.

17

Existence—Being transcending relative phenomena...

Fielding stormed into the hangar, dropped to the ground and placed both hands on the president's heart. For the first time since his wife's death, General Roy Fielding lost complete control. "What have I done! I killed him," he screamed.

Fielding noticed the remains of Venton's covered body lying next to the president's. The general could only see part of his head—very little else remained. He fought an impulse to thrash the corpse, to desecrate it. Instead, he admonished, "What the hell is he doing here? I want this body removed NOW!"

"Sir, Venton died trying to save the president. If it weren't for him, everybody in the compound might have been killed. He's a hero," the sergeant said.

The general noticed Saul lying over Duffy's body. "Oh my God, no, I'm so sorry, son." Fielding placed his hand on Saul's shoulder and felt a strange, sticky density. Then Fielding saw a glow like a cloudy halo emanating from Duffy's body. Saul looked up at Fielding with a spaced out, angelic expression.

Fielding moved his hand above the president's body and felt a similar soupy density. He leaned back and squinted. "Do you see it?" he questioned, looking into the eyes of the soft-spoken sergeant.

"Very much so, sir. It's beautiful, isn't it?"

Brook's left hand was around Igor's shoulder while his right hand rested on Tommy's chest. Dina put her hand on top of Brook's. She felt something sticky, almost glue-like. The reporter's head turned slowly, surveying the clans sitting in communion around departed children. Wailing had turned into soft sobs and weeping whispers.

Brook looked up to see an astonishing sight. In disbelief, he took Dina's chin and gently pointed her towards it. Igor respectfully picked up his camera as Brook nodded approval.

Above every lifeless body was a living light wavering in a milky glow. Loved ones around the bodies were enmeshed in it.

Tom Brook felt a light surrounding them. "Dina, it's your son. He's all around us," Brook realized, directing her attention to the subtle glow. "I think we can feel him, maybe even communicate with him. It is him."

As the light engulfed her, Dina cried out, "I *can* feel him! And he can feel me!" Igor ran to help bewildered families make contact with the sticky essence of their loved ones.

Faith was reborn.

The ED was beating like a heart again. Its skin was now attached to the sides of Leon's face—the child looked like he'd been through a botched face-lift. His expression was grim; it had determination written on it as he throbbed along.

"How can anyone know what Leon is experiencing?" Snow asked Josie, watching Aaron teeter from heel to toe. "How can we tell Aaron what to do when we're all on different journeys?"

She gave him a grateful look. " Whatever Aaron chooses to do, I won't stop him." She took a deep, shuddering breath. "Please don't let me stop him, Walt."

Snow whispered, "Don't let me stop him either." They smiled at each other and went back to watching the lights. Snow's mind drifted. *There has to be an Eighth Key! Something is missing.*

Zelia sent the answer, but Josie was too distracted to receive it.

Walking down the line of his fallen troops, Fielding drank in every face; he could feel their soupy auras hovering around his knees. When he discovered Albert Feinstein's small body looking bashful and innocent, Fielding flushed with delight. "It's probably exactly as you theorized, and you're experiencing it right now. Aren't you?" Fielding smiled, realizing he was no longer an atheist; he believed in something, although he didn't know what. Albert Feinstein tried to penetrate the barrier of matter. He was about to reach Fielding with an urgent message when Fielding bellowed, "The organism—It's changing!"

Fine filaments of pure, white light sprung from the organism's globe. The wispy strands fluttered about, waving and thrashing, increasing in number and size. Within seconds, thousands of light tentacles were erupting out from the ED.

The dancing arms of light reached for Snow, pulling his awareness beyond the veil of consciousness. Snow began to speak in a trance. "*Existence—Being transcending relative phenomena. Devoid of attributes or characteristics. . .the origin and cause of the manifestation of the universe and the essence of souls. . .Vibrating creative force emanated from God manifesting as space-time and cosmic forces regulated by the three continuant attributes. Inertia causes it to manifest the universe. Transformative influences are instrumental causing changes to occur. The luminous (attracting) attributes unveils the life essence in nature, influences the processes of evolution and eventually returns the three attributes to a state of equilibrium.*—Roy Eugene Davis." Snapping out of his channel, Snow was not aware that he had been talking.

BAM! A loud noise shook the hangar. Josie pulled Snow back as the organism's light tentacles grew another three feet and began to wrap around each other in groups of three. They looked like hissing DNA strands.

Aaron was now completely engulfed in the braided light tentacles. His face radiated a hyper-bliss and he writhed in a continuous, full-bodied orgasm.

"I kinda wish I was with Aaron," Snow joked in his Woody Allen voice.

Josie laughed so heartily through her tears that they had to double their grips to hold on to each other. As they shook with laughter, the organism began to shake, then rumble.

The three braided light tentacles were swinging wildly but there was a pattern to their escalating sound and motion. Then the organism emitted a rolling roar which jolted Fielding from Albert's second communication attempt. The general snapped to attention, thinking aircraft were approaching—he could smell the fuel.

The ED began to shake defiantly, and Aaron was thrown to the ground, where he stayed. The sound was maddening, but neither Snow nor Josie felt fear as the tentacles reached for them, touching their chests, creating a tangible tickle. Josie and Snow plunged into ecstasy.

"It's time!" Leon proclaimed above the rumbling. "Do it now!"

Thousands of three-stranded tentacles flew from the organism in every direction, leaving residues of light (and a spinning fairy) in their wake.

One light tentacle attached to Duffy's aura, causing bubbling light. As her aura became more defined, the bubbling essence increased in density. Fielding watched Duffy's aura wrap itself around her lifeless body in a loving embrace. Light particles, like children's sparklers, spewed from her two-inch bullet holes.

Saul began shaking violently. Fielding thought he was having a seizure and tried to contain him, but he began to tremble as well. They were two shivering masses holding onto each other when Duffy's body slowly rose, her eyes popping open as her lips moved. "I'm back, dudes! Wow! That was awesome!"

Saul and Fielding froze in dumbfounded wonder.

One by one, dead soldiers began to squirm. Fielding rushed up and down the line touching each of them, letting them feel the warmth of flesh. (Touch was what Duffy needed when she beckoned a bewildered Saul with a seductive wink and a busty jiggle.)

Albert Feinstein was the last to come to. He was closest to the door and the people rushing in could hear the faintest, meekest sound. "Heeya ho, Heeya ho," he uttered sweetly, as he remained motionless with his eyes open. Everyone in the room started to chant through their tears of joy.

Boyd Venton even continued singing as the president gently squeezed his hand and pulled him into a sustained embrace.

Brook watched Igor filming the new phenomenon. The energy fields of all the deceased children had risen twelve feet off the ground and were merging into a singular soup. A soothing hum, like an "Om" emanated from the communal aura.

"Our children are trying to show us the *truth!*" Brook illuminated. He paused to consider his revelation, then said, "We are not separate from each other. We all come from and return to the same source. Please, look,

look what our children are telling us! It's so beautiful," Brook cried aloud as he slumped over Dina's son.

As people beheld the undulating rhythm of the collective aura, a few softly begged God to release them so they might join their departed in what seemed an everlasting dance of light. Igor filmed several intimate close-ups, then returned to filming the massive, pulsing field. His camera was perfectly positioned to record the two thousand tentacles piercing the collective energy field, producing sparks of light like a thousand cameras flashing at once.

Brook watched as the horde of tentacles, writhing in ecstasy, continued to penetrate the outer edge of the collective aura. Slowly, the huge energy field began to lower and separate into parts. Brook could see the three-stranded lifelines attaching to individual auras, becoming more defined, then slowly descending until they touched the edge of each lifeless body.

One woman passed out when she saw her daughter's decapitated head begin to grow back.

Dina could see her son's essence become richer and more dynamic. Brook was touching the boy's chest when a light tentacle penetrated Tommy's aura, right through Brook's hand. A rush of energy shot up Brook's left arm and into his heart. It was the child's first playful joke! The boy's aura sparkled, as did Brook's love for the Soul who had just touched him.

Dina began trembling as she watched her child's eyes flutter and his charred skin change from black to normal. Brook felt Tommy's heartbeat beneath his hand. Impulsively, the boy lunged into his mother's arms drawing Brook into the embrace. The child smiled at Brook knowingly.

The outer-zone was a riot of delight. Every human killed was brought back to life! Euphoric hordes of townspeople and anti-zoners rejoiced, dancing and singing in harmony with the deafening sound of screeching squirrels, chirping birds, and barking dogs.

Brook had to yell into his mike. "This is Tom Brook, very much alive from the outer-zone. I have a story that is. . ." He was speechless for the first time in his reporting career. Igor winked back, indicating that he was capturing Brook's perfect angle. Tom Brook broke into unbridled laughter that was sent around the world at the speed of healing light. He couldn't stop, and his producer at CNN didn't want him to. The world had never seen or heard a laugh like that.

Duffy and Albert were huddled on the ground with the soldiers. Falco and Venton were in the center of the happy crowd. The president sat humbly on the outside, his mind racing with thoughts about helping humanity. Fielding sat beside him in erect silence.

Across the room, Aaron struggled. "I think it will release him now," Aaron said, as he felt around the edges of Leon's form.

Josie found solace when she realized that she and Aaron were both following their instincts, even if it took them in opposite directions.

By now, Leon was completely encased by a clear membrane of skin. His expression was blissful, but frozen; he seemed both dead and alive, transformed.

The organism glowed peacefully. No one, except Aaron, sensed the gradual increase in its brightness. It was becoming too intense to look at directly, so Aaron had to angle his glance down to where he could still see Leon's feet. The organism continued heating up until Aaron had to move away from it. He wondered why Leon wasn't burning up.

The ED began to tremble. The light dimmed and it began shaking so rapidly, Aaron couldn't discern its edges; Leon was a blur. When the shaking increased to an even finer intensity, Leon and the organism appeared to be all vibration, no substance.

Snow returned to Josie just as the organism began to pulse in and out of form. "It's over," Snow said to himself. Josie heard.

Aaron was standing three feet away when the ED sputtered, then transformed into a shaft of light, becoming an endless tube with particles racing through it. Aaron looked up the shaft, which extended forever. He looked down and saw the same.

Everyone in the outer-zone saw the transformed ED pierce the clouds. Everything stopped. Even the plants seemed transfixed. Naturally, Igor was the first to see it and he panned up into infinity; Brook's laughter orchestrated the breathtaking images.

Leon was trapped within the tube of light. The boy's amorphous face looked excited. Slowly, Leon's fading form moved up the tube as if he were being sucked away.

Aaron knew this was his moment! He charged, leaping into the tube, piercing its center where rushes of upward energy whirled like a wind tunnel. He grabbed at Leon's foot, but his hand passed right through. Thrashing wildly, Aaron swam through the currents until he was beside his son. He embraced him. Love radiated! *WHOOSH!*

The tunnel sucked up into itself, enfolding past the roof, beyond the clouds. In an instant, the organism was gone, along with Aaron and Leon.

Josie and Snow froze like statues with jaws sculpted open. The hangar was still. They could feel the weight of the silence as they squeezed each other's hands harder and harder until they had to let go.

"Leon, where are we?" Aaron asked joyfully. They were hovering before a wavering entrance that appeared to extend forever, in all directions.

"This is the final gate. I'm going home, Dad."

"I'm coming with you."

"You can't. This is where Souls return after they've experienced life in all its material and spiritual forms. This is the last stop! Here, there is no self, no individualized nature, only singular existence being. I'm returning to God."

"Is your life over?" Aaron asked, feeling devastated for the loss of his son.

"You may think of it as an ending, but it's also a beginning. There is nothing more beautiful or perfect. I am being granted ultimate freedom, Aaron."

"How can you be free, if you won't exist?"

"Aaron, there are no words to describe this transition."

"It's hard to imagine life without you. Josie and I will—"

"Aaron Ardo's body no longer exists," Leon explained. "You will return to Earth in a new one; soon you will be a baby in someone's arms." Leon's energy field bubbled as the portal began to fade. "I have to leave, but I will always be in your heart, especially in your next life." Leon's field became more brilliant. "Thank you, Aaron. You were my Earth anchor. You enabled me to have my adventure." Leon's connection with the portal was fading. With his last bit of material essence he called out, "Farewell, Aaron. Your next life will be a glorious one."

Aaron felt an explosion of love as Leon entered the shimmering void and disappeared.

Aaron hovered. He watched the portal's fading bleeps. They were losing intensity, as was his energy field which pulsed along. In and out, in and out, in and out, Aaron and the portal throbbed when, on a mutual upbeat, Aaron soared through the forbidden gate the instant before it snapped shut!

Every Angel wing fluttered. Modeen sighed, "Oh my!"

18

Where's the echo...

The plants and trees glowed with the radiance of an Eden and the president took it all in from the front seat of Fielding's jeep. The leader had insisted that Fielding drive slowly, enabling them to savor what might be a fading paradise. Like a child on a family trip, the president pointed at everything and bubbled with excitement. Without warning he leaned out the window and screamed, "Stop!"

Fielding slammed on the brakes.

"Can you hear the birds?"

Fielding listened. "It's like a symphony."

"The birds know something special has happened and they're taking it in, just like we are." The president took a deep, fulfilling breath. "Let's make a pact to remember how beautiful it is." He extended his pinky and Fielding met him halfway; locking fingers, they said together, "I pledge," just like they had done in college when they had joined the same fraternity.

Fielding took a restrained breath and looked around. He was a maze of conflicted feelings when a flurry of sounds came from a nearby tree, causing him to reach for his pistol.

"It's just the birds," the president said, laughing. "Look! They're flying away; they want to give us space. Animals understand boundaries better than humans do. Did you know that some birds can sleep and be on guard for predators at the same time? One side of the brain sleeps, and its corresponding eye is closed; the other hemisphere is awake, and its eye is open. Some fish can do that too. I wonder why humans can't?"

Two young doves swooped down from the branch, cooing as they dove. One landed on the president's shoulder, the other on his lap.

"Yes, I will protect you," the president said sweetly. "No more trees will be needlessly chopped, no more clearing for cattle. No more," the president said emphatically.

The birds took off and joined two older birds circling above. The president and Fielding watched them soar deep into the E-Zone woods.

"Give me your hand," the president said in a hushed voice.

Surprised by this curious request, Fielding reluctantly moved his hand forward and the president took it, holding it gently. Instantly, feelings began to flood the president's mind, a soup of love, anger, fear, rigidity, integrity, goodness, and loneliness. Suddenly, specific information began to fill the president's consciousness: how Fielding had protected the Ardos, how he had used Tom Brook to manipulate the media. He felt the general's inner struggle and knew his questionable actions had been done selflessly at great personal risk.

"I know why you manipulated the press. I know everything!"

"Sir?" Fielding snapped.

"I know you did it for America, and I'm glad you did."

"How did you find out?" Fielding asked.

"Since being brought back to life I pick up thoughts and feelings from people. I'm a new person, literally reborn," the president said.

Fielding rejoiced in this new development with another pinky lock; it inspired him to unburden himself. "When I first encountered Leon, he took my consciousness back in time 550 million years. Incredible as that journey was, it wasn't what caused me to break the rules. It was the feeling after. It was love! I felt incredible love for Leon. Whenever I thought about that child, Sylvia would pop into my mind. Her voice urged me to help him; it's what she would have done." Fielding drifted into thought. "I had to protect Leon. It was destined," he asserted, shaking his fist.

"I understand," the president replied.

"I wish I did. I'm not pleased with the results," Fielding confessed, his eyes misting. "Sam, I question my decisions. It's weighing on me." Roy Fielding dropped his head, unable to look the president in the eye. "The organism is gone! Think of what it could have done for humankind. Maybe a world without wars," Fielding said with remorse.

"Don't give up on that new age so quickly." The president's eyes twinkled. "The E-Zone isn't gone. It's alive within the people who were there, and especially within, what shall we call them, the resurrected ones!"

"I like that name," Fielding said.

The president cleared his throat. "We have to do a very thorough follow-up related to the E-Zone effect, and particularly the resurrected ones. Roy, I want you to head this investigation. I want you on my cabinet, in on everything. Consider yourself duly appointed and the investigation officially launched."

"Yes, sir," Fielding responded, allowing delight to soften his penetrating eyes. Memories of Albert singing "Heeya ho" rippled through his heart. "I want Albert Feinstein to head the scientific teams. Besides being the best man for the job, he's a resurrected one."

"Perfect," the president responded. "Let's head for the bomb sights; I want to see the damage. We'll implement a cleanup ASAP. I don't want reminders of the chaos, only the beauty, Roy. Only the beauty."

As Roy Fielding drove to the bombed school, he laid out an approach to the follow-up investigation while the president offered stunning additions. Both men thoroughly enjoyed the process, and by the time they'd reached the school, a basic plan was confirmed. Their good mood was dampened by what they saw.

"It looks like a war zone," the president lamented, his face twitching. Impressions began to impinge upon him. He could feel the energies of the slain children lingering like wispy clouds. He gasped. One child had suffered excessively, and the president could feel the agony along with the rapture of the child's rebirth. He could also feel the collective joy of all those witnessing the rebirths.

The leader whispered to the breeze as it gathered steam, "The E-Zone is alive."

"Where does something go when it disappears? Where's the echo of its essence?" Albert Feinstein questioned. Duffy was listening to him as she puttered about her living room. "The ED's energetic counterpart has to be somewhere; nothing is ever lost! If it transformed beyond recognition, where is the organism's transformed version? What is the organism's transformed version?"

"I miss Aaron and Leon," Duffy admitted with a moan. "They're not coming back."

Saul slumped into the couch. "I think you're right, but this E-Zone thing isn't over; there's lots to be done. We should assemble a team or something."

"You're right, sweetie. I'm surprised Fielding let us leave."

Albert considered. "He told me that people needed to reconnect with their families. To him, we're soldiers on leave. He'll call us back if he needs us."

"I'd love to be called back," Duffy confessed.

Saul nodded, affirming his similar desire.

Albert acknowledged, "If I'm in, you're in; the two of you are indispensable."

"Then we're in! There's no way they're not having you back. You're Fielding's favorite," Duffy declared, waving a prophetic, teasing finger.

Albert's mind flipped to the dancing communion with the organism. "Thanks for letting me stay with you guys. The thought of being alone is unbearable, which is odd since I'm a notorious hermit."

"No act of kindness, however small, is ever wasted," Duffy and Albert chanted simultaneously.

"Wow, that was far out!" Saul's eyes darted between Duffy and Albert, who were stunned. "Every inflection was identical; it sounded like you guys rehearsed."

"That didn't feel normal," Albert said, peeking into Duffy's hazel eyes.

She smiled and agreed. "I just had the strangest thought. Who's feeding your cat?"

"What?" Albert replied, wide-eyed. "How did you know Gabby popped into my mind? Our experience and your eyes reminded me of her psychic talents. That cat can sense the instant an unexpected treat is coming. She's amazing. I was also thinking about my ex-wife, who's watching Gabby; she loves the fat little stinker. Duffy, do you realize your question covered my entire thought process at that precise moment?"

"Hey dude and dudette, something is going on here," Saul pointed out. The string bean, ready to pop, pulled Duffy and Albert into an embrace. "I think the two of you are joined somehow. When you were dead—wow, that's weird to say—anyway, your bodies were right next to each other. Your energy fields mingled, maybe merged. This is fantastic!"

Duffy and Albert felt an outpouring of love for Saul. Few men would rejoice in his soul mate's intimate connection with another man. They engulfed Saul in hugs and kisses. "Tickle-fest!" Duffy declared, as they each took one side and knew exactly where to tickle for maximum results. Saul begged for relief, which he got after an ample dose.

Albert broke the panting silence. "You know, I just got the most overwhelming craving for some—"

"Organic carrot juice," Duffy finished.

"Yes!" Albert cried. "And I don't even *like* carrots!"

The three laughed as Duffy started for the door, eager to get some carrots fresh from the magic garden. "This is big," she claimed, wiggling her breasts as she reached for the phone before it rang. "Yes, sir," she said into the receiver.

Saul and Albert watched her mouth drop. "Yes, sir," she repeated, miming amazement back to them. "It's the president. He wants to ask Albert a favor."

Albert nervously pointed to himself, while mimicking the word, "Me?"

Duffy brought him the telephone and reassured him, "Just be yourself. The prez is a sweetie-pie."

"Hello, Mr. President . . . Okay, Sam." Albert gave Duffy and Saul a thumbs up. "Well, sir, we were just talking about that exact thing. . . . I would be honored. In fact, there is nothing I'd rather do and no one I'd rather serve under." Gaining courage, Albert asserted, "Sam, there are two people, Duffy and Saul Rainbow, I need them . . . He has? Okay, sir. I'll expect General Fielding to contact me with details. . .You are very welcome, sir."

Duffy knew everything. "They want you to head the scientific teams to research the E-Zone aftermath." Duffy looked at Saul and cheered, "We're in! Fielding requested us!"

"I didn't think Fielding thought twice about me with all he had going on," Saul said. "I guess Fielding has eyes in the back of his head."

"And in the back of his heart," Duffy and Albert blurted simultaneously.

The three laughed.

"Three carrot juices coming up," Duffy affirmed, dancing toward the kitchen. "Tonight we celebrate."

It was strange to be home sitting in her favorite spot while music came from behind Aaron's closed door. It wasn't planned, but after Josie and Snow left the compound, he'd driven her home and stayed over in the guestroom.

Walt Snow had awakened early, tired yet unable to sleep. He had been drawn to Aaron's office and the short stories that were laying on the desk. He didn't think Josie would mind that he had read them.

Josie knocked on the door lightly, then opened it. "Want some coffee? I can make pancakes."

"No thanks," Snow answered softly. "I gave up coffee in the zone. Now I eat fruit in the morning, but I'm not hungry. Remember that Harvey Diamond book *Fit for Life*? It was circulating around the compound. I'm doing the program. Do you know about it?"

"That was my book, an autographed copy!" she contended with regal grandeur.

"Autographed!" Snow pronounced, with even more grandeur.

After a good laugh, Josie added, "Did you know that Harvey Diamond and Aaron were best friends? We all used to live in glorious Sarasota, Florida, and now we spend most winters there." Josie's face softened. "Harvey was the first person to call when Aaron's unique departure hit the media. I love Harvey—he's so, so spiritually playful," Josie said with a twinkle. "Christian is his new first name. I love saying it. Christian Diamond," she affirmed.

"Christian Diamond," Snow copied, as his stomach growled.

"I'm ravenous," Josie admitted. She looked around the office and remembered the countless times she'd been hungry when Aaron had been too involved to stop. "When Aaron was writing, he wouldn't eat until dinner. Most days he wouldn't get out of his pajamas."

"Josie, I had no idea he was such an extraordinary fiction writer; his short stories have everything. They're like *Keys of Light* in story form with action, lovable characters and plot twists. I love them."

"I do too," Josie said as her eyes dropped.

"You know, Larry King would do anything to help Aaron. The world needs these stories. I could—"

"Let's not rush into anything right now. It took Aaron a year just to edit *Positive Pursuits*."

"It showed. It was a masterpiece and a gift to humankind."

"I know," Josie said, as her eyes welled.

Snow moved toward her cautiously, gently placing his arm on her back. When he felt she was comfortable, he gradually pulled her into an embrace, where she released gushing sobs.

"I can't believe they're gone," she managed to utter between rushes of release. "I don't know w-w-where they are! At least when someone dies, you know they're dead. But I don't know what, where . . ."

"We're going to find out," Snow promised. "Meanwhile, I'll be here for you. I love you."

"I love you too," Josie responded, with no fear of implication.

The two held on tight as confused feelings blossomed into more sobs. They were brought back to reality when the telephone rang. "I'll get it," Snow offered, prying himself away. "It's Duffy; turn on CNN."

Josie searched for the remote control and found it just in time.

"I'll call you back," Snow said.

"This is Tom Brook, reporting from what was the E-Zone. Look around." Igor panned lush greenery and a budding field of wildflowers. "The E-Zone is still thriving in body, mind, and spirit. What are the 'lasting' effects of the E-Zone? Why have resurrected humans acquired special gifts? It's all a mystery. And to solve it, the president has assigned renowned scientist Albert Feinstein.

"Announcements concerning more staff appointments will be forthcoming from the project leader, the newest member of the president's cabinet, General Roy Fielding. The general tells me that many people who were working at the compound will be invited back. This project, from the president's standpoint, is an absolute priority. His administration's mandate is to make the E-Zone's gifts available to every American.

"Public support has been overwhelming. Euphoria Zone mania is sweeping the world. Books, films, and TV shows are coming, but the president wants more. He wants the world to share in the tangible miracle.

"Finally, this will be my last report for CNN. I'll be taking a sabbatical to become press secretary for the E-Zone Follow-Up Program. I look forward to working with the media in that capacity. This is Tom Brook, wishing everyone involved in this extraordinary adventure the best of luck and my utmost support. Thank you, Jane, and back to CNN center."

As soon as the report ended, Duffy was back on the telephone. "Walt, do you want in on the project?"

"Yes, definitely, but what can I do?"

"Can I tell him?" Snow heard Duffy whisper.

"Definitely," Albert replied.

"Walt, the kids at the school are experiencing some far-out side effects—Leon stuff, know what I mean? Well, Albert wants you to head up their education and coordinate it with the scientific area and their investigation and stuff. Got it?"

"I sure do. Wow! Tell Albert I'd love the opportunity under one condition—Josie can assist me."

"Albert says anything you want, you got. Carte blanche. And that's straight from the prez himself."

"Duffy, I love you," Snow said, his heart fluttering.

"I love you too. Saul loves you, and Albert loves you," Duffy gushed out. "See you later. We're coming over with some treats to celebrate, if it's okay."

"Awesome okay." Snow hung up feeling Duffy's sweetness lingering in his mind. He shared the conversation with Josie, who felt conflicted but interested. They drifted into honest talk about her grief. By the end of the conversation, Josie was onboard and even more excited than Snow. She finally accepted that her husband and son, who had been her entire personal universe, had helped create the miracles. These miracles were their legacy and she wanted to maximize it. What better way than working with children!

It was after dark when Saul, Duffy and Albert arrived at the dome with fresh baked carrot cake. After it was joyously devoured, Duffy decided to call the president. Albert and Snow were reluctant to disturb the leader, but they couldn't stop her. "He said Albert could call him! He gave Albert his private number. Awesome!" When she began the conversation with, "Hello, prez dude," everybody broke up laughing, including the president.

Duffy got right to the point. "We all agree on something and wanted to check it out with you." She winked at Snow. "Walter will be heading the school follow-up program and he thinks the best deal would be to set up school in the hangar where the scientific teams will be. We thought everything could kinda work together and . . ." Duffy covered the phone for a second. "He loves it," Duffy whispered to her breathless playmates. "Oh, Sam, Albert feels you should be on site as much as possible. Your empathic thing . . . Yes, sir, we love you too!"

Duffy dropped the telephone and let out an unrestrained hooray. "He is so awesome! We'll all be together!"

Albert then called Fielding, who loved the idea so much he code-named it, in Duffy's honor, the Rainbow Plan.

When Tom Brook was asked to be the press secretary for the E-Zone Follow-up Program, he immediately wanted to approach Dina with a proposal but he had decided to wait for the perfect moment. After hearing the news that the Rainbow Plan was in effect, he knew he couldn't wait any longer.

"Tommy will be there and so will I. Please join us! I need a press assistant," Brook pleaded with Dina, who was resting in his arms.

"We'll need lots of help," Igor agreed.

"I'd love to," Dina began, "but only if I can really contribute. You know I don't have a college degree, I'm self-educated . . . Wait!" She sat up and looked at Brook intently. "You're not hiring me because you can't bear being apart from me, are you?"

"Well, let's say it's both," Brook admitted.

"You'll be invaluable," Igor insisted. "Dina, you have a great memory and a way with people. You're a natural press assistant."

Brook pulled her closer just as Tommy bounced into the room and climbed into both their arms. Sensing the moment, Tommy flung Igor the catcher's mitt. "Have fun, kids," he said with an impish wink as he pulled Igor out the door.

"I'm in love with that kid," Brook confessed. "He's so much himself and so good without being syrupy sweet."

Dina nodded, pulling him into her warm, green eyes.

"I don't want to wait," Brook heard himself say.

"Hmm?" Dina murmured, moving in for a kiss.

"Say yes."

"Yes," Dina responded immediately.

"Okay," Brook said. "I think we should get married in the hangar, at the exact spot where the ED rested. How's next month?"

Dina sprang from his lap and brushed lush, blonde hair off her face. "I guess we're not talking about a traditional wedding!"

Tom Brook laughed unrestrained, as Dina pounced on him, kissing him wildly.

"Save that for later," Brook said teasingly. He got up hesitantly, then ran outside and took the ball and glove from Igor.

"Show me what you've got," Tom Brook called out as he threw the ball back to Tommy. He smiled as the boy mimicked picking up a rosin bag, chewing tobacco, and spitting. Tommy held the ball ready for his signature windup, which was a lot better than his actual pitching ability.

Igor heckled from the sidelines.

"Here comes a fastball. Think you can handle it?" Tommy hollered.

"I'll try. Give it all you've got," Tom encouraged as Tommy began his windup and threw. "Ouch!" Brook howled, throwing his glove to the ground. "That was incredible." He shook his beet-red hand. "I didn't know you could pitch like that. Wow!"

Tommy looked equally surprised. He'd always had some strength, but no accuracy. "Lucky pitch," he teased.

Brook glanced at Igor as he threw the ball back and returned to a crouching position, but this time he held himself like a professional catcher. He'd played a lot of ball in school, and except for first base, catcher was his favorite position.

"Okay," Brook called out, "you got any other pitches?"

"A curve," Tommy responded, continuing his elaborate pro mimicking.

Tom Brook radiated. He'd experienced love at first sight but never thought it could apply to a child. "Let's see what you got, Tommy boy."

Tommy's comical windup resulted in a wild release. Brook saw how the ball started high, gradually curved, and dropped in a perfect arc that accelerated right into the center of his glove.

"My God," Brook said, "that was the best pitch I've ever seen." Tommy looked surprised. "Your mom told me you stunk at sports; she was joking, huh? Try it again."

Tommy let loose another perfect pitch.

"Amazing," Brook declared. "Pros can't do that! How . . ." Simultaneously, the two Toms had the same thought.

"You think?" Tommy responded.

"Let's try an experiment," the reporter suggested, as he scratched his head. "Throw one ball with your eyes closed, and think about your beautiful mom. Then throw a second pitch with your eyes closed while you think about the ball going right into my glove. You got it?"

"Two eyes-closed curves coming up," Tommy said, indicating he understood the experiment.

Igor watched, totally entertained by their antics.

Brook pounded his glove on his way back to the makeshift home plate—a white paper plate with a rock holding it down. "Think about your mom and throw."

With no shenanigans, Tommy launched his pitch. It started wildly, like the others, but kept sailing, landing a good ten feet to the right.

"All right," Brook called out, as he tossed the ball back, "now think about hitting the center of my glove."

Tommy let another ball sail. It started wildly, then arced, and dropped right into Brook's motionless glove.

"Holy cow," Brook roared, as he shook his hand from the sting. Tommy ran to Brook and hugged him.

"I'm big league material, huh?" the boy said cutely, softening what he was about to share. "When I was dying, I felt incredible pain across my legs—there was a steel beam on top of them. I thought that if I could get up, I might be able to help some of the kids. I didn't know my legs were crushed when I tried to pull the beam off." The child's eyes misted. "Anyway, after a long time, a real long time, the pain got really, really bad, so I tried to move the beam with my mind. That, and the pain, were my last memories before I-I died."

Brook's heart was in his eyes as he pulled the boy in close.

Dina came bouncing out with fresh-squeezed organic orange juice. "What's going on?" she asked, handing them drinks.

"Your son is telekinetic. It looks like the ED's resurrection has left a very positive gift."

"Watch this!" Tommy commanded. He threw a cotton ball on the ground, and with minimal effort, caused it to rise two feet off the ground. "Gravity!" Tommy thundered, and the ball fell to the floor.

Tommy took his mother's hand as he lifted the glass in a toast. "To Leon, Aaron, and the ED."

"Wherever they are," Dina added.

"Whatever they are," Brook agreed in a lustrous voice.

"Forever they are," Tommy avowed, looking to the heavens with his new, penetrating mind.

"Amen," Igor said.

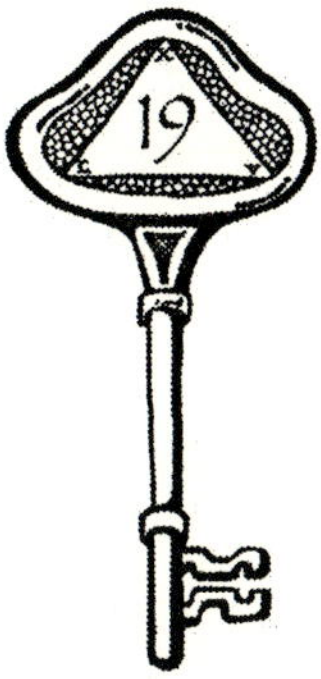

When you're in Soft Control...

The school's logistics were Snow's priority and he worked on them feverishly. He envisioned partitioned classrooms with a large open space sheltered from the scientific area. He sketched out a detailed blueprint and was feverishly working on his third draft when Josie offered a different approach.

"Let's empower the kids to create what they want," she said, waving a copy of *Positive Pursuits* opened to the chapter on Soft Control.

Snow knew that *Positive Pursuits* was a bible written just for this circumstance. He took the book and started to read aloud, "*When you're in Soft Control, results are instant. You can start at the end and be finished.*" Once he decided to allow the kids to make the decisions, his work was done!

He also began to read more of Aaron's stories, paying special attention to the games that preceded them. Aaron's dance exercises intrigued him, and Snow found himself panting as he played Freak Out: feeling an emotion, then expressing it by moving "every muscle" in his body vigorously. It looked like contorted modern dance, but it felt great. Josie had entered when Snow was expressing "rage" and she joined him in movement madness that resulted in them collapsing on the floor, feeling anything but rage.

During this period, they had many conversations about Aaron's theories on cognitive development—how Aaron integrated physicality and dance into every learning situation. Snow was awestruck by the extent of Aaron's research which indicated that "expressive" movement improved mental and conceptual ability. Snow reviewed some games from a chapter in *Positive Pursuits* called: Balancing Beginnings. With that complete, they were ready!

Meanwhile, Duffy and Saul were busy contacting the resurrected schoolteachers and a chain calling system was implemented to contact the kids. Timing was essential—The scientists were scheduled to arrive the next day and school was to begin the day after that. Hearts and souls were aflame.

Fielding had been so excited, he had spent the night at the hangar. Up before dawn, his boots clanked against the musty hangar floor, setting off echoes in the vast empty space. Albert Feinstein arrived shortly after dawn and paced nervously as he watched Saul and Duffy entertain the two hundred scientists as they gathered outside. Duffy had them in stitches as she dramatized the night the disheveled fugitive Fielding had come to their door. They were transfixed as she described how a fairy, who lived in her cleavage, had led the way. Her bouncy breasts were again the main attraction, although she'd dressed down, per Fielding's direct order.

Obeying his psychic impressions, Albert decided that the team leaders should begin setting up their areas. Duffy picked this up psychically and indicated to the scientists that they could enter the hangar. Duffy and Saul led the way.

Since Albert found his psychic connection with Duffy distracting at first, he made her stay as far away from him as possible. He wondered exactly how much Duffy could pick up and quickly found out when he had the thought, *Can she read my mind when I'm having raunchy fantasies?*

Instantly, he received his clearest Duffy transmission. *Only when they're about me!*

Albert broke out in laughter as Duffy initiated a long, surrendered hug. Thus began a new level of closeness, which Duffy called, "a sensual, platonic affair." (Duffy and Albert continued getting intuitive flashes throughout the day which they shared with each other. Very quickly, Albert learned how to manage their connection and the more he learned, the more he wanted her near. She was his psychic volume control, and he was enjoying it turned way up.)

Outside the hangar, Brook was getting a shot of the president for an immediate release to the major networks. This would dispel any "air of secrecy" and begin the process of building public support. Brook chose to feature the president, whose popularity was rocketing to over eighty percent.

Dina and Tommy arrived just as Brook finished the shot.

"Mr. President, this is my assistant, Dina Ashley, and her son Tommy,"

The president shivered as Dina and Brook's love energy rushed through him. "I am delighted for the two of you. We need heart-connected teams. Most of my time is spent with people in bitter opposition. Democracy is an adversarial system designed to cultivate opposing opinions. Unfortunately, opposition may not result in enlightened solutions since power prevails, and power seldom yields goodness and truth." Realizing he was rambling, the president stopped. "Remember this, Dina," he said, looking at her lovingly, "it's not how much experience you have—it's how much you can experience. You're going to be a great newsperson. I know it! Anything I can do to help, just ask!"

Dina nodded humbly, feeling amazingly secure.

The president felt drawn to Tommy, who was delighted by the leader's kindness toward his mom. "Hum, you're one of us, huh?"

Tommy understood and began a nod that turned into a royal bow.

"Whoa, I'm not king yet," the president chuckled.

"Monarchy can be a pretty good system," Tommy declared with one of his signature winks. His perfect timing made them all laugh.

Still laughing, they entered the hangar in search of Fielding, who appeared instantly.

Brook didn't waste a second. "Sir, I would like to film freely, providing nothing be released without your approval. Footage not suitable today may have future educational, historic, or press uses. I'll have Albert Feinstein brief my staff about comportment around the scientific area."

Fielding's response was wide-eyed and instant. "We have nothing to hide; this is an open process."

Nodding agreement, the president leaned down to Tommy. "What do you think, boss?"

"Once a Miracle begins, it never ends!" Tommy said with another prophetic wink. (From that time on, the president and Tommy would be together frequently, despite their busy schedules.)

Brook wanted lots of interviews with scientists and doctors so he'd have diverse footage for the opening release. Besides, it was the very first day and *you only get one of those,* he thought as he sent Tommy to alert the next person to be interviewed. Tommy took it upon himself to prep the subject emotionally and technically. When Tommy was involved, things fell into place like the ball that found the center of the glove every time. The release was actually composing itself.

Albert and Fielding experienced the same flow and finished a week's work in a few hours. Fielding noticed that when Duffy was nearby, Albert's insights surged. So the general arranged chance meetings at strategic moments throughout the day. Albert named them "Duffy Escapades" because they resulted in adventurous fun and revelations. (By the end of the day, Duffy Escapades were infamous throughout the compound.)

Since most of the scientists were still working through the evening, Fielding decided to take the opportunity to bring everyone together as a community. They all gathered by the podium resulting in several minutes of boisterous chatter. Spontaneously, the president, Tommy, and Duffy took the stage and became an impromptu vaudeville act. The president was quite a clown as well as a straight man for Tommy—Duffy played off the two of them using her assets to everyone's delight. Their big number was an improvised song called *The E in E-Zone means Awesome*. It was totally preposterous but it rhymed and the audience laughed and joined in with verses and harmless heckling.

Igor filmed the show while Brook and Dina sat entwined in front of him. Dina was overflowing with giddy giggles—She was working at a fantasy job, in love with a celebrity and watching her son perform with the president.

As Brook watched the show, he realized that the old Brook would have been intimidated by Tommy's closeness with the president. Instead, Tom Brook felt simple, easy joy. For the first time in his life, he liked himself.

Anticipating thousands of children arriving the next day, Fielding decided to stay up all night and work. He sensed that everyone felt the same and wondered why people weren't needing sleep. "Perchance to dream," he whispered to himself whimsically.

The morning was crisp with sounds of life. Birds flapped about chirping brightly as they nested on the hangar roof. Neighborhood dogs lined the outside fences, clawing as they barked; a white kitten claimed ownership of the empty boxes behind the hangar as she rattled through them making purring squeaks.

By the time the school buses converged upon the compound, the science area was already brimming with activity. Snow simply directed the children and teachers to the back of the hangar. The president emerged from his command post, Fielding's old office, and was overwhelmed by the energy radiating from the children. He was just learning how to open and close his psychic receptivity like the aperture of a lens.

Snow took his place on a makeshift podium and observed the children sitting like so many undisturbed candles glowing in a shrine. Josie fidgeted behind him, feeling out of place and not yet sure of her new stance.

He began simply: "I am your principal, Walter Snow, and this is my associate, Josie Ardo." He turned to invite Josie forward.

As she stood up, she heard the buzzing sound of voices spread across the room. Two young girls were the first to rush toward her, each grabbing a hand and kissing it gently before attaching themselves to her calves. Josie's eyes moistened. It had never occurred to her that in the children's eyes, she was a celebrity or benefactor. Snow allowed space for Josie and the children to savor this moment.

"We're going to co-create the school of our dreams," Snow assured. All heads moved forward in absorbed wonder. "We are going to begin each day with Soft Control Brainstorming. I will ask a question and anyone can offer a very brief answer. No answer will be judged right or wrong. We simply want to get volume, meaning as many answers as possible." Snow pointed to three teachers sitting at their desks ready to write each answer on a separate index card. "After this session, we'll sort the cards into a conceptual model. Aaron called this Creative Synergy. From this beginning framework, initial decisions and directions will be charted, all created from 'your' ideas."

Josie smiled as a few more children crept up and sat beside her. One little boy stroked her ankles. It tickled. As she held in giggles, love rose from her feet into her longing eyes.

Snow read his first question: "What do you want the physical school to look like?"

Before he could clarify, a fiery, redheaded child called out, "All of us together in one big room, just like this. No walls!" A murmur of approval spread across the room.

"Very good," Snow affirmed, praising the child for a brief and specific answer. "Now let's have more answers to the same question." Silence. "We want to get everyone's opinion so we can form a consensus. Don't be shy," Snow urged.

A little boy jumped up. "That is everyone's opinion, Mr. Snow, sir." He was so charming that Josie nearly swept him up in her arms.

Snow's eyes darted back and forth, surveying the crowd before turning to Josie with a childish grin. "Great," he said. "Let's get on with question two. Remember, for best results, lots of opinions are necessary. How many days a week shall school meet, and what time do we begin and end?"

A radiant teenage girl stood. "We meet six days a week, begin at nine, and leave whenever we're finished."

"Interesting," Snow replied, resisting a comment on the logistics of leaving whenever finished. "Any other ideas?" Snow asked enthusiastically.

A popular teacher stood up and the kids applauded respectfully. Her voice matched her meaning. "*All green plants are tender and yielding. At death they are brittle and dry. When hard and rigid, we consort with death. When soft and flexible, we affirm greater life.*"

"That's Lao-Tzu, a favorite of mine," Snow responded. "I assume that was confirmation of the previous idea with no end time." Snow saw two thousand heads nod in agreement. A few more children rushed over to Josie.

"Next question," Snow continued like a buoyant game show host. "What would you like to learn?"

An athletic boy stood up followed by his younger twin brothers. The first one said, "I want to learn about what's happening inside of me."

The twins nodded, then all three said in perfect accord, "I want to learn about God."

The room buzzed, then applauded. The three brothers bowed as if they were a single Soul.

A boy with glasses and slicked back hair stood up. "I want to learn about them." He pointed to the scientists at the other end of the room.

"Yeah," many voices cheered.

A girl stood and offered, "I want to learn about pure consciousness and the steps required in going from it to matter and individualized spiritual essences."

"Huh?" Snow couldn't connect those words with the fresh, pink lips that had uttered them.

The girl simplified. "I want to learn about God, too, but I want to know how it all works."

"Oh." Snow was getting his first inkling that these resurrected children were intellectually beyond him. His eyes misted with joy as he scanned the room, eagerly awaiting more responses.

Just as Dina and Igor were approaching, Tommy jumped up; he was the first child to be recorded on video. The children laughed because he had cotton balls stuck in his hair. One fell to the ground as he said, "I want to explore being more loving, open, playful, flowing, creative, non-judgmental, peaceful, and trusting because all these things increase my connection to myself and to you." He spanned the audience with his arms like a gracious leader.

Snow turned to Josie with a smile that spread like a Halloween pumpkin. She'd never seen his face so open, not even in the E-Zone at its peak. "What a beautiful statement," Snow acknowledged. He resisted his urge to discuss it so that more ideas could surface.

The next comment echoed through the room. "I want to fully actualize myself and help others do the same," a teen ventured as he smiled at his girlfriend.

Snow had a revelation. This wasn't a school, it was to be a center for planetary renewal—an unfolding temple built on the ground that the organism, Leon, and Aaron had paved. Expansive optimism permeated Snow as he inquired, "Anyone else have a comment—anything about anything?"

"I want to . . ." The little girl paused; she should have been searching for the words but had no such look on her face. She simply stood there calmly. Then she whispered, "learn about silence."

Snow's mind flashed to the *Fourth Key of Light*, where experiencing the silent void was discussed. He recalled Leon saying that within the silence one can have a direct experience of God. *The Keys and God are a thread to all the children's statements.*

"Wonderful," Snow encouraged, as he scanned an ocean of glowing eyes, each a resurrected treasure holding a key. There was silence. Snow briefly closed his eyes and took a deep wondrous breath; when he opened them the children had organically flowed into meditation, and their collective energy drew them in, deeper and deeper.

Snow followed the irresistible force and immediately saw himself in a boat on a raging river. He saw children lining the shore, and he looked at them intently as he paddled. The soft, sweet currents flowed innocently toward the rapids. He rode through them easily, maneuvering to the shore next to the magic mountain. Snow climbed the steps leading up the cliff. His hand slid between two large rocks at the crowned peak and he easily pulled himself up to the flat mountaintop.

He saw no vista, nor was Mo swinging from a tree. Today the Archangel was sitting in a lotus position in front of the portal gate. His back gently touched the gate's ebbing light; his body was aglow. Copying Mo's posture and attitude, Snow sat facing him. The principal closed his eyes and rested within the silent void.

Time dissolved into Mo's sweet voice. "I'm glad you found me again. Now you know the way."

"I am also glad," Walter Snow said, not realizing the enormous implication of Mo's statement. The swirling vortex sparkled. "I want to enter it," Snow confessed, looking past Mo into the light.

"Your energy field is too dense. You would be spit out like a pit," Mo explained, laughing at his gross but apt analogy.

"I need to find Leon and Aaron, or at least find out what happened. Josie needs to know so she can put their . . . their . . ."

"Deaths," Mo prompted. "Death is a beautiful word. You can say it."

"Well, I'm not sure what to say because their departure was so. . .so—"

"Out of the ordinary," Mo contributed with a smile. He was enjoying filling in the words when he offered, "Ask me your questions."

"Where are Leon and Aaron? Are they coming back?"

"Leon is never returning. He has returned to the All. It was his dream, and it finally came to pass. In time and beyond, dreams of union with God always come true. The ED, as you call it, has also returned to the All, and for your information, it was not an extraterrestrial. It was an interdimensional. Your scientists will not learn anything tangible about it, but allow them to discover this for themselves. Through their process, they will acquire some inspiring truths to spur humankind."

"What's happened to Aaron?" Snow asked forthrightly.

"That is a more complex matter," Mo considered, staring at his fingertips which met in the meditation mudra. "I am unable to tell you about Aaron's essence; it is experiencing cosmic complications. I can tell you that his body is forever gone—dead, as you call it."

"Aaron is dead?" Snow repeated soberly.

Mo looked to the heavens. "Aaron's immortal Soul is having a spiritual adventure with an indeterminable outcome. Tell Josie he is on a privileged journey that no Soul has ever experienced. A fitting end to his extraordinary incarnation."

The Master wiggled his fingers and said, "Rejoice. Love dominates the dimensions Aaron now inhabits. Love was the force that connected Leon to the organism. Love created the healing miracles and resurrections." Mo leaned forward. Snow copied. "Let humanity know that the organism, whose name is roughly pronounced Ibidob Bodibi, did not consciously resurrect your people. Ibidob was so overcome with love for Earth humans, that the force of this love created the healing."

Mo smiled. "Humankind should know that some of Jesus' healings occurred in the same unplanned manner. Overwhelming love creates miracles without anyone's consciousness directing it. Love has a mind of its own," Mo heralded, as the gate sent forth a fiery flash in agreement.

"Cherish these moments; mortals rarely experience the marvels of love." The Archangel sent a swell of light before stating, "Return to your school. Let the children lead the way. Your start is wonderful. It is divine!"

Snow's eyes opened just as the children emerged from their inner voyages. Each child was glowing and the light formed a unified field above them like the collective aura that had hung above their dead bodies just weeks ago. Several children could see the aura—others raised their hands and could feel it—some simply knew that something was hovering above them like a loving cloud.

Snow could not see it, but he knew. "Love is in the air," he sang to two thousand nodding heads. "Let it rain," he rejoiced.

"Let it rain!" the children responded in a single voice.

Snow threw fifty beach balls into the crowd of children, offering no instructions. Mayhem ensued as the kids batted the balls around, using them as props in adventurous, creative play. Pent-up energy was released, relationships organically formed and a sense of individual freedom was established during this unstructured play. (*Beach Ball* became a morning ritual and its importance would be explored for years to come.)

About thirty minutes later, just as a lull developed in the group play, Josie started the structured portion of the day with expressive games to open the voice and body. Two thousand children simultaneously exaggerated the sound of "Wow," while visualizing the one thing they wanted most from life. Aaron's expressive games unified the children and modeled the expressive freedom the school hoped to embody.

Snow and Josie were ready to take the ultimate risk. It required a total letting go! Using Aaron's Soft Control methodology, Snow simply said, "Break into groups of any size." No further instruction was offered.

It was chaos for awhile, what Aaron had called *evolutionary flux.* Gradually children flowed into specific interest groups. Art, music, theater, writing, philosophy, and science—subjects that stirred the spirit were emerging within these loose federations which Josie named Passion Groups. One group even went from group to group, spreading ideas like buzzing bees. Josie could feel a divine hand reaching from the void guiding them as each group realized the same purpose: to actualize the E-effects that were evolving within them. Simply, to understand and share the miracle.

A way to explore one's potential was to be in a Positive Pursuits group, so everyone was delighted when one formed. They named themselves *Sacred Theatre* and Aaron's book was their bible. (A six-year-old girl had wanted to read it so badly that she learned to read in one week under Tommy's tutelage.) Josie spent a good part of the day with this group and her acting skills soared. She was an inspiration to the kids as they were to her. When the president, Fielding, and Brook happened into the theater section, the Sacred Theatre ensemble was performing an improv mob scene about people experiencing a miracle. The energy was so strong that the president needed to be held up. Even with his aperture shut, it was almost too intense to bear.

"The Euphoria Zone, the 'effect,' it's here," the president said, pointing a trembling finger at the resurrected children. "Can you feel it?" He turned to Fielding, then to Brook. "Can you feel it?"

Like God, like Artists...

Snow continued to synthesize Aaron's work and the Keys into an educational system which connected with the president's vision, all of which melded with Albert's latest revelations. Everything was converging, but into what, no one knew—or cared!

School began to spiral upward at an outrageous speed with no one in control. One day during the lunch break, Snow posted a quote from Aaron's book that he hadn't understood before: In an empowered, creative environment, right ideas will implement themselves. And that is exactly what was happening the day Walter Snow realized he had nothing to do! Happily, he went to the remotest corner and began writing.

The president joined him and they explored their shared passion: to translate the E-Zone magic into real advancements for the entire country. Aaron's ideas were center stage.

"It's breathtaking," Snow assured, waving his ragged Positive Pursuits book at the president. "Josie's agreed to provide us with Aaron's unpublished work; it's a gold mine. Listen to this. Aaron created a program to transform culture through the school systems. He called it Renewal for

Life. It's very simple." Snow read from the sheet: "One hour during every school day children learn the skills they need to live a happy, healthy, and fulfilled life. Daily dedication to learning life skills in a loving, creative setting will transform our culture."

Snow put down the sheet and added, "Aaron felt that *Renewal for Life* training should continue through public school, college, and beyond. . . And here's the piece de resistance. . .its philosophy applies to any group: families, businesses, schools or even to an entire civilization." He handed the president a piece of paper. "This is a list of topics *Renewal for Life* addresses." The president scanned it with his empathic mind magnetized to the page:

Renewal for Life Curriculum
HOW TO:
* *Be happy*
* *Communicate effectively*
* *Love yourself and others*
* *Benefit from high integrity*
* *Have vibrant physical health*
* *Foster growing human relationships*
* *Deal with emotions—rage to euphoria*
* *Increase peace of mind and reduce anxiety*
* *Identify and express your God-given creativity*
* *Discover your life's purpose and find joy in work*
* *Raise a happy, healthy, growing family to do all of the above*

"It's like a Handbook for Life," the president said as he leaned back and transported himself into a world where everyone knew such things. "Amazing how much we emphasize intellectual development," he said dreamily. "It's a fixation, like our fixation on sex, violence, and money." He handed Snow the sheet and asked, "Why don't we teach our kids to love? Why don't we?"

"People believe it's the parents' job, not society's job," Snow suggested.

"Parents can't teach what they don't know. A cycle of knowing has to begin somewhere. Aaron's program would create that positive cycle. It would change every aspect of life."

"That's why we don't do it!" Snow suggested, staring at the president with newly-acquired piercing eyes.

The Powers That Be, the president thought as he shivered. He wouldn't utter the words.

Snow handed him a ten-page list of *Renewal for Life* benefits. Ironically, the first one was "accelerated intellectual development." The leader scanned the list: his eyeballs rolled back in their sockets. "Aaron Ardo was a genius."

"*Is* a genius," Snow offered.

The president nodded. "Did the genius detail a curriculum?"

"Better. He details a system to create it so it can never be out of date. And he shows us how to train the teachers. Teachers become growth facilitators, and they train students to be the same."

"A growth chain," the president observed.

"Exactly! According to Aaron, *We can create a forever evolving chain of learning if we do it with healthy teachers the healthy way.*"

"What's the healthy way?"

Snow pointed to the school. "Behold Aaron's way! Loving environments that create themselves because the people within them are empowered to create." Snow took a breath. "This school is alive, Sam. I'm not running it. It's a living organism," Snow gasped and held his mouth. "Organism," he repeated again, causing shivers up both their spines.

They were still tingling when the Sacred Theatre Ensemble appeared. Tommy was the ensemble's leader and danced out from the chorus line explaining, "Since life did not come with instructions, Sacred Theatre proudly presents, the Handbook of Life."

"This place is magic," the president proclaimed, clapping and adding hysterical hoots and whistles. Fielding joined them and stayed to watch the show.

"The whole world could be this way," Snow enticed. He stood up to participate in an interactive show where anyone could create a rule for the Handbook of Life, as long as they said it in a funny voice. One of Aaron's major theories was that playfulness increased health, well-being and creativity. Chapter five in *Positive Pursuits* was entitled, "Playfulness is Genius Business." Tommy facilitated masterfully, and loving mayhem ensued with unlikely depth from unlikely sources—no one stole the show; no one was in control. Aaron Ardo's ideas were spreading like wildfire and so was something else.

From the far side of the hangar Albert Feinstein came running toward them yelling, "Something unbelievable is happening." Albert ran to the piano and kneeled, lifting it off the ground with one hand. Fielding went bug-eyed. Albert breathed heavily. "Resurrected people are acquiring 'new' E-effects, like physical strength." He grabbed Fielding's hand and challenged him to a stand-up arm wrestle and won.

"Glory Be," the president exclaimed. "Are there other effects? How quickly are they spreading and evolving?"

"We can't predict that, yet. But it looks like E-effects will continue to evolve."

"Fantastic!" Fielding and the president said simultaneously. They exchanged quizzical glances.

Albert couldn't contain himself: "That's not the big news. There's more! It's huge!"

"Hold that thought, I need to walk," the president interrupted. Fielding put a supportive arm around him as they walked away from the school toward the scientific area. The president felt instant relief, enabling Albert to continue.

"The incredible gifts are not restricted to resurrected people. Anyone who was in the Euphoria Zone, particularly at its peak, is a candidate for E-effects. The clinic received over a hundred calls this morning, mostly from Fairview townspeople. They reported feeling younger, happier, and even wiser. Listen to this." Albert was breathless. "The husband of a woman with Alzheimer's called; he told me his wife had been glancing at the newspaper and hours later she began reciting every word on the page from memory." Albert laughed. "A woman who couldn't remember her own name suddenly has a photographic memory!"

"If you've received a hundred calls already," Fielding proposed, "statistically speaking, this thing could skyrocket."

"Statistically speaking," Albert nodded enthusiastically, "it's awesome, dudes!"

Tom Brook began an outreach program using the media; anyone who had been in the E-Zone was encouraged to participate in the compound's emerging programs. Between the townspeople and the military alone, the count exceeded ten thousand. Projected numbers were ten times that.

Albert Feinstein's priority was to employ resurrected doctors and science staff from Archmont Hospital. He trembled when he imagined doing research with resurrected medical personnel. They would head the hottest area of study, the positive health effects from E-exposure.

The potential of this health research made it easy for the president to acquire a billion-dollar budget to build a research facility as big as all their dreams.

Yet amidst the growing reports of vibrant health, Josie was suffering with nausea, achy muscles, and congestion. Walter was concerned. Upon his urging, Josie had a physical examination from Dr. Rector, a resurrected one. He suggested that the stress of Josie's unparalleled situation could account for her symptoms. Still, extensive blood tests were sent to a lab outside the compound.

Snow realized, *Now is the moment to tell Josie about Aaron and Leon's fate.* Though he was hesitant to do so he forged ahead, feeling that the closure could possibly relieve her symptoms. Josie experienced a huge emotional release; however, the catharsis did not relieve her physical discomfort. It did bring them closer to each other and to Aaron, whom they could now discuss with ease.

They continued to stay up nights at the hangar talking about ways to adapt Aaron's ideas to the school. One night they had a breakthrough related to a system Aaron had called Shifting Higher.

"Aaron guaranteed huge results," Josie said, "and it takes only one minute a day. If all the kids did it together the results could be unimaginable." Josie had a realization, "Shifting Higher is the *Sixth Key of Light* in action because it uses polarity to heal. You rate yourself in different areas of life using polarized key words."

That thought caused Snow's mind to leap. "Have you noticed how vibrant language is in the hangar," Snow commented. "I asked a physicist how he was doing and he said, 'Besieged by the radiance of your effulgent light.' Language seems heightened, mirroring people's heightened consciousness. I've named it Higher Language."

Snow watched Josie turn pale. "Aaron created a system with that exact name," she said softly.

For Snow, this was a miracle and an omen. "You know all about Aaron's Higher Language, don't you?"

"A lot," Josie nodded.

"Please tell me!" He dropped to his knees. "Tell me, tell me," he begged like a spoiled child, then did an outrageous exaggeration of a baby crying.

She loved his theatrics and rewarded him with a wink before she spoke. "Aaron proposed that language, besides being a barometer of consciousness like we're experiencing here, can be a tool to expand consciousness. *Language is the foundation of thought, thought is the foundation of reality—change your words and you change your 'reality'.* I think that was the first sentence in the article."

Josie paused as warm remembrances of Aaron washed through her. She allowed the sweet feeling to reflect on her face as she recalled, "I'll never forget when Aaron invented Higher Language. He was having an extended creative orgasm; every ten minutes I'd hear a scream, and he'd come running out of his office to tell me, in ultra-high speed, his latest revelation. This went on for weeks and I was getting worn out." She smiled sweetly. "I can tell you a few of the Higher Language rules. But I can't go into the whole system now; it's too involved. It's at least an eight-week course."

Snow nodded as Josie explained, "Higher Language is based upon becoming aware of what you say. Awareness of your word choices becomes your Sadhana, your spiritual discipline. When you break a Higher Language rule—at that moment, you rephrase what you've said. It's a self-training process. Here's one of the big rules," Josie offered.

Snow's pen was touching the page, ready.

"*Avoid using pronouns, particularly 'I', with a negative—I don't, we can't, they won't,* and *I'm not*. Here is a good example of re-phrasing into higher language," Josie explained. "Instead of saying, *I don't want to go*—say, *I choose to stay. I choose* is a higher vibration than *I don't want*. Aaron had seven higher phrases, one for each chakra. *I choose* was one of them, chakra five I think."

It was coming back to her, particularly the intensity in which she and Aaron had pursued the system. "I'll never forget when Aaron came to me and said we had to stop. The Higher Language system opened the unconscious, as Aaron predicted, but it did it too quickly and we were freaking out. Leave it to Aaron to create something that worked too well. Anyway, Aaron corrected the system but we never got into it again. He always meant to do something with it."

The following morning during the assembly at school, Snow's eyes were sparkling with adoration as he watched Josie share the basics of Higher Language. An eight-year-old child captured Josie's deepest intent with a metaphor: "Language is a dance of birth and death, every word a lifetime. Let your radiance be reborn into words."

Snow quoted a line from a poem he'd written, "Like Gods, like Artists—we make our way!"

"We make our way!" two thousand voices thundered back with fiery intent.

As Josie glowed with the light of discovery, from across the room a nurse peered sideways at her and could see Josie's aura in detail. Rings of color with distortions became increasingly vivid.

The following day, dozens more could see the rings of light around people. Albert was so excited by this new E-effect he abandoned scientific method for a quickie experiment. He wanted to know if each aura reader, looking at the same subject, saw the same thing. The test was conclusive. Everyone was seeing the same thing.

The next experiment tested whether aura readers could "manipulate" the energy field in order to produce healing. Since every reader had reported seeing dark spots in peoples' auras, Albert designed experiments to see what would happen if these spots were removed. About twenty doctors and nurses who could see the spots removed them by simply pulling them out of the aura. Certain hand movements seemed to revitalize the treated area.

Patient responses were astounding

Albert sought people with severe health challenges who had not been exposed to the E-Zone. The same blockage-removal experiments were performed and the results were spectacular. In most cases, awestruck attending physicians confirmed complete remissions. Word spread and people began showing up in droves; the experiment was organically transforming into a revolutionary clinic. Every moment was "a dance of birth and death" on many levels.

Fielding could not have done a better job of guiding the clinic's expansion. He was gliding across uncharted waters with Albert at the helm—and a lot of help from Duffy Escapades.

During this turning point, Saul was a solid railing beside tenuous steps. He was uncanny at providing obscure scientific supplies which he scavenged throughout the D.C. area. When Saul's van entered the compound, the scientists ran like children chasing an ice cream truck. One day Saul installed the music to "Pop Goes the Weasel" on his van emulating an ice cream truck; when all the scientists came running, he handed them frozen cones. The scientists laughed so heartily that they dripped chocolate all over themselves.

Boiling with possibilities related to the healing miracles, the president sought Snow's council. "We could share these methods with the world right now, but . . . the Powers That Be."

"Even the Powers That Be can't control evolution. Culture leaps!" Snow contended.

"Maybe we can give culture a kick in the behind," the president asserted as he thrust his foot forward. Snow copied.

"Normally when something's wrong we go to the opposite extreme to fix it. Let's not be extreme. Instead we can find the center, the heart," Snow said, his eyes widening. "Duality is a trinity!"

"Duality is a trinity?" the president questioned whimsically.

"Yeah, both sides share a center where the two sides meet. This invisible line, the middle path through the heart of reality, is the place where the pendulum stops. A one-sided coin. We need to find it!"

Looking into his inspired eyes, the president realized that Walter Snow was expanding the Keys.

That night, while Snow wrote feverishly about the Keys, the president stood by the exit hugging people as they left the hangar. The touch provided him with powerful impressions, which were magnified by everyone's sleepy state. When Saul and Audrey finally left, their hugs overwhelmed the leader. As he watched them teeter off like wobbly angels with drooping halos, he saw their auras entwine as if each were holding the other up. A smile of amazement set the presidents face aglow.

Zelia watched from a distant dimension and vowed never to return.

21

The greatest of these is love...

The E-Zone's healing miracles were documented brilliantly by Brook and Dina with Igor's usual magic. And it got even better after the curious twist occurred. Igor had filmed Dina talking with an old man who had lived near the compound his entire life. When Igor showed Brook the footage, they both agreed that she was the best interviewer they had ever seen. Brook then became the producer and Dina took his job as the project's interviewer and spokesperson.

It was common to see her questioning a subject while Brook gazed on. They were lovebirds infecting everyone. When Tom Brook had asked the president if he could marry Dina on the spot where the organism had been, the president not only said yes, he offered to perform the ceremony. Brook then asked Fielding to be the best man and the general actually sobbed his acceptance. (An hour later, Fielding met a nurse seer named Cindy Canter and fell insanely in love.) Love was in the air.

The wedding began taking on a life all its own. Duffy had "awesome-licious" healthy food plans which she kept secret from everyone except Albert and Saul, her assistant cooks. The president was in bliss, meandering outdoors watching the birds and daydreaming of his wedding oration. It would mark, for him, a new beginning.

Tommy had a "rocking idea" for a wedding video where he would impersonate his father-to-be. He began imitating the reporter in every way, even down to the socks (soft, one hundred percent cotton, loose at the top so they wouldn't chafe). Tommy's explorations came to life when he used Aaron's theater games related to character development, particularly one called *Copy a Subject*: Tommy simply followed Brook, copying his walk and movements as precisely as possible. Although it was hilarious to see the miniature mirror version, particularly when they were eating, it was serious business for Tommy. After days of laser concentration, he had felt a shift and could feel the reporter in his muscles. He could now become Tom Brook at will.

Brook loved the process, aware that Tommy, in his infinite wisdom, had created their passageway into a family. They had grown very close as the child produced and starred in the "Awesome Wedding Video." The title derived from Duffy's incessant affirmation, "This is gonna be the most awesome wedding video."

When the day of the wedding arrived, Tommy took the lead. "This is CNN's Tommy Brook, reporting live from the wedding of Dina Ashley and Tom Brook."

"Fantastic," Igor assured. "You look hot on tape!" Igor shifted to the standard Brook camera angle, and the boy's image popped. "It's no coincidence," Igor said, adjusting the light.

"Do I really look like him?" Tommy asked, as he displayed his blue pinstripe suit, the Brook trademark.

"You *are* him," Igor assured, as he gave Tommy the "I got the right camera angle" move and laughed. "Let's get some establishment shots," Igor said, coaching Tommy. "We can go outside and film the hangar; maybe the president will get some birds to fly around the doorway. You've got to establish location, but you can do it creatively."

Tommy listened intently to Igor's instructions. (At Tommy's request, Igor was teaching video production in the Sacred Theatre passion group.)

"Remember, stay alert; capture the unpredictable," Igor prompted.

"Got it," Tommy responded with Tom Brook's intonation.

"Darn, you're good," Igor affirmed. He moved slowly toward the exit, getting a shot of the screened-in area where Dina was dressing.

Inside the dressing area, Dina and Josie spoke softly.

"Nervous?" Josie asked.

"Not as much as you," the bride answered, tucking a rebel strand of hair into the antique blue barrette that Josie had just given her.

"Wow, I am nervous," Josie said, taking a deep breath. "It's only been a few months since I lost Aaron and Leon but it seems like a lifetime ago. I think all the romance around here is pushing my buttons."

"What's going on between you and Walter?"

Josie paused to think; she wanted to be clear. "Morally, because my loss is so recent, it doesn't feel right to consider romantic feelings. Walter and I have had this friendship chemistry from the moment we met." Josie brightened and said, "He's changed so much since the school began. You see the way he nurtures those kids. He smiles so much he's getting lines around his mouth."

"His face looks so different since he lost that weight; it's oval now," Dina added, adjusting her sash. "He's a hunk, and so distinguished with that wavy white hair."

Josie agreed with a sexy smile. "And now that the hunk spends so much time with the president, he's deepening. He's becoming more introspective, like Aaron was."

Dina gasped. "You're in love with him! This is great!"

"Shhhh, you're a troublemaker," Josie countered. "I'm also madly in love with a thousand kids; and I love you and Tommy. You know if Leon had been a normal kid, I'll bet he would have been a lot like your son." This thought brought a shared delight and a shift in direction.

"Josie, do you ever think that all this, the E-Zone and the miracles, were all Leon's doing? Look at what a gift he has given humankind. I know that nothing can make up for your loss, but do you comprehend the gain?"

Josie nodded. "I do."

"Better not say those words today," Dina joked as she fluffed her wedding dress. "Maybe it's none of my business but your relationship with Walter is beautiful and you shouldn't deny its natural evolution."

Josie's voice was vulnerable. "I know you're right, it's just too soon for romance."

"Not for him," Dina teased. "He's in love with you." Josie's eyes widened as Dina continued, "When I interviewed him, every other word out of his mouth was 'Josie.' My first interview rule is to go with what excites the subject, so I was obligated to question him, in depth, about you. Well, that boy is smitten."

"You're projecting," Josie rebounded. "You're so blinded by 'Brooky-poo' everything looks ga-ga."

"I've never been more clear," Dina said in a strong voice. "I'll admit love is in the air but that's because love is inside of us crying for expression. This is hot off the press. Seers can actually *see* love! It looks like starlight shooting out from the heart area. They claim they can see stars radiating in greater resonance to each other which means they can actually *see* romance, maybe predict it."

Dina closed her eyes and envisioned Tom Brook. (The star in her heart glowed so brightly the Angels stirred. Dimron looked away.) "Albert believes that people with resonant hearts have similar Soul pasts and the older the Souls are, the stronger their resplendent bond. I think that's the phrase he used." Dina approached Josie, gazing into her eyes, not wavering until they entered a warm embrace. "You and Walter are old, resonating Souls; I can feel it. You don't have to rush into anything, but don't rush away from it."

"I won't," Josie conceded, recalling a line from one of Aaron's short stories. She flipped into her actress mode and recited dramatically, "*Chosen are those who choose love.*"

"Yep," Dina agreed, as a very odd realization popped into her mind. "Gosh, this is spooky." She laughed slyly and said, "Did you know your son's full name "Leon Ardo" spells Walter's middle name exactly, Walter *Leonardo* Snow?"

"No, I didn't," Josie replied with a smile. "Hmm!"

"Mr. President," Tommy said in Tom Brook's deep reporter voice, "you are performing the wedding ceremony today and my audience wants to know if you have credentials. Do you have a minister's license? Is this marriage legal?"

"Well, I did take contemporary religion at Yale," the president confessed, wiping imaginary sweat from his brow. "Oh yeah, oh yeah, in the sixties I got a reverend's license from the church of *You Got Cash—We Got God*. I think it's still good!" The camera shook as Igor restrained a giggle; it enhanced the effect.

"Mr. President, this reporter would like you to share your opinion of the betrothed."

"Tom Brook wins big because he gets two treasures, the enchanting Dina Ashley, plus, and this is huge, he gets Tommy Ashley. That Ashley boy is quite a prize; I'm told he's in six passion groups, more than any other kid in school."

"Reports have it he's up to eight and facilitates one of them."

"See what I mean," the leader acclaimed. "Tom Brook is a celebrity and a hero. And I must say he is doing a fantastic job as press secretary for the E-Zone. In fact, my press secretary is retiring, and I'm a thinkin' . . ." The president put his finger to his lips and moved toward the camera. "Shhh , I want Tom to find out that he's my next press secretary while he's watching this wedding video. Dina and Igor, you're coming too."

Igor glowed.

"Back to the betrothed," Tommy said with Brook's deep intonation.

"Dina and Tom are going to make a great couple and great parents." The president's face turned earnest. "Our nation needs healthy families and this wedding marks the first E-Zone created family. It could be a beacon for America." The president stared into empty space.

"Mr. President, rumor has it that 'family' will be the subject of your marriage sermon, a sermon we hope will be shorter than the state of the union address during which this reporter fell asleep."

Straining to stay in character, the president replied, "I pledge to keep my discourse brief, but expect surprises."

"Surprise is a way of life in the E-Zone. This is an amazed Tommy Brook reporting live from the awesome wedding of Dina Ashley and Tom Brook."

Igor faded out. "Fantastico! Let's get the bird shot now. Mr. president, if you don't mind."

"I'll try." The president positioned himself in front of the hangar doorway, then looked over his shoulder to the rooftop and sang, "Here birdies, come to Daddy."

Within seconds a dozen doves swooped down and hovered above the president's head. Igor got great footage, then directed, "Slowly move away; I want to get the birds alone." Most of the birds remained, fluttering above the door. "Wow!" Igor exclaimed, causing the birds to scatter, inadvertently creating the perfect ending to the sequence.

Tommy and Igor waited by the hangar door for their next subject, who was late. They understood why when General Fielding strutted up with his beloved Cindy Cantor on his arm. He looked like a bruiser walking a primped toy poodle. (Aura readers could see a rainbow arc connecting their hearts, no matter how great the distance between them.)

"On your mark, general," Tommy commanded.

Fielding snapped to attention and saluted his director. "Can Cindy join me?"

"Not in the first shot, sir. This is a solo mission." Tommy cued Igor. "Get ready," he alerted Fielding.

The general tried to erase the grin that spread across his face.

"General Fielding, you are the groom's best man and rumor has it you used him to manipulate the press. In fact, Tom Brook was your puppet during the early E-Zone days. Right?"

"What?" Fielding replied.

Tommy maintained a serious expression, and the general finally realized what was happening.

"He's a pistol," Fielding said, flinging a loving glance at Cindy before responding. "Tom Brook is not a puppet," the general emphasized. "He is a straight-shooting reporter and he was my source because I trusted him. Besides, the SOB hounded me day and night." Forgetting he was in front of a camera, Fielding explained, "When you're in the military, you develop a second sense about the character beneath the surface of a man—what emerges under stress. On the surface Brook was ambitious and conceited, but I knew he had a solid core. And history proved me correct. When the going got tough, and it got very tough, Tom Brook was at the front, shining." Fielding's face softened, "I think of him like a son," he admitted.

Tommy flirted. "That would make you my grandfather, right Grandpa?" Loving, prophetic shivers shot up the general's stiff arms. Cindy blew a sensuous, puckering kiss as she moved forward, fixing her perfectly coiffed red hair.

Tommy took the cue. "This is Cindy Cantor. Cindy, I'd like to ask you about—"

"This wedding is going to be so awesomely spectacular," Duffy Rainbow interrupted, dancing right in front of the camera. Igor went in close just as Duffy demanded, "Watch this!" She squeezed her eyelids shut and Albert Feinstein came dancing over.

"You rang," he said with comic flair before noticing the camera and stiffening. Duffy continued her mental machinations, and an attractive nurse trotted over and stood beside Albert. Igor captured Albert's face lighting up, then panned to the girl who was doing the same. You could almost see Cupid fluttering between them.

"Is romance in the air or what?" Duffy said, taunting the camera when Saul's ice cream bells beckoned. "He's back! This is so great!" Duffy bounced away as fast as she had come.

Tommy worked the energy and said, "I want to talk to these lovely ladies." Albert and Fielding moved to the side and watched like puppies in a window. "Miss Cantor, you know Dina Ashley very well, what do you think of her?"

Cindy didn't skip a beat. "What I love about Dina is her ability to be present for others amidst this chaos. I don't think I've ever met anyone so heartfelt yet steady, except for . . ." Cindy looked over to Fielding, who twinkled like a lone star.

Tommy honored the moment.

Wedding activities were escalating around them. Two soldiers mistakenly walked into the shot prepared to paint a gold circle that was to delineate where the organism had rested. Igor and Tommy continued to film, capturing their conversation.

"I wish I'd spent more time with Leon when he was here," the sergeant said.

"Yeah, me too. Think he was an angel?"

"I don't know. He spent his last days right where you're standing. Can you feel anything?"

"Naa, that's the president's job," the soldier said respectfully.

"I stood next to the president when he first arrived," the sergeant recalled, pointing to the entrance of the hangar where Duffy was supervising the unloading of wedding supplies. "Leon was about to do his Jesus thing. I remember the look on the president's face, boy that was something. I'll never forget it."

"Wow, that was a piece of history only you witnessed."

"Maybe," the sergeant replied, enjoying the wondrous possibility. "We better concentrate on this circle. I'll hold the string in the center; you draw the circle in chalk. Then you can paint it gold. You have some art ability, right?"

"You bet, Sarge. I'm a regular Rembrandt."

Igor faded out the shot when Tommy signaled. The child spoke to the camera, merging what was in his heart with Tom Brook's deadpan style. "No one has forgotten our benefactors. Behind doors, during quiet moments—the few we have around here—we talk about Leon, Aaron, and the ED. They are alive within us, yet remain a mystery." Tommy looked straight into the camera with unblinking eyes. "Glorious mystery, that's what marriage and the E-Zone are about. This is Tommy Brook for CNN with two words of advice: Enjoy it!" Tommy dropped a cotton ball and made it hover in front of his chest. Igor went tight until the white puff consumed the entire frame, then he gradually faded out of focus.

Going wide, Igor panned the preparation activity. With Duffy and Saul orchestrating, there was a healthy blend of focus and looseness. Decorations went up in a free-form modern art style. Soldiers carried in tables for the feast, creating a crude circle. Scientists busily cleaned their work areas. In the back, the Sacred Theatre troupe reviewed their presentation, which, like everything else, was not rehearsed. Tommy captured it all, ending the sequence with a shot of the president and Snow sitting in their remote corner, forging their New World into words.

Hundreds of birds watched from their front row rafter seats; the white kitten peeked from behind a crate—even two mice peered from invisible openings, sniffing the aroma of Duffy's organic, veggie lasagna.

Dina and Josie waited behind the screen for their cue. As Josie bent to straighten Dina's train, she lost her balance.

"You're dizzy again?" Dina questioned, feeling concern.

"Let's say I'm dizzily excited about two people I love marrying each other." Josie hugged her, careful not to muss either of them.

Tom Brook and General Fielding waited behind a second screen while Tommy dashed in and out with updates. "Everybody's here, including the president, and he looks pumped," Tommy said as he skidded to a stop, then turned to leave.

"Wait. I've got something to tell you," Brook called to him. "I want you to know that I love you as much as I love your mom and I'm pumped about being your dad."

"I'm pumped too," Tommy admitted, his face turning a boyish pink.

Fielding cleared his throat, "I'm pumped and I'm just the honorary grandpa." Both Toms chuckled and looked at Fielding with adoring eyes as he spoke. "You two are so alike. You both have the kind of rebelliousness that grows into something great. Dina's gonna love every minute." Fielding lifted an imaginary cup and toasted, "To a magical future!" They raised their arms and quaffed the invisible brew just as the music began.

The orchestra, composed of a synthesizer, guitar, three horns, and a string section, started out playing a simple melody. The melody slowly matured into layers of counterpoint amidst increasing volume that peaked into a lush, sustained note. The unadorned melody continued as a line of children entered, their faces glowing from the light of the candle each held. They sang with angelic sweetness.

Tears of joy and wonder cleanse the air, here and everywhere,
Open hearts see God, as doves take flight,
Open lights illumine even the darkest night,
Tears of joy and wonder cleanse the air, here and everywhere.

Solemnly, the president entered the circle of gold. He looked up and smiled at the birds—they ruffled back, shifting on their perch. The orchestra and voices increased their volume.

("It's time," Modeen informed the wonder-struck Angels.)

"It's time," Tommy said, peeking out from behind the screen, verifying that Igor was filming. Tom Brook took a deep breath and smiled at the boy. Fielding gave both Toms loving pats before nudging them forward. Together, the triad emerged from behind the screen in perfect step with the music.

"I never realized Tom was so handsome," Josie said as she reported the action to Dina. "It's time."

Dina nodded and moved forward. Josie took her position and stepped out. Dina hesitated, leaving Josie in full view alone.

The children's voices filled the room.

Tears of Joy and wonder cleanse the air, here and everywhere,
Open hearts converge as doves take flight,
Infinite flames merge into a single light,
Tears of joy and wonder lift us beyond sight, cleansing everything.

Dina stepped out, locked arms with Josie and they walked toward the flower-laden altar where Brook waited. Josie stepped to the side as Dina walked to her mark.

The president raised his arms into the shimmering collective aura as the light tickled his fingertips, tantalizing the feelings that waited to be released into words. "Family is the Soul of a nation—the unit of measure by which a culture is weighed. But it is more.

"Family is divine evolution. Two people unite and have a child, whom they raise to do the same—a miraculous chain of life. Have you ever wondered why there must be a male and female to create a child? Why did God make it that *two* are required to make *one*? Could it be that the number two contains a special truth? What is this truth?"

An older couple knew and entered the wedding circle with one spontaneous step. Only a few people saw them.

"Love is the truth! It is the reason for *two*. It is what makes every living thing vibrate." The little mouse sniffed and snuggled up to its mate. "Love is the one force that exists in this and all other dimensions. Though we do not know the myriad of worlds beyond our sight, love is there. Where angels dwell and matter swells into invisible dark voids, love is there. Love is the thread between here and everywhere; it unites it all. That is what our children mean when they sing, *Tears of joy and wonder cleanse the air, here and everywhere.*" Twelve children spontaneously sang that single line in perfect harmony. "Family is where love is born and raised." He thrust his fist into the air. "I pledge to uphold the divine importance of family from this moment on and forever."

Larry King realized this message was like the one he'd received when Leon took him to the distant world. Beside him, Albert and Sue headed for the circle

"Consider the honor of marriage. Of the infinite Souls, one looks into your eyes and says, 'My precious life I share with you. Let's plant God's seed.' It takes two to make one, and one to make two," the president declared. He beckoned the bride and groom forward and invited them to peer into each others eyes as he said, "Of the infinite sparks of God's consciousness, I choose you." He was beaming when he asked, "Is this union chance? Or God's divine plan? Perhaps there is a third choice, the middle path. God's divine happenstance!"

Couples everywhere stepped over the golden line and stood beneath the increasing halo of light. The president watched in rapture. His planned speech was abandoned for the spirit guiding him. "Listen to our children," the president said warmly.

As he raised his arms, the choir knew exactly what to sing. *Tears of joy and wonder cleanse the air, here and everywhere. Open hearts see God, as doves take flight,...* Thirty doves swooped down from the rafters coming aglow in the collective halo, creating a ballet of flickering light above the president's head. Children's voices rang out, *Infinite flames merge into a single light. Tears of joy and wonder lift us beyond sight, cleansing everything.*

As a bird's wing tickled his head, the president raised his voice above the soft singing, "Family leads us to the light; it holds us as we shake with joy at the sight. Family catches us when we fall."

Thirty more couples stepped across the line.

The president was looking into Fielding's eyes when the general felt Cindy Cantor's soft hand wrap around his arm. Fielding's eyes shot golden joy, creating a bridge to the president that would never be broken. Cindy saw the light singe between them; her powers as a seer expanded at that moment. The leader tried to stop it, but tears of joy and wonder flowed from him. With drenched eyes, the president watched fifty more couples cross the golden line. Following their lead many same-sex couples stepped into the circle. The president began sobbing uncontrollably, but managed to call out between heaves, "Love reigns supreme!"

Tommy came to the rescue, his voice ringing in the president's echo,

Though I speak with the tongues of men and angels but have not loved,
I have become as a sounding brass or a clanging symbol.
And though I have the gift of prophecy,

and understand all mysteries and all knowledge,
and though I have all faith so that I could remove mountains,
but have not love,
I am nothing.

And although I bestow all my goods to feed the poor,
and though I give my body to be burned,
but have not love,
it profits me nothing.
Love suffers long and is kind; love does not envy;
love does not parade itself,
is not puffed up, does not behave rudely,
does not seek its own,
is not provoked, thinks no evil;
Does not rejoice in iniquity but rejoices in truth.
Bears all things, believes all things, hopes all things, endures all things.

Love never fails.
But whether there are prophecies, they will fail;
whether there are tongues, they will cease;
whether there is knowledge, it will vanish away.
For we know in part and we prophesy in part.

But when that which is perfect has come,
then that which is in part will be done away...
And now abide faith, hope, love, these three;
but the greatest of these is love.— 1 Corinthians 13

The president's voice rang above the breathless silence, "*Love never fails.*"

Walter Snow's hand moved upon divine command and wrapped around Josie's. Gently he beckoned her forward with an ever-so-slight movement of his wrist. Josie resisted. Lovingly he tightened his grip, then loosened it in resignation. Josie responded with a reassuring rub of her thumb and a squeeze.

From the back where they watched over everything, Saul motioned to Duffy who skipped along like a child keeping up. They had used the same made-up last name but had never been married. "It's time we had little Rainbows," he whispered, kissing her as they stepped into the circle of gold.

The president raised his arms and the children began to sing again.

The sweetness of their voices caused a shift in Josie, creating an overwhelming impulse to step across the line; she pulled Walter Snow along, impelling more couples to enter the marriage circle. The aura above the blissful couples shifted to vivid violet.

Snow pulled Josie's face around with a gentle touch to her chin and gazed into her eyes. His heart fluttered like the birds that flapped above them. A soft voice entered their magical field, "I think you should know," a young, female doctor was saying. "I saw your blood test results today while I was cleaning up. You should know!" The doctor grasped Josie's shoulder as she repeated, "You should know!"

Josie turned and gave permission with a nod; Snow looked away, unable to breathe.

"You're pregnant," she said.

Josie didn't flinch. "I'm infertile. It's impossible!"

"It's possible," the assistant assured her with eyes aglow. She was a seer and was looking at the fetus as they spoke.

Walter Snow's cry for joy ruptured the silence. "Josie Ardo is pregnant; she's having a baby!"

The president's fist soared above his head as he and everyone in the room shouted, "Leon strikes again!"

A remarkable peace descended on the tightly-packed circle of gold as the president spoke his final decree: "You are now recognized as beloved partners in the light. God bless you. And God bless your children; they will be miraculous." Upon those words, the president's empathic ability expanded into prophecy and he could see the future in mosaic images. He looked up as birds flew from their perches.

Love brightened the collective aura like a Hollywood special effect. The two mice scampered across the floor and became official pets. The white kitten nuzzled a homely black hound while spotted doves blessed the shoulders of everyone. Seers saw arcs of luminescent glow connecting everything.

Epilogue

"Now you can understand my passion for these Earthlings," Modeen said, glowing so brightly the nine hundred Angels surrounding him could not be discerned. "These newlyweds are blessed with E-Effects which their children will inherit—the E-Effects will evolve for generations! This is the beginning of a new seed, and you will be the first to cultivate it."

Modeen paused and gleamed brighter than he ever had. "My beloved, I have chosen you to be the guardian angels for the magical children that will be born! Imagine a planet filled with Leons," Modeen said lightheartedly.

The novice Spirits merged in collective splendor—the traditional acknowledgment for such an honor.

"There is more. It is the heart of my master plan, the reason for your special training and all the delicious angel candy. AhhhhhEeeeeeee," the Master roared, "Proclamation of Divergence!" Light billowed as Modeen rallied, "You will be Angels unto human eyes. Those you indwell will see you and know you!"

Modeen allowed a moment for the unprecedented reality to settle, then bellowed, "The spirals, made from creation's light have changed the cosmos forever; you can now traverse the physical plane." In that instant, the spiral implants dissolved but their powers remained, and every Spirit felt the blessing. Nine hundred Angels united into a five-pointed star, then transformed back to individuality with a blast. Modeen was dazzled.

"Imagine what humans might achieve after they've felt the soft touch of angel wings. Imagine what angels might learn." Modeen's voice raged in triumph, "Rejoice! You are harbingers of a new era—Angels and humans together!"

An agitated flutter rustled through the luminous field. Modeen addressed it. "Many of your brethren have wondered why a Spirit prone to defiance resides within this legion. Well, Dimron, your rebellious essence will be put to use! You are assigned to Josie Ardo's child. The adventure is just beginning."

The Master's communication link was disturbed by a penetrating thought wave, and all the Angels watched as Walter Snow's *out-of-body* self climbed to the summit grasping a notebook entitled, *Eight Keys of Light.*

"It's time," Modeen said.

Mo was a blinding haze outlined by Angels, but even that divine vision failed to divert Walter Snow who marched toward the portal, then turned to Mo offering the sweetest pumpkin-face smile. Courageously, he stepped through the gateway in search of the *Eighth Key of Light.*

Snow saw a blur of lime green and shocking pink, it tickled and he felt a flutter.

"I'm Zelia," the fairy said, as she finished aligning his energy field. "I'll be your guide when you enter this side. Are you ready?"

Walter Snow emitted a bold "yes," just when Josie leaped into the gate and nestled beside him—she felt a tickle and a flutter.

Faster than the speed of love, the threesome soared into blazing light.

The End . . . *is ENDLESS . . .*

ABOUT THE AUTHOR

Alan Lee Breslow innovates personal growth systems and is a Master Facilitator—having led thousands of workshops teaching his methods. His popular inventions include: *Writing Healing Stories*, which heals unconscious negative patterns by writing and reading metaphorical short stories— and *Higher Language*, which elevates consciousness through word choices. Alan also composes music, teaches creative development, and makes independent films. With his wife, Maia, they have produced the documentary, *You're a Genius, Stupid*, based on Alan's favorite invention, the *Intuitive Acting Method* (referred to in the novel as Positive Pursuits). Alan believes, "Everyone is an adventure waiting to happen." Welcome to the Euphoria Zone!

Contact The Author

Lectures, Workshops and Week-End Programs:

Authors Alan Lee Breslow and Maia Shaffer would like to create the Euphoria Zone in your organization, school or fundraiser. They are available to co-create customized programs.

Media Products:

The documentary, *You're a Genius, Stupid!* (Positive Pursuits) and other growth oriented media products created by the author are available:

Website:
www.keysoflight.com

E-Mail:
Euphoriazone@AOL.com

or
Write the author at:
Alan Breslow
P.O. Box 18574
Sarasota, Fl, 34276-1574